The Queen of Second Chances

D. M. Barr

CHAMPAGNE BOOK GROUP

The Queen of Second Chances

This is a work of fiction. The characters, incidents and dialogues in this book are of the author's imagination and are not to be construed as real. Any resemblance to actual events or persons, living or dead, is completely coincidental.

Published by Champagne Book Group
2373 NE Evergreen Avenue, Albany OR 97321 U.S.A.

~~~

First Edition 2021

pISBN: 978-1-77155-403-9

Copyright © 2021 D. M. Barr All rights reserved.

Cover Art by Robyn Hart

Champagne Book Group supports copyright which encourages creativity and diverse voices, creates a rich culture, and promotes free speech. Thank you by complying by not scanning, uploading, or distributing this book via any other means without the permission of the publisher. Your purchase or use of an authorized edition supports the author's rights and hard work and allows Champagne Book Group to continue to bring readers fiction at its finest.

www.champagnebooks.com

Version_1

For my father and favorite senior, Harry D.J. Barclay, who continues to live independently, and to my brother, Gordon, who watches over him and ensures he remains free from harm.

Chapter One

I couldn't take my eyes off the man. He came barreling into the recreational center at SALAD—Seniors Awaiting Lunch and Dinner, Rock Canyon's answer to Meals on Wheels—as I sat in the outer office, awaiting my job interview. He was tall, but not too tall. His expensive suit barely concealed an athletic physique that fell just shy of a slavish devotion to muscle mass. Early thirties, I estimated, and monied. Honey-blond curly hair, blue eyes, high cheekbones, chiseled features, gold-rimmed glasses, and of course, dimples. Why did there always have to be dimples? They were my kryptonite, rendering me powerless to resist.

I nicknamed him Adonis, Donny for short, lest anyone accuse me of being pretentious. He was the stuff of every girl's dreams, especially if that girl was as masochistic as yours truly. Men like that didn't fall for ordinary girls like me, gals more Cocoa Puff than Coco Chanel, more likely to run their pantyhose than strut the runway. I leaned back on the leather couch, laid down my half-completed application, and prepared to enjoy the view. Then he opened his mouth, and the attraction withered like a popped balloon.

"I want to speak to Judith. Now. Is she here?" The sharpness of his voice put Ginsu knives to shame. It was jagged enough to slash open memories of my mother's own barely contained temper when refereeing sibling disputes between Nikki and me. Well, at least until she prematurely retired her whistle and skipped town for good.

The attendant working the main desk looked fresh out of nursing school and had obviously missed the lecture on dealing with difficult clients. She sputtered, held up both hands in surrender, and retreated into the administration office, reemerging with an older woman whose guff-be-gone demeanor softened as she got closer. Her name tag read, "Judith Ferester," the woman scheduled to conduct my interview. She took one look at Donny, sighed as if to say, *Here we go again*, and plastered on her requisite customer service smile.

"Mr. Prentiss, to what do we owe the honor of this visit?" she asked in a tone sweet enough to make my teeth hurt.

"Judith, I thought we had this discussion before. I trust you to take care of my nana, but day after day, I discover goings-on that are utterly unacceptable. Maybe we shouldn't have added the senior center, just limited SALAD to meal delivery. Last week you served chips and a roll at lunch? That's too many carbs. This week, I find someone is duping her out of her pocket change. No one is going to take advantage of her good nature, not under my watch."

I half-expected him to spit on the ground. Was such venom contagious? I didn't want my prospective employer in a foul mood when she reviewed my application. I really, really needed this job.

"Mr. Prentiss," Judith answered, her patronizing smile frozen in place, "I assure you that your championing of our senior center was well founded. The reason your nana isn't complaining is that she receives the utmost care. She is one of our dearest visitors. Everyone loves her."

"Tell me then, what is this?" Donny—scratch that, Mr. Prentiss—drew a scrap of paper from his pocket and flung it onto the counter. I leaned forward to make out the object of his disdain. Then, thinking better of it, I relaxed and watched as this melodrama played itself out.

Judith glanced down at the paper. "This? It's a scoresheet. They play gin for ten cents a hand. We monitor everything that goes on here; your grandmother is not being conned out of her life savings. You have my word."

Prentiss shook his head so vigorously his gold-rimmed glasses worked their way down to the tip of his perfect nose. He pushed them back with obvious annoyance. Even when he was acting like a jerk, his dimples were captivating. Would they be even more alluring if he smiled? Did he smile…like, ever?

"It's not the amount that worries me. It's the act itself. Many seniors here are memory impaired. How can you condone gambling between people who aren't coherent? Could you please keep a closer eye on things? Otherwise, I'm afraid I'll have to take my nana—and my support—to the center I've heard about across the river."

Without waiting for Judith's response, Prentiss departed as brusquely as he'd arrived. Ah, the entitlement of the rich. Walk over everyone, then storm off. He never even noticed my presence. Just as well, considering my purpose for being there. Even if I wasn't sorry to see the back end of his temper, his rear end was pleasant enough to watch as he exited, I noted with a guilty shudder.

Judith shook her head, rolled her eyes, and let out a huff. Then she noticed me. "I'm so sorry you had to overhear that. I'm the director here. How can I help you?"

"I'm Carraway Quinn. Everyone calls me Carra. I have an appointment for the recreational aide position."

Judith typed a few keystrokes into the main desk's computer. "Ah yes, Ms. Quinn. Carraway, like the seed?"

"Something like that," I said with a smile.

They always guessed, but no one got it right. Some man would, one day. That's what my mother said a million years ago, when she still lived within earshot. One man would figure it out, and that's how I'd know he was the one for me. Not that it mattered right now. I had bigger problems than finding a new boyfriend.

"Tell me, would I have to deal with people like that all day?" I tilted my head in the direction of Prentiss's contrail.

"What can I say? He loves his nana." Judith shrugged, staring at the door. "Though I've never seen him lash out like that before. He's usually so calm." She quickly shifted into public relations mode. "Jay Prentiss is one of our biggest contributors. It's only because of his generosity that we have this senior center and can afford to hire a recreational aide." She beckoned me into the inner office. "Shall we proceed?"

I followed, but I had my doubts. I belonged in the editorial office of a magazine or on a book tour for my perennially unfinished novel, not at a senior center. This job was my stepmother's idea, not mine. Calling it an idea was being generous; it was more like a scheme, and the elderly deserved better than someone sent here to deceive them. I was the embodiment of what Jay Prentiss worried about most.

The interview lasted less than ten minutes, as if Judith was going through the formalities but had already decided to hire me. I was to start my orientation the following day. I shook her hand and thanked her, all the while wishing I was anywhere else.

Afterward, I wandered into the recreation area, where I'd be spending most of my time. The room was dingy, teeming with doleful seniors watching television, playing cards, or staring off into space. A few complained among themselves about a jigsaw puzzle they were unable to finish because the last pieces were missing. I wondered how many had lost their spouses and came to the center out of loneliness, their children too busy with their own lives to visit. It was a heartbreaking thought.

Jay Prentiss was complaining about carbs and gambling when he should have been concentrating on ennui. The seniors' dismal expressions told me they were visiting SALAD more out of desperation than opportunity. It was clear they needed an injection of enthusiasm, not some aide looking to unsettle their lives. It came down to my conscience. Could it triumph against my stepmother's directives and my plummeting bank account?

Chapter Two

Jay Prentiss fumed as he drove back to his office, frustrated by the SALAD altercation but angrier at himself for losing his temper over picayune details like carbs. He cursed his inflexibility and perfectionism, but when it came to protecting his nana, the sainted woman who had raised him, he lost all reason. The jangle of his cellphone deepened his irritation. He hated talking while driving, even though his speakers easily broadcast the caller's voice without him ever having to take his hands off the wheel. It was a distraction, and Jay preferred to concentrate on one thing at a time. That's how you succeeded, without everything becoming muddled and confused. Multitasking was the devil's plaything.

Worse, the dashboard displayed the caller's name, Meggie Murant, his administrative assistant. He knew he should answer, but he didn't want to talk to anyone until he recovered his usual calm demeanor. With his staff, he needed to project strength and leadership, not the histrionics that his grandmother's caretakers always evoked.

The gods of technology routed the unanswered call to voicemail. Not a fan of prolonged curiosity, Jay played the message at the next red light. "Mr. Prentiss? I'm sorry to disturb you, but a Ms. Gemi Dibble arrived a few minutes ago without an appointment. She seems very distraught. I put her in the smaller conference room, and I'll make sure she has plenty of coffee and cookies until you return." *Click.* He bristled. A surprise, just what he needed.

Jay's first reaction was to floor it, but he forced himself to maintain the fifty-five mile per hour speed limit. Ten more minutes wouldn't worsen Ms. Dibble's problems, whereas a hefty ticket and points on his license would definitely affect his. It never paid to cut corners. Never.

For half an instant, he thought about Meggie and her big, brown, hero-worshipping eyes. Her crush on him was more annoying than endearing. With a giant tattoo on her shoulder—even if a jacket masked it during work hours—she was not his idea of the quintessential lawyer/future politician's wife. No, his bride, if such a woman existed, would be inkless, unpierced, size four, and impeccably dressed. In a word, perfect. Adriana, his current girlfriend, was the closest he'd come, but even she had recently revealed some unfortunate imperfections beneath her flawless exterior.

Fifteen minutes later, he pulled up outside Hudson Valley Legal Associates, home to Prentiss Elder Law and a few non-competing firms that sublet from him. The renovated Queen Anne Victorian was the showplace of Rock Canyon. Seven years into private practice he still felt the same frisson of pride he'd experienced on day one, when he was merely a determined law school grad with a bank loan and a dream.

Jay's two office mates raised their heads as he pushed open the creaky front door. One of them was Meggie, dressed in an unfortunately tight chartreuse suit. The other was Solomon, the senior black and tan bloodhound he'd inherited from his grandmother when her townhouse community unexpectedly started enforcing their forty-pound-pet limit.

Meggie reached for the phone. "I'll call the handyman to see if he can do something about those hinges, sir."

Meanwhile, Solomon, with his typical air of indifference, looked up and sniffed twice, debated if he should expend the energy to greet his substitute master, decided against it, then laid his head back down on his plush doggie bed.

"No need, I have some WD-40 in the back. I'll deal with it later." Jay adjusted his red-and-blue striped tie to ensure it was taut and hanging straight.

Then he knelt by the side of the reception desk to scratch Solomon under his big, floppy ears. The act of petting Nana's dog was often his sole stress release during a hectic day. The dog maintained his aloof stance, reluctantly wagged his tail twice and let out a giant fart. Serves me right, thought Jay, rising off his knee. *Sometimes it's best to let sleeping dogs lie. Especially this one.*

"Please tell me about Ms. Dibble. What's got her in such a panic?" he asked Meggie.

"She said she read that interview you gave to the *Guardian* a few weeks back and hoped you might help her. She refused to offer any details."

"Perfect. And what time is my next appointment?"

"You're free for another two hours." Meggie batted her eyes and winked.

Jay stiffened. "Buzz the intercom in about ten minutes so if I need one, I'll have an excuse to end the meeting early." He silenced his cellphone and headed toward the conference room without waiting for her response.

Ms. Dibble rose as Jay introduced himself and extended his hand. She was a slender, dark-skinned woman in her mid-fifties, wearing a colorful hijab and exuding a determined air. She greeted him by placing her hand over her heart rather than shaking his hand.

"Mr. Prentiss, I need you to help me," she started without preamble. "I think my sister is robbing our mother blind, but no one believes me—not even my mother."

"I see." He gestured for her to sit. "What gives you that impression?"

Ms. Dibble plopped back down, tears brimming. "I can see you're already dismissing me. Just like everyone else."

He creased his brow. "Not at all, I assure you. Remember, I've been doing this for a long time. I see many siblings squabbling over future inheritances, claiming their parents are being unfairly manipulated. I need to hear all the facts before rendering a judgement. That makes sense, right?" He smiled, hoping some extra warmth might waylay her lack of faith.

"I guess so." Ms. Dibble eked out a weak smile. "You need to understand, I've been my mother's primary caregiver for the past ten years. She's eighty-four, and her knees are bad, so she spends most of her day in a wheelchair. Lately, her memory seems to be going as well. I work ten-hour days, so I called my sister to see if she would help, at least send some money because my mom's health insurance won't cover a full-time aide."

She looked down at her lap and wrung her handkerchief. "Next thing I know, Siti's moved from Las Vegas into my mom's home. My sister—Allah forgive me for saying this—she isn't a good person. She only calls when she's looking for a handout. She hadn't phoned for a while, so I figured she might have a steady job and, for once, be willing to give something back."

"Has she paid for any of your mother's expenses since she's returned? Taken on any of the burden?"

"Not that I know of. Since Siti moved in, my mom seems out of it all the time, like she's overmedicated, so she's been in no condition to tell me. And I can't find her checkbook or bank statements anywhere. I asked her about it while my sister was out of the room, but she snarled and accused me of being jealous, upset that now I had to share her love." Ms. Dibble closed her eyes as if the darkness would erase her mother's allegations. "I'm worried, Mr. Prentiss. I don't know what my sister is capable of, but even if it's nothing, I'd feel better having her out of the picture. I don't have much spare cash, but if you'd consider accepting a few dollars each week out of my paycheck..."

"Let's see what we can do to help your mother before we worry about payment."

It was a difficult situation. He'd only heard one side of the story. Who was to say Gemi wasn't the guilty party, trying to force Siti out of town so she could keep the entire inheritance for herself? He'd seen it before. Yet, Jay considered himself an excellent judge of character, and Ms. Dibble seemed sincere.

The conference room extension rang. Why was Meggie calling instead of using the intercom, and why five minutes early? "Excuse me, I'll get rid of this caller, then we'll figure out our next step."

He picked up the receiver and frowned as Adriana's insistent nagging greeted his ear. "Darling, did you pick up the tie for our dinner tonight? You absolutely must wear something that reflects Senator Mitsky's favorite colors—red and yellow, or his hobbies—fishing and hunting, remember? If you don't wear something to break the ice, you won't have a thing to talk to him about. His personality is as dull as children's scissors—"

"I'm sorry, I'm in the middle of a client conference. I'll get back to you later." He disconnected the call with a twinge of satisfaction.

He was ashamed to admit it, but despite her long black hair, perfect body, stylish wardrobe, and influential political connections, incensing Adriana by doing the opposite of anything she asked had become his new favorite hobby. Unfortunately, he wasn't sure how much more of her micromanagement he could endure. Like her calling on an office phone when he hadn't answered his cell. How had she gotten the conference room extension, anyway? Had Adriana sweet-talked Meggie into putting her through? The same way she'd repeatedly tried to talk her way into moving into his condo?

He pressed the intercom. "Meggie, no more interruptions." Then he returned his full attention to Ms. Dibble. "I apologize. What I was going to say is that unfortunately, what you're describing is not all that unusual. It's estimated that about ten percent of the senior population experiences elder abuse, and financial exploitation is at the top of the list. Sadly, the cases are likely underreported."

Ms. Dibble squinted. "So what can we do?"

"The tricky thing is, unlike physical mistreatment and neglect, financial abuse is hard to prove. The victim often hands over money willingly, especially since the abuser is typically a loved one, like a child or a sibling. Tell me about your sister. What's important to her?"

"Money. Money's all that's ever mattered to Siti. When we were little she would dream up these clubs for me to join and then swindle me out of quarters as membership fees. She'd buy herself gumballs with the dues, then the imaginary club would mysteriously burn down, no refunds. She says she moved to Vegas for the abundance of work, but I'm sure every night she works the casino patrons, blowing on men's, *ahem*, dice for good luck and a chip or two."

Ms. Dibble's description gave him an idea. "She likes to gamble?"

"Absolutely. I'm sure she loses more than she makes. I don't know how she stays afloat."

"That works." He swiveled his chair around, drew a pad and pen from a cabinet, then set them in front of his client. "Please print your sister's full name, home address, all her phone numbers and email addresses, and her birthdate. I'll also need her place of employment if one exists. Then underneath, add your full name and contact information, including your email address and phone number."

She scribbled the requested information and pushed the pad back to Jay's side of the boardroom table. "What are you going to do?"

"I have a colleague who may lend a hand, show your mother exactly how much her welfare means to your sister. In the meantime, don't stop doing anything you're doing. Keep visiting your mom. Don't let on that anything has changed or that we've spoken, agreed?"

Ms. Dibble nodded. "I appreciate any help you can give my family. I've read about you, Mr. Prentiss. You're a good man."

He wished her well and watched her exit into the foyer. Then he pulled out his cellphone and punched in his ex-college roommate's number. *Greg owes me a favor for hiring his kid sister, and he's always up for a prank or two. Let's see if he can pull this one off.*

Chapter Three

Back at our tiny apartment on the outskirts of Rock Canyon, I found my roommate Kiki and her Aunt Jaime inhaling a bag of Pepperidge Farm Milanos. They'd left three for me. Great, exactly what my diet needed. I wedged in between them at the kitchen table and bit into one, longing for a sugar high to numb my anxiety.

"How'd it go, Carra?" Kiki's tone was casual, but her eyes bespoke our mutual concern.

Once my inheritance ran out, her accounting salary wouldn't be enough to cover our monthly expenses. I had to contribute something to keep us from being kicked to the curb. Unfortunately, you can't pay the rent with job rejections, which is all I'd been bringing in since we both graduated from Emerson in May.

Aunt Jaime raised her brows expectantly.

"They offered me the job. I deliver food trays in the mornings—that part is unpaid because everyone volunteers—and help the recreational director in the afternoons. All starting tomorrow. But the whole thing's not sitting right with me."

"You're going to take it anyway, right?" they asked in tandem.

Kiki reached for one of the remaining cookies, but I slapped her hand away. Desserts were a delicacy in our nascent empty-purse era, and these were mine. "Thanks for bringing the goodies, Mrs. Goldfinch. Very sweet of you, excuse the pun."

"I've told you a million times, call me Jaime. So tell us, what's the hiccup?"

Jaime had more on her plate than a few cookies. I had no intention of piling on my woes or divulging the real reason I'd applied to work with the elderly, but when she laid her hand on mine, my dam of resistance broke and out flowed a torrent of misgivings.

"I'm a writer, an artist. Artists should spend their time creating, not babysitting seniors. There's no magic to it, no imagination. But more importantly, I feel like a fraud. They think they are hiring a caregiver. What qualifies me for that?"

Jaime leaned over and hugged me. Even though I'd had two, count 'em, two mothers in my life, she was my third, my Carol Brady, always there to talk me down from my daily dating or academic crises. This year had been a doozy for her, but being Jaime, she always stole a few hours here and there to drive up and visit us as her husband underwent extended cancer treatments at Memorial Sloan Kettering.

"Remember every final exam you worried about?" she asked. "You aced those, and you'll figure your way through this challenge too. In fact, I can't think of anyone better to add some spice to SALAD, so to speak. Take their programs and sprinkle on your special pizzazz. Leave your mark."

I blinked. The job didn't seem so bad the way she described it. And the seniors did need something fresh to rejuvenate their spirits. I just hadn't realized until Jaime's comment that I could be its source. Even if that agenda didn't mesh with the real reason my stepmother wanted me working there.

"Spend a few months at SALAD, see how it goes," she continued. "You're young. The world is full of opportunities for someone who can write well—even if it isn't as a novelist or magazine editor. While you're there, why not offer to write some of SALAD's copy? Every company needs fresh content for their websites, brochures, and newsletters."

"That would take some long-term planning skills. Not exactly something Ms. Spur-of-the-Moment excels at." Kiki scowled in my direction. "Which is a pity, considering we only have enough rent money to cover the next few months."

Jaime sighed. "I'd take you in, but unfortunately, four people would be a stretch in a one-bedroom condo. You're both survivors. You won't need anyone's help."

"I guess I'd better think of something special to offer the seniors. All while I apply for copywriting jobs," I said, trying to temper the hurt of Kiki's accusation while grasping at the hope Jaime was flinging out. They were both right. It was time to make some drastic changes. If not for me, then for the sake of my roomie. At graduation, Kiki and I made a pact to stay together. Somehow I had to hold up my end of the bargain—without sacrificing my soul.

Chapter Four

As I tossed and turned that night, wrestling with guilt, I thought about yesterday's meeting in the glass-walled conference room of Rock Canyon Realty that had brought me to SALAD in the first place.

From the day mega-agent Melanie Wright defected to open her own brokerage, RCR had become part morgue, part roller derby, the remaining dregs mournful as they jockeyed to become top agent. Included among them was my stepmother, Beatrice. Once known as "Queen Bea" of the mobile home market, she was hell-bent on branching out into residential resale. She'd recruited both me and Nikki as a key strategy in her expansion scheme.

Out of breath and a half-hour late to the meeting she'd called, Bea finally scurried in, her skirt two inches shy of respectable and her dark hair escaping from her bun in all directions. With her signature stack of folders under her arm, she looked as frantic and harried as always—like a forgetful scientist who'd discovered, and immediately misplaced, the cure for cancer. She set the files on the table and stood behind the manager's podium, attempting to inject some formality into the discussion.

"Before I start, I want to congratulate Carra on passing her licensing exam and finally putting commerce over creativity. You can't pay the rent with hope, honey, but you can pay it with the proceeds of a big, fat commission check. You'll see."

Typical Bea. She knew my sore spot and insisted on irritating it further by spouting homemade aphorisms.

I shot Nikki an *I warned you it would be like this* glance and received a mouthed "Hang in there" in response. Who was I kidding? There was no one to blame for my predicament but myself—and this damn mental block keeping me from finishing my novel. I had tried to force myself to make the agents' and publishers' requested edits, but month after month, their Revise and Resubmit notes sat in my email, unanswered. So, I'd applied for publishing and editing jobs, anything to pay the rent. No luck. Hence real estate, the last refuge for millions of recent grads like me who'd attacked the job market armed with nothing but enthusiasm, an English degree, and a growing pile of unpaid bills.

"I've devised an exciting project for our little team. A new niche—the senior market. They're aging out of homeownership and, in Carra's vernacular, we're the perfect ones to help them start a new chapter in their lives."

"By displacing them?" The words slipped out, an involuntary reaction to the acrid taste welling in my mouth. "I would think they'd be more comfortable staying where they are, where they raised their families and built a lifetime of memories. Why not help them make some simple adjustments—like adding grab bars in the showers?"

"Where's the profit in that?" chided Bea, batting her false eyelashes as if to fend off any dispiriting remarks. "And what's so horrible about offering seniors a fresh start? Not to mention cashing in on all their equity to cover the cost of assisted living. Nursing care is expensive. For many of the elderly, it's not safe to stay home on their own. We'd be doing them a favor."

Bills, food, car repairs. Reasons to stay the course swirled in my mind. "Fine." It was futile to argue with a stone wall. "What did you have in mind?"

She turned to my sister. "Nikki, I want you to volunteer at the rehabilitation center at Saint Agatha's. The older stroke patients can no longer climb stairs, they'll need to swap their multi-level homes for ranches and one-level condos. Some younger accident victims now find themselves paraplegic. Concentrate on them if you can. Their insurance payoffs may allow them to buy up. If they're feeling sorry for themselves, they may be more generous with their budgets."

Outrage seeped from my every pore.

"Don't give me that look, Carra," said Bea. "This is business. We're providing a service. No one is selling anyone anything they don't need or can't afford. Got it?"

I threw myself back against my chair and stared at the ceiling, biting my tongue. *Bills, food, car repairs...and rent.*

"Now Carra, I've set up an interview for you tomorrow as a recreational aide at Seniors Awaiting Lunch and Dinner. The staff is mostly comprised of volunteers who deliver meals to the housebound, but they also have a center crawling with widows and widowers killing time and seeking companionship. That's where they're looking for help, and they're willing to pay for it.

"This should be an easy sale for you, convincing them to

downsize, trade their oversized houses for retirement homes and assisted living. You should also seek out the directors at those fifty-five-and-over communities, see if they'll pay you a commission for anyone you refer. That way, we can cash in on both sides."

I sat on my fists to refrain from banging them against the boardroom table. I did not put myself through four years of college to con someone's grandparents out of their home. "I know nothing about being a recreational aide."

She batted those eyelashes again. "I checked. At this entry level, there are no special courses or accreditation needed. Use your common sense. Hand the geezers a pair of blunt scissors and some construction paper. Snowflakes for winter, ornaments for Christmas, dreidels at Hanukah, and Easter eggs in the spring. Host a Bingo game. Nothing to it. And subtly make it known that you sell houses in case anyone's looking to move. It'll be like taking candy from a baby."

"Sounds about right, both wear diapers." Nikki never missed a chance to get in a dig. "Bea, how long do you think it'll take before we get a bite or two? I have my eye on a lease for a little red roadster, but I need around $5,000 for the down payment."

"I'm counting on both of you to come up with your first clients within three months. That puts us at the beginning of November, which is perfect timing because that's when real estate sales usually slow down. With your help, our business shouldn't take that seasonal dip."

"And if we come up short?" asked Nikki.

"I'm covering your salary through Halloween. Which means I'm investing twelve weeks of payroll to help you sharpen your selling skills, on top of what you'll earn at the rehab and senior centers. After that, it's commission only. You'll eat what you kill. We'll meet again after your appointments. Good luck!" She gathered her files and bustled out of the room.

"Why does she drag all those papers around?" I asked my sister. "She never looks at them. Isn't everything stored on computers these days?"

"I think they're her security folders. With the side benefit of making her look busy. A necessary illusion, I fear, since Judy at reception told me no one is hiring her these days for anything except mobile homes."

"So how can she afford to keep us on salary for three months?" Nikki shrugged. "Dad must have left her more than he left us. God bless him. Speaking of parents—"

"Don't even go there, Nikki." I hit the table for emphasis. My sister might look like a slightly older replica of me, but on this topic we'd entrenched ourselves on opposite sides of the fence.

"But she's been begging."

"You want to embrace our birth mother for walking out on us, that's your business. I refuse to provide the cure for that woman's belated guilt." I pushed back from the table.

"You don't remember her like I do—overwhelmed, unable to cope. She did what she thought was best for us. Until you deal with this, give her another chance, you'll never be free of how her leaving affected you."

"Overwhelmed? That's a lie and a cop-out, Nik. She was flighty, and she got bored with her marriage and children. Case closed."

I stormed from the conference room without another word. No matter how bad things get, you don't walk out on your husband and kids. And if you do, you don't attempt to wheedle your way back into their good graces over a decade later.

Perhaps she'd heard about our inheritance. Too late, lady, nearly all spent. Whatever was left would likely run out right around Bea's deadline. Which meant if I wanted to continue living with Kiki, I'd have to oblige my stepmother by preying on seniors. Otherwise, I'd be celebrating New Year's Eve at the local homeless shelter.

Chapter Five

I glowered at the large double oak doors leading into SALAD. There was still time to make a break for it. I was debating which was worse: what waited for me inside, or Queen Bea's reaction to outright mutiny. My buzzing cellphone delayed that decision.

"Not as bad as you thought, right?" Nikki's Pollyanna tone was especially cloying on this, the first day of our perverse marketing assignment. I'd almost forgiven the recent mention of our birth mother. We were sisters, after all. We had to stick together.

"I wouldn't know. I haven't convinced myself to go inside yet. How about you?"

"It's depressing, just what you'd expect from a rehab facility. Quadriplegia isn't exactly something you celebrate. They said they were grateful for any volunteers though, so I'm in."

"Nikki, this is a terrible idea. They're going to find out what we're up to and bounce us out on our ear."

"Oh please. Suck it up, Ms. Ready-for-Anything. You are the most adventurous person I've ever known."

"Adventure is one thing; this is practically fraud. Bea was crazy for suggesting it."

"Don't underestimate Bea. With prospecting, she's got a sixth sense."

"Yes, all hail our almighty stepmother and her sales schemes. Anyway, I'm doing it, all right? But no one said I've got to be happy about it. Bea is a user, but I'm not. And deep down, Nik, you're not either."

"We're not using people. Think of it as making friends. An outstretched hand to an old woman or two. They've got to move sometime, you know. If you happen to run into them as they're making that decision... Oops, gotta run. Dr. Adorable, the head guy, is on his way back. Later."

I shook my head in disbelief, clicked off my cellphone, then stuffed it back into my pocket. How could Nikki and Bea possibly think "working" the senior and disabled markets was ethical? It put them right up there with Henry Potter at Bailey Building and Loan, calling in mortgages on impoverished souls who were learning that perhaps it wasn't such a wonderful life after all.

My characterization wasn't entirely fair, I conceded that. It couldn't have been easy for Bea, losing our dad to pancreatic cancer and providing for two teenagers on her own. Real estate was such a competitive business. Too often, she came home complaining about other agents stealing her clients. Or having wasted days and tankfuls of gas schlepping clients to hundreds of homes, only to have them buy a "For Sale by Owner" and leave her with nothing but a thank you card.

Real estate was her obsession, I got that. But it didn't justify siccing two cash-strapped stepdaughters on feeble, arthritic seniors. More than an "Agent of the Year" plaque, what Bea needed most was the companionship of a nice man who could share her life and, hopefully, her expenses.

Judith had scheduled my orientation for 11:00 AM in the staff lounge, but my hesitation had already made me five minutes late. I braced myself for the worst and pulled open the door.

A few elderly men and women filled the lobby, chatting on cheerful persimmon leather couches, no doubt meant to brighten the building's dour atmosphere. Their faces equally leathery and well lined, they glanced up hopefully as I passed, perhaps momentarily mistaking me for their plump, twenty-something granddaughters. I nodded in response, noting their expressions turning bittersweet, as if swept away by wistful memories of fifty years back when all the options of the world lay at their feet.

Near the staff lounge entrance, I spotted a woman sitting alone in the corner, sniffling as she concentrated on her knitting. I was already late, so what would another few minutes matter? I sidled up next to her and took a seat. "What beautiful colors. Is that going to be a blanket?"

The woman looked up, the unexpected attention eliciting a grateful smile. "Actually, it's going to be a sweater for my grandson. How sweet of you to ask."

"I wish I knew how to knit. I've heard it's very relaxing." Interacting quelled my apprehension. Could this be the essence of the job—making the seniors feel less isolated?

"Miss Quinn?" a voice with an edge called from the lounge door. "We've been waiting."

Judith stood with her arms crossed against her chest. This was not how I'd wanted to begin my employment, displeasing my supervisor before I'd even signed my W-2.

"Better not keep Miss Snippy Pants waiting," the knitter said with a smirk, a conspiratorial gleam in her eye. Clearly she was no stranger to breaking a rule or two. "Come back later," she whispered, holding up her completed rows, "and I'll fill you with *purls* of wisdom." She giggled at her own pun, a signal that at heart, she was much younger than her gray perm and wrinkles might suggest.

"I'll make a point of it," I said, walking toward Judith and the sting of my first reprimand.

The staff lounge was comprised of one tiny room squeezed in between Judith's office and the main recreation area. It was barely large enough to house a supply closet, let alone a folding table surrounded by six chairs. Built-in shelves held a coffee maker along with creamer, sweetener, tea bags, and mugs bearing past fundraising slogans like, "SALAD—Lettuce Squash Hunger!" and "SALAD—Beet Senior Malnutrition." *Subtle.*

Already at the table sat a bespectacled, fidgeting Asian American man who looked about my age, dressed in pastels, a butterscotch fedora on his head, and an orange cravat around his neck. He looked like an anxious, nerdy reject from some hipster art school.

"Carra, this is Hainfroy," said Judith. "He is the Recreational Director and will be your immediate supervisor. I want to take a moment to explain a little about our program. I apologize if this is repetitive, but it's important enough to review a second time."

Hainfroy glared silently in my direction. Did he fear I'd been hired to replace him?

"SALAD has three main avenues of income: government funding, private donations, and the small fees our members pay toward daily transportation and refreshments," she explained. "Losing any of these sources would prove devastating, especially now with county budgets in the red and legislators looking for any opportunity to trim fat."

Judith paused dramatically to emphasize the full import of her warning. "Therefore, we dedicate everything we do here—every activity, every verbal exchange with our members—to keeping them calm, happy, and coming back week after week. We don't encourage outside interests, controversial activities, or anything that might upset the applecart, so take time to review the programming we've painstakingly implemented and decide how you'll divide the workload. When that's done, please come to my office, Carra, and we'll discuss your meal delivery assignments for the rest of the week. Any questions?"

"No, that's fine," I said, donning the illusion of professionalism.

"I'm sure we'll learn to work together successfully under your carefully constructed framework." *Gag.*

"Let's hope so. You'll be on probation for the next three months. Then the position becomes permanent. I'll expect you to be more punctual from here on out. Will that be an issue?"

"No, ma'am."

"I'll leave you to it then." She stood and headed back to her office.

As soon as we were alone, I turned to my new manager. "Hainfroy, it's nice to meet you. Tell me, what do people actually call you?"

"Hainfroy," he said dryly.

"Oh. Sorry." Judging by his tone, he was squarely on Team Judith.

He looked at me askance. "I was an arts and communications major at Ithaca. Exactly what qualifications do you bring to SALAD?"

I hadn't realized I was in for a second interview and it took every ounce of self-restraint not to counter his haughty attitude with a snappy pun like, "I was an English major at Emerson, but that's the tip of the *iceberg*," or "I dunno, I thought I might *toss* my hat into the ring." Instead, knowing I had to make this relationship work if I wanted to keep my job, I gave the submissive route a try.

"Wow. Ithaca. That's impressive. I applied to their creative writing program, but they turned me down."

His eyes narrowed, suspicious of my ploy, but his posturing softened slightly. "Ithaca *is* a competitive school…"

"You must be very talented. I'm sure I'll learn a lot from you."

He straightened his shoulders and pulled back slightly. "I am. And you will. Not that we needed a second person. We've been carrying on fine up to now."

If this was the Wild West of senior care, I was the uninvited newcomer who had obliviously wandered into the local saloon expecting a nod and a beer instead of a roomful of hostile stares. Well, if Hainfroy wanted a gunfight, he'd found one. The key to victory was to convince him I wasn't the new sheriff in town, looking to usurp his position.

"Please don't tell Judith, but I'm quitting as soon as I snag a writing gig," I said, flashing my warmest smile. "In the meantime, I'd be happy to make your daily life easier if you'll let me."

He twisted his mouth in disapproval, but something in his eyes told me he'd welcome the help. He was on the brink. I knew the one question that would push him over.

"Can you share any photos of your work?"

That did it. He drew out his phone faster than Wyatt Earp at the O.K. Corral and scrolled through some of his paintings and sculptures.

"These are quite good, Hainfroy," I said with sincerity, relieved that my earlier, hollow compliments held some validity.

"I guess you can call me Froy, since we're going to be working together. At least for the short term."

"Thank you, Froy. I appreciate that." *One obstacle out of the way.*

Froy opened a folder, revealing a color-coded schedule. "Let's go over the daily activities. Judith doesn't want us to make any changes, just divvy up the work." Then he lowered his voice. "I must warn you though, sometimes it's like grade school around here—cliques, fighting, pranks. You'd think that by seventy, they would have outgrown this stuff."

As Froy reviewed the agenda, I realized to what extent Judith had understated its mundaneness. Just as I'd witnessed the day before, it was simplistic, tedious, and antiquated. Mostly game time, group television viewing, the occasional magician or other uninspired choice of performer. Nothing that would excite anyone. I had to agree with Froy's assessment. One person could easily handle the workload, which begged the question: why had they hired another? Especially when they didn't want to make any changes to the programming?

It was clear the best way to brighten these seniors' lives—and solidify my employment—was to ignore Judith's directives in favor of Aunt Jaime's and add more innovative content that would require a team to administer. Make myself invaluable to the center and its participants and, by doing so, keep the bill collectors at bay. I still had my apprehensions about my co-worker, but I suspected if I convinced him any innovations were his idea, we'd be okay.

"Froy, you're so creative, and this is a great opportunity to make your mark. Together I bet we could make some tiny improvements that everyone would enjoy. When Judith sees how good your ideas make her look, she'll come around, I promise." We brainstormed for a few hours, our plodding progress hampered by Froy's recurrent whines and trepidation. Regardless, I left the staff lounge more confident of my ability to make a difference at SALAD.

Based on all I'd just learned about Judith's micromanagement and inflexibility, I knocked on her door, dreading the second half of my orientation. She invited me in and handed me the addresses of five homes I was to visit every morning after picking up their meal trays from the distribution center. All were located close to my apartment, so it seemed very doable. After deliveries, I'd have a few hours free before assisting

Froy in running the afternoon recreation program.

"You must understand, there are certain do's and don'ts when visiting our clients and they are non-negotiable." I pictured Judith as a peacock, fanning out her plumage, so impressed was she with her own importance. "SALAD limits your job to knocking on clients' doors, handing them their trays, then continuing onto the next delivery. If they don't emerge after a few minutes, knock again, leave the food on the porch, and move on.

"If they answer and make a request, like asking for medication or home repairs, make a note of it and let us know after you complete your rounds. We have people we can send over. Whatever you do, no long chats. You haven't been certified to counsel these seniors or perform maintenance work. We could get sued if unskilled workers give out medication or advice, or cause damage to clients' homes. Is that clear?"

"Crystal." That was that. In November, I'd just have to break the sad news to my stepmother: SALAD prohibited chatting with clients, much less giving out unsolicited real estate advice. She'd be disappointed, but them's the breaks. "Is there anything else I should be aware of when visiting them?"

"Our drivers deliver lunch and dinner, but if anyone asks about breakfast, we've had a budget increase, thanks to Jay Prentiss, and we can now add a box of cereal and milk at the beginning of the week."

The mention of Jay's name aroused visions of dimples I didn't need distracting me at that moment. I thanked Judith for her time, then snuck back into the rec room to observe the center's patrons, especially the women. One of these hobbling older ladies was Jay's nana, and I needed to know which. If I accidentally slighted her, it could mean the end of my SALAD days and the salary I desperately needed until better positions presented themselves.

I walked through the room, smiling at anyone who noticed me while studying their faces and mannerisms. A few introduced themselves and asked who I was looking for. Unfortunately, in the sea of silver, no one displayed the Prentiss dimples nor temper. I guessed the nana search would have to wait until D-Day—the "D" standing for "Dupe"—when I'd be forced to start doing Bea's bidding, if not on my rounds, then at the center.

Chapter Six

Jay pulled into the underground parking garage of his high-rise condo building at exactly 6:00 PM. There was something so satisfying about arriving directly on the hour. Even the leash-tugging war instigated by Solomon's refusal to move hadn't created an unwanted delay. That's because from the day Jay had taken charge of his nana's obstinate bloodhound, he'd started setting his office clock ahead by ten minutes. Forethought always reaped dividends.

As man and dog rode the elevator to the thirty-second floor, Jay shuddered at what awaited him inside his two-bedroom apartment. Adriana would be furious he hadn't picked up the tie for tonight's fundraiser. Senator Mitsky was going to have to settle for the ties Jay already owned. If Roberto Cavalli wasn't good enough for the Mitsker, then he could go pound sand.

Jay hated the compulsory nature of these formal events. Why wasn't a strong work ethic and moral character enough to get into politics? Why did everything revolve around who you knew and who you were willing to turn yourself inside out to impress?

Adriana lived and breathed networking. A political science major at Georgetown who dove into public relations right out of college, she was every aspiring congressman's wet dream. It looked so good on paper. Unfortunately, Jay existed in the three-dimensional world, not the printed page. A world where Adriana had convinced him of the logic of giving her a key to his apartment and, in doing so, had turned his riverfront refuge into a never-ending sparring session.

He wasn't sure why she was rubbing him the wrong way lately. They were both adherents to the "Doggedly Pursue Your Goal" philosophy of life. That's how you got things done. Soulmates, really. And yet...

As he reached for his set of keys his cellphone rang, rerouting an after-hours call made to his office. "Prentiss Elder Law," he answered as Solomon plonked himself down to sleep on the hall carpet.

"Mr. Prentiss, you are a miracle worker!" It was Ms. Dibble.

"Hello, it's so nice to hear from you. How are things going?"

"Siti left late this afternoon. How did you do it?"

He stood stunned, unsure of what to say. "Uh…I have my ways."

"Well, I can't thank you enough, Mr. Prentiss."

He paused a second to regroup. "You're very welcome. I advise you to use this time to get over to your mom's, change the locks, and bring her to the bank first thing tomorrow morning to straighten out her finances. Hopefully your sister hasn't taken much. Her leaving so quickly was fortuitous because suing would have been more difficult, especially if your mom gave her the money willingly."

"I'm sure you're right. How much do I owe you?"

"You don't owe me anything. Take care of your mother, and yourself, and enjoy your time together."

"Thank you," she said, her voice breaking before she hung up the phone.

The call both gladdened and puzzled him because he hadn't done anything yet in the Dibble case. He'd concocted a crazy idea to have his old Princeton roommate call from Vegas and inform Siti she'd won a $10,000 prize in their casino's lottery, but only if she claimed it in person by 10:30 that night. They'd schedule the call so there'd be only an infinitesimal chance she'd make it, based on Vegas flights that were perpetually delayed. It would have been a clear way to test Siti's priorities and establish whether or not her mother's welfare meant more to her than her personal finances.

Greg was all for the idea, but in the end Jay talked himself out of it. Good lawyers didn't pull impulsive pranks, he decided, especially ones that were so risky, inappropriate, and so far outside his comfort zone.

Her leaving suddenly was almost too easy. Let's hope it doesn't come back to bite me in the butt.

Adriana was waiting in the living room, hair up, adorned in a shimmering one-shoulder black gown with a slit up the side—classic politician-wife chic. She held up two ties, one in each hand. Marring the green one was a hideous pattern of lures and multi-colored fish, the other was red with a gold shotgun motif. "I figured you'd forget, so I picked these up. They're no-name brands but I don't suppose that will matter because the design itself will capture his attention. I'd wear the dark gray Brioni with the white Tom Ford shirt."

Jay shook his head as he removed Solomon's leash. The dog trudged into the bedroom, as if looking to separate himself from the argument that was sure to follow. "I don't need you to pick out my wardrobe like I'm some eight-year-old heading off to my first communion. I am perfectly capable of dressing myself, and when I do, I won't be choosing either of those monstrosities. The green one is an eyesore and as for the other, whatever made you think I'd wear anything featuring firearms when I support gun control?"

Adriana didn't budge, nor did her frozen smile. "Honestly, darling, it's not about you and your policies; it's about the senator. I don't think anyone at the dinner will worry that you haven't coordinated your necktie with your political views. You need Senator Mitsky's support if you're going to run for the House next year. He must notice you. We need this."

Right on schedule came the return of the temple-throbbing that accompanied any visit from his girlfriend. Jay crossed in front of Adriana to store the leash in Solomon's drawer alongside his nail clippers and slobber cloths, then loosened his necktie at half-speed—anything to delay their inevitable squabble. His personal life was becoming far more complicated than his elder abuse practice and he was growing tired of the stress.

"It's been a long day. I think I'm going to sit this fundraiser out." He walked past Adriana into the bedroom to hang up his jacket.

Without looking, he pictured her dropped jaw and crossed arms.

"You can't..." she pleaded, trailing after him. "The tickets...they were $500 apiece. We can't not go."

He spun around to find her in the exact position he'd imagined. "Then you go. Convey my regrets. I'm sure you'll carry it off just fine. Why not wear one of these lovely ties?"

She remained silent, no doubt biting her tongue as she debated how far she was willing to escalate this fight. At this point, he really didn't care if she broke things off. It would be a welcome relief, especially if he didn't have to be the one walking away. Ending relationships was not his strong suit.

"Fine," she said after a few beats. "Fine. I'll make your apologies. Bad migraine headache. Took some meds, went to bed early to sleep it off. Do me a favor though. Don't embarrass me by posting on social media tonight. Think you can manage that?"

It seemed like a fair compromise, even with her passive-aggressive delivery. If he couldn't sever the relationship cleanly, at least he could buy himself a few hours of quiet. "Sure thing. I'm going to read, walk the dog one last time, and turn in early."

"Then I guess you won't mind if I spend the night at my apartment."

Threat, ultimatum, or punishment? Jay hesitated before answering. Adriana was treading on thinner ice than she imagined. One or two more moves and she'd fall right through. Still, he didn't have the stomach for any more arguing. Not tonight.

"Whatever you think is best, sweetheart. Have a good time."

She threw the ties on the dining room table and left without another word. The click of the door latch reminded him of the sound of handcuff ratchets springing open as a sense of freedom filled the room.

Chapter Seven

Torrents of rain blurred my windshield as I began my 7:45 AM drive to SALAD's distribution center, located two blocks from their headquarters. It was an early start but not too early to preclude an inspiring text message from my stepmother to "Dig up some leads!" Nor an imploring look from Kiki as she handed me a mug of steaming coffee, accompanied by the electric bill and a rousing pep talk: "I know you expect to hate every part of this job. I hate mine too. But we've got to get on top of these expenses." Nothing like starting a new job by unwrapping a congratulatory gift brimming with expectations and guilt.

The building's gray bricks looked even more depressing against a dismal sky, perfectly reflecting my mood. Volunteers hurriedly dodged raindrops, pushing shopping carts loaded with trays to their cars and loading their trunks with senior sustenance. They looked determined, eager to start their day. A few even stopped mid-scurry to high-five each other. Of course, they were there to feed the homebound, not try to uproot them. I pulled up the hood of my rain slicker and headed out.

The inside of the distribution center hummed with the efficiency of an assembly line. An avuncular-looking Hispanic man, balding and rotund, greeted me by the door. His name badge read, "Hector."

"May I help you, Miss?"

"My name is Carra Quinn. I'm supposed to pick up trays for five seniors." I reached into my pocket and pulled out the list Judith gave me the day before. "These are my drop-offs."

He chuckled. "Not sure I've heard them referred to as drop-offs before. By noon, I think you'll be calling them something else. Can I see some identification, please?"

I pulled out my driver's license. He took it into the back to scan, returning with a cart containing ten trays, along with some miscellaneous boxes. "The red ones are lunches and the blue ones are dinners," he explained as he handed me back my ID. "The other cartons have supplies of cereal and milk that you should keep in your car in case anyone requests them. Also, some bottled water; the elderly get easily dehydrated. Remember, ring the bell, hand them the trays, then move onto your next house. Some of these folks are lonely and will want to chat, so invite them to stop by the center. Tell them we can provide transportation if they need it. Make a note and let me know. But don't hang around, okay?"

SALAD was so anti-lingering they should switch their catchphrase to "Lettuce Leaf Quickly." Swallowing a smirk, I signed a manifest acknowledging I'd accepted the delivery, then pushed the cart back out to my Honda. The shower had passed over, rays of sunlight now streamed through the clouds and reflected off puddles.

I noticed a rainbow in the distance. A superstitious person, like my birth mother, might have read it as a sign. For me, the lack of rain was just one less hassle to complicate my day.

The first stop was three blocks north, over on Ahearn Court. The house had seen better days. Shingles were missing from the roof and the cracks in the driveway resembled a circulatory system carved in asphalt. The once-white fence had grayed, with gaps where pickets were broken or missing. A lone decorative wagon wheel, propped up against the front steps amid a tangle of overgrown grass, screamed of abandonment. I wondered if two months ago, before I'd started the real estate salesperson's course, I would have noticed any of these flaws. Now I couldn't see past them.

I pulled a lunch and dinner couplet from my trunk, along with the manifest to help me address the homeowner by name. Mrs. Michaela Geraghty. Hopefully she'd taken better care of herself than she had of her property. I took a deep breath and rang the bell.

Inside, a walker scraped slowly but audibly against the hardwood floors, so unsurprisingly, it took a few minutes before Mrs. Geraghty cracked open the door. Cigarette fumes, mingled with the musty scent of mold, assailed my nostrils. She was frail and stooped, no taller than 4'11" with translucent skin that revealed the purple network of veins underneath. When she looked up, apprehension shone in her eyes. "Yes?" she rasped in a tobacco-addled voice so strained my heart ached for her efforts.

"I'm Carra Quinn, and I'm delivering food from SALAD. Would you like me to drop it off inside so you don't have to balance the trays while using your walker?"

"That…would…be…nice." Every word exhausted another hard-fought breath, evoking a stream of coughs at the end of each sentence.

I gently pushed open the door and walked gingerly past her toward what I hoped was the kitchen, dodging dust balls the size of tumbleweed in the narrow passageway carved between piles of boxes, papers, and paraphernalia stretching up to the ceiling. It figured that my first stop would have to be a hoarder's house.

"Leave... them... on... the... counter... please."

What counter? Was there a countertop under the pots, pans, and leftovers on either side of the sink, itself overflowing with unwashed dishes and silverware? "You don't want me to leave them in the fridge?" I asked without turning around, shielding her from the concern in my eyes. How did people allow their lives to get so cluttered? Was it an inability to let go of the past?

"It's... broken. The... counter... is... fine."

The thought of an elderly woman living alone in this hovel without a working refrigerator made my face burn. I knew the guidelines—Judith and Hector had made them very clear—but sometimes rules were like clay, meant to be molded to the situation. I wasn't about to leave 8 Ahearn Court without asking a few questions. "Mrs. Geraghty, don't you have anyone who can clean up for you, or call a repairman to fix your fridge?"

"You... are... so... kind... to... ask. The... last... girl... never... did. I'll... be... fine."

The previous volunteer must have been as heartless as the Tin Man. I couldn't sit idly by while Mrs. Geraghty lived in squalor, which made my next decision an easy one. "If I come back over the weekend and clean up a little, would that be okay with you?" I asked, resting my hand on her hunched shoulder.

She looked up at me, her eyes glistening. "That... would... be... wonderful. Thank... you."

"I'll come by Saturday, around ten? Have a good day and enjoy the meals, Mrs. Geraghty. I'll see you tomorrow."

I heard her whisper, "God... bless... you." as I let myself out.

Who cares if I won't have time to write or look through the classifieds on Saturday, I rationalized as I walked back to my car. I'll ask Kiki to help, lighten the load. And Bea must have a handyman or two on speed dial who wouldn't mind doing some pro-bono work in exchange for all the referrals she'd thrown them over the years. No one at SALAD needed to know.

It started to drizzle again as I drove to my next destination, over on Walters Lane. Janet Scott, according to the manifest. I hoped the meeting would prove less heart-wrenching than the Geraghty episode, especially since this house, a Colonial with Tudor trim, looked to be in much better condition.

The surrounding chain-link fence bore a "Beware of Dog" sign in bold, crimson letters that made my heart palpitate. I didn't hear any barking when I knocked; however, a good sign for a terrified volunteer who had been bitten as a child. A red-headed woman in an electric wheelchair answered the door. Age spots discolored what had clearly been a beautiful face in her youth.

"I'm assuming you must be from SALAD?" she said in a British accent. "I'm Janet. Come, get out of the wet. Follow me, and I'll show you where to leave those trays."

She motored through the living room toward a modern kitchen, replete with granite countertops and oak cabinets. Again, my training reared its ugly head, transforming my inner dialogue into a real-estate classified, accompanied by visions of a drooling Bea.

"This is a lovely house," I said, noting the lack of dust and clutter as I placed the trays on an empty shelf in the Sub Zero. But I couldn't help noticing the picture frames scattered in both the kitchen and living room, featuring the loving faces of a brace of golden retrievers. Large doggie cushions filled two corners of each room. "Your dogs are so beautiful."

"They were, yes," said Janet, wistfully. "I lost them last year, right after my husband passed. Social Services convinced me that between the accident that put me in this chair and my depression, they were too much for me to handle on my own. It has been a very trying time all around."

"I'm so sorry for your loss." And I was. I imagined living in this big house all alone, longing for the voices and activity that had once filled each room. The dogs, had they remained, might have alleviated her depression.

"It's such a large house. Have you ever thought of…?" I tried to force out the word "downsizing" so I could honestly tell Bea I had tried for the listing, but my better judgement prevailed.

She cruised over to my side, seemingly oblivious to my unfinished sentence. "Their names were Fallon and Carson, like *The Tonight Show* hosts. They were our children. Keith and I took them everywhere. Such clowns, always trying to make everyone laugh."

I leaned against the counter, not sure what to say or do. Grief and loneliness clouded her eyes, and I longed to suggest something to make her whole. "Is there anything you can do to get them back?"

"I tried, believe me. Once I came out of my funk I called the animal shelter, but some Connecticut family with three kids had already adopted them." She looked down at her lap. "At night, I ask God to watch over them and make sure their new family is treating them right."

I sensed she was tearing up, and now I had an inkling why Judith and Hector had been so adamant about not hanging around to chat with the clients. My comments may have stirred up dormant feelings and worsened an already shaky situation. I needed to make a graceful exit without appearing rude or disinterested.

"Dogs are the best," I lied, recalling the strength of their jaws and the sharpness of their teeth. "I have to finish my rounds, but next time I'd love to hear more."

Damn, that wouldn't draw any boundaries. Apparently I sucked at this distancing stuff. Still, I could justify the discussion because while deepening relationships wasn't in SALAD's playbook, it certainly was in Bea's. Wasn't I here working for both?

"That would be lovely. I'll make tea next time, and we'll have a chinwag." Janet's words oozed hope. She needed more than a meal delivery. She needed a friend. Then I remembered something helpful Judith mentioned during orientation.

"Janet, I work at SALAD's senior center every afternoon, helping to run an activities program. We provide transportation. Why don't I have you picked up tomorrow? We can talk more then."

She beamed. "That's a wonderful idea. I'll give you my number. That way, you can let me know what time I should be ready."

Janet's smile warmed my soul. Maybe I wasn't so terrible at this after all.

My third and fourth stops of the day were less eventful. There were notes on the door instructing the SALAD driver to leave the trays on the porch, ring the bell, and leave. It felt a little off-putting after the kindness expressed at the previous stops, but I complied with their wishes. My fifth and final visit was to Mr. Simon Garrison on Putnam Court. Like Janet's Tudor, Garrison's home was one that would make Bea salivate, an adorable Cape with a well-maintained exterior, like a little dollhouse. He opened the door before I could even knock, and his effusiveness was almost overwhelming.

"Is it SALAD time already? I guess it is! Welcome!"

"Grandpa, Grandpa, SALAD time, SALAD time!" cried two twin toddlers who ran up to me, each hugging a leg.

Garrison didn't look like he'd passed up many SALAD trays. He must have weighed over 450 pounds, and he waddled rather than walked. He lured the kids away with the promise of fudge, allowing me to make my way into his kitchen to drop off my delivery.

"Grandpa is going to read us *Alice in Wonderland* today on his phone!" Moppet Number One jumped with excitement.

I knelt to address the speaker on his own level. "How fun! Books are my favorite thing." *If only I could revise and sell one.*

"Oh yes, really fun," added his not-as-eloquent sister. "In *Alice in Wumberwand*, there are wabbits and queens and cats and caterpiwars. But I wish Grandpa wed to us instead."

Simon turned red and looked away. "I play them the recording of the book off Audible on my cell. They like the different voices and sound effects. Would you like to join us?"

"That sounds wonderful, but I have to head back to the center. Can I do anything for you? Set up an optometrist appointment, perhaps?"

The second the words left my mouth I knew they'd been a mistake. Simon's face turned even redder, and I suddenly realized that perhaps the problem wasn't his eyesight, it might be that he didn't know how to read. The last thing I'd meant to do to this pleasant man was embarrass him. Time to regroup.

"As long as you're downloading from Audible, I recommend *Harriet the Spy*. It was one of my favorites growing up. And now, unfortunately, I must run. Enjoy your grandfather, kids, and the recording. Say hi to Alice for me."

I pushed back a wave of nausea and sprinted to my car. Now I understood even better the importance of maintaining my emotional distance. There must be some way to help Simon Garrison, so he could read and understand the world around him and become closer with his grandkids. But how, until he admitted to his illiteracy? I started the car and prayed none of my morning's missteps would come back to haunt me.

My cellphone rang as I pulled into SALAD's parking lot. So predictable.

"So?"

"So what, Bea?"

"So, did you deliver the food?"

"Yes, I did. Thanks for asking." I continued stringing her along, waiting, waiting…

"So?"

"So…?"

"Are any of them interested in selling?" Ah, there it was. Right on schedule.

"You wouldn't want to list any of these," I lied, conveniently forgetting that two of the three houses I'd been inside would probably attract a lot of buyer interest. "They're mostly in disrepair. Remember, these people can't maneuver around well enough to get to the supermarket, much less fix up their houses. And my guess is, even if they could pick up their own food, most wouldn't be able to afford it."

"An even better reason for them to move someplace smaller, more manageable. Don't kid yourself, fixer-uppers attract investors like flies. Try again. Three months goes by quickly. You're going to want to sock away some money. The best way to do that is to pick up a few listings."

Where was a wall to bang your head against when you needed one? She meant well, and I was grateful for her help, but how was I going to tolerate another ninety days of *Bea-siegement*? "Nice chatting, but I have to get going. My shift's about to start."

"Work on those folks, Carra. I can't subsidize you forever."

"Love you too. Bye."

When I reached the recreation area, it became clearer why they had hired an assistant. The room was more crowded than the previous day, teeming with silver hair and polyester. Fifty or more seniors huddled in small groups, bent over jigsaw puzzles and games of Gin Rummy, Checkers, Scrabble, and Backgammon. Sixties soft rock streamed through an iPhone attached to a speaker. Froy was running around as if his purple pork-pie hat were on fire, handing out cups of fruit punch.

I stopped him long enough to evoke an eye roll worthy of a diva in distress. "Hey, Froy, here I am, right on time, and I'm excited to start what we talked about yesterday. Where's the equipment?"

He pointed to the front of the room. "Everything's where you asked, but I don't think this is going to work, Carra," he rambled, face flushed. "We should reconsider. They're already involved. I'm not sure we can—"

I refused to forego my big introduction because Froy was risk averse. If we permitted the seniors to remain ensconced in their own activities, there wouldn't be much of a job left for me. They had to need me as badly as I needed the salary.

"I know it's hokey, but it's worth a try, right? If it fails, you can claim I blindsided you, and I'll back you one hundred percent. None of the blame will fall your way."

Blissful ignorance clearly appealed to Froy's survival instinct. He nodded and returned to pouring juice, albeit in a less frenzied fashion.

I sucked in a calming breath and walked to the front of the room. I'd spent half the night mentally rehearsing this scenario. A lot hinged on the next few minutes. If I fell on my face, figuratively or otherwise, I'd lose credibility with Judith, Froy, and most crucially, with the crowd. I took out my cellphone and substituted it for the one now playing the instrumental version of *Nights in White Satin*. Then I hit play.

As Pharrell Williams' *Happy* blared over the speaker, I grabbed one of the two hula-hoops Froy put out for me and started twirling it around my upper arm. Slowly, members raised their bifocals from game boards to watch the show. I repositioned the hoop around my waist and started swiveling it while singing and snapping my fingers. Then I added a second one and gyrated my hips while keeping both in play.

Applause filled the room. A few seniors stood and shuffled back and forth to the beat. When the song finished, they cheered for more.

Slightly winded, I fought to catch my breath as I unplugged my phone from the speaker and switched on a cordless microphone. The room quieted as an expectant audience waited to hear what I'd do for an encore. I noticed Judith staring from the back of the room but couldn't decipher her take.

"Hello everyone! I'm Carraway Quinn, your new assistant recreational aide, and thank you all for that wonderful welcome. I guess those hours spent jumping through *hoops* to graduate college have finally paid off. So now I'll be seeing how I can help a-*round* here." The audience groaned. "Bad, right? But I assure you, my intentions are better than my puns. Hainfroy and I want to make the recreation program an even more exciting part of your lives. But we need your help. Tell us what activities you'd like to see us run at SALAD. Wave your hand if you have a suggestion, and I'll bring the mic around."

The room buzzed with seniors murmuring among themselves, but none thrust their hands into the air. It was clear that up to now, no one had bothered asking any of the patrons what they wanted, and they were unsure of how to react. Seconds passed and seemed to stretch into hours. My stomach fell as I stood there waiting, my face growing hot. Judith's mouth turned downward, her brow furrowing. Even Froy focused on his juice cups, mentally separating himself from the debacle. But I was in no mood to accept defeat.

"Anyone, really. Every idea is welcome. And the first five people to share their ideas will get a special prize I'll bring tomorrow." The mention of unauthorized awarding of gifts prompted Froy to cease his punch pouring.

Even Judith raised an eyebrow. Ugh, I'd have to figure out something tonight. A few books? Or some cookies? Unless reading was difficult for them. Or they suffered from diabetes and avoided added sugar. Oh God, what had I gotten myself into?

I noticed one withered, upraised hand to my left. I recognized the plucky respondent as the knitter who befriended me during my orientation. She sat alone on the couch, wearing a stylish vintage Chanel jacket and skirt. I wondered if her apparent wealth was the reason no one else sat nearby. Were the others shunning her out of jealousy? I walked the mic over and held it near her mouth as the room quieted to hear one brave person's response.

"Hello, sweetheart. I'm Helen Sutherland. We've spoken before. Guess you got the job." She winked, flashing a playful glint from behind tortoiseshell frames.

"Hello. Helen, thanks for being the first to raise your hand. What programs would you like to see us implement?" The audience buzzed again, so I cleared my throat into the mic to cut the rudeness. "I'm sure all your fellow members are eager to hear."

"I'd like to see us do more things as a group, like put on a show, or volunteer at a soup kitchen to help others less fortunate than ourselves."

"Those are wonderful ideas, Helen." And they were. My mind was already considering the possibilities.

She pushed the mic aside for a private word. "Don't worry yourself about the prize, honey. It's unnecessary—but fast thinking on your part." Another wink. At least I had one ally at SALAD.

Once Helen broke the ice, others followed, suggesting book clubs, game tournaments, excursions to local attractions like the zoo. The temperature of the room soared, fueled by the crowd's pent-up desire for variety.

The one naysayer determined to pierce the positivity was Blanche Schmidt, a scowling woman with a pinched brow and a sigh on perpetual loop. Blanche countered every suggestion with, "That won't work," and "I don't much care for that." Where had I heard such negativity before? Had I accidentally stumbled upon Jay Prentiss's beloved nana?

Luckily, the enthusiastic crowd drowned out Blanche's contrariness, at least until Judith slithered over and unceremoniously removed the microphone from my hand.

"Ladies and gentlemen, we appreciate your suggestions. The activities committee will take all these recommendations under consideration when planning next year's schedule. Thank you again." Then she turned off the mic and addressed me privately. "Please report to my office during your break. In the meantime, no more surprise announcements."

My spirit wilted as I watched her leave the room. It had gone so well. What was her problem? Was my job on the line even before the end of my first day?

Froy edged up beside me as the seniors returned to their individual endeavors. "That was impressive, Carra. I've never seen these people so engaged. Where did you pick up those mad hula-hoop skills?"

I shrugged. "Just something I used to do when I got bored as a kid." I gestured toward the departed Judith with a tilt of my head. "What do you think got into her craw?"

"She's kind of a control freak. You need to run everything by her before it happens."

"Why didn't you tell me that yesterday, when we discussed this approach?"

He looked past me. "I guess I didn't think she'd be observing when you did it. She almost never is."

He appeared earnest, but perhaps I'd been too trusting. From this point forward, I'd think twice before confiding in anyone connected with SALAD. I helped Froy hand out the juice cups, anything to keep my mind off Judith and my scheduled scolding. The seniors were very receptive, asking about my background and previous jobs. I chatted about Emerson and my writing ambitions.

"Excuse me, Miss Carra?" An African American woman playing Parcheesi with her friends beckoned. "My name is Georgia Martin. I overheard you mention something about being an aspiring author. I'd love to write a memoir, leave my legacy behind, but I'm not sure where to start. Can you teach us?"

"Sure, great idea. Let's discuss it tomorrow…" My voice trailed off with the "if I'm still working here" left unspoken.

A memoir writing class, I mused. What an easy, affordable idea. Not to mention a way to keep my skills sharp, even if I wasn't using them to revise my manuscript as editors had requested. And the memories! How could they fail to resurrect some happiness into each of these seniors' lives?

Once my break rolled around, I marched toward Judith's office, a convicted felon bound for the firing squad. I knocked twice, and Judith's strident tone invited me in.

"What was that all about?" she started before I could even take the seat across from her. "Prizes? Excursions? Not only did I warn you we had methodically planned our programs—and they were to remain unchanged—but even if we did choose to enhance them, where would we come up with the funds?"

I scrambled for an answer as she sat back in her chair, shaking her head and looking up at the ceiling, as if God would provide a clue.

"I plan to bring in the prizes myself. Little knick-knacks I can pick up at Odd Lot. The excursions…what if we charged a small fee?"

"Many of our members can barely afford to come here, much less cover the cost of field trips. Now that you've raised their expectations, we're going to take a hit when we disappoint them. I guess

I should have mentioned this. Oh wait, I did. Repeatedly."

Her sneer reduced me to the size of a chess pawn, redoubling my determination to stand my ground. This was now about more than just a salary. These older people needed something to animate the few years they had left. Their exuberance over a simple hula-hoop dance proved that a little innovation at SALAD could go a long way. Frankly, there was something addictive about their applause and appreciation. It was nice to feel needed, maybe for the first time ever.

"Don't worry. I swear I won't let the center lose face, and I won't disillusion our guests."

Judith lifted a single eyebrow. "How, exactly?"

"I'm more resourceful than you imagine. Give me a week, and I'll set things straight."

Chapter Eight

"So how are you going to fix it?" my sister asked after I described the fiasco of my first day at SALAD.

She'd stopped by the apartment for a joint debriefing while Kiki listened and commiserated. Discussing SALAD while making salad—classic. I stooped over my veggies, looking down partly so I wouldn't chop off a finger and partially because I didn't want to reveal the uncertainty in my eyes.

"I stopped by the five-and-dime and picked up a few prizes. Colorful kitchen magnet sets, less than three dollars apiece, and I figured they'll be perfect for hanging grandchildren's pictures on the fridge."

Kiki was unimpressed. "Great, that's fifteen dollars you can't contribute to the rent this month."

"I'll be short more than that if I lose this job, so it's money well spent." I put down the knife, desperate to redirect the conversation. "How was your day at the rehab center, Nikki?"

"Not as bad as I'd feared. The patients are grateful and the director—who's the spitting image of Chris Hemsworth—seems to appreciate my help. Not that I'm doing much, just taking medical histories, filing papers, and a little candy striper activity like going room to room, handing out books. I asked a few people if they needed to move to one-level homes. One sounded interested."

"You felt no guilt?" I found it hard to believe she was so brazen about taking advantage of people in dire straits.

"Not in the least. I'm not forcing them out of their homes. I'm offering options. Nothing underhanded about any of that."

I sighed. Nikki and I had different opinions on the matter.

"Back to your dilemma. How are you going to implement those programs you got everyone so excited about?" Nikki understood the value of deflection and that the best defense was a strong offense.

I returned my gaze to the cucumbers and tomatoes. "I love the idea of a formal dance, and it doesn't have to be pricey. No need to hold it at night, it can be a teatime affair in the rec room. I'll download some seventies and eighties ballads and turn the lights down. Hang some crepe paper banners. You both can help." I glanced over my shoulder to gauge their reactions.

Kiki pursed her lips. "How did I get roped into the decorations committee?"

"Oh, that's nothing. You're also coming to Mrs. Geraghty's on Saturday. We're going to clean up her house a little."

"Why is that?"

"Because I promised, Kiki. Well, I promised my help, but I know that do-gooder heart of yours won't let me go it alone."

"Nothing like using my altruism against me."

"Ayn Rand says there's no such thing as altruism. We do good things because of the benefit we derive from them. Like feeling self-satisfied. So I'm actually doing you a favor. You'll come, right? I can't do it alone, and if you saw how she's living…"

"Yeah, I'll go."

I looked over at Nikki, wondering if she'd make it unanimous.

"Not me. I promised Bea I'd help her sort through some files. But you two enjoy."

"I'm sure it will be heaven on earth." My spear of guilt proved no match for her shield of apathy, so I chose another tactic. "I want to pick your brains. Most of my ideas are affordable: the dance, some easy-to-organize game tournaments with cheap prizes. Someone even suggested a memoir-writing class. What I'd love to organize though, are some excursions, but I can't figure out how to fund them. If we do one a quarter, I think that's more than enough. But I checked out bus rental costs and entrance fees. Each outing would run around $1,000 for a group of fifty."

My sister raised a brow. "That's money you really don't have. Maybe Bea would spring for it. Especially since this whole thing was her idea." *Ah Nikki, the eternal optimist.*

"I called and asked her. She said sure, as long as I took it as an advance on my salary. So no, she won't *Bea-queath* the funds."

"Sounds like you'll have to think of something to line up some donations," Kiki said.

Donations. A lightbulb blinked and a possible benefactor came to mind. The meeting might be unpleasant and require a bit of courage, but the most worthwhile quests always did. I reached for my phone and searched for contact information.

Chapter Nine

Jay glared at the intimidating number of case files mounting on his desk. They were all color-coded and stacked in chronological order of appointment date, just the way he liked them. If only there were fewer of them. Mr. and Mrs. Moehrie were awaiting the final draft of their will. The Zellers wanted to discuss their long-term care options. Mrs. Parks was still searching for an appropriate memory care facility for her Alzheimer's-addled mother. And Eddie Rios was hot to sue his late father's nursing home for homicidal negligence. So when the intercom buzzed and interrupted his train of thought, Jay's entire body grew rigid.

"Mr. Prentiss, there's a Carra Quinn here to see you." Meggie's sultry voice dripped like melted chocolate, making every comment sound like a proposition.

He thumped the intercom button as if the extra force might convey his irritation to the unwelcome visitor. "Sorry, I'm not seeing anyone without an appointment today."

A minute passed. "Mr. Prentiss, she says she works at SALAD, and it's about your nana."

Jay's skin prickled. If this concerned his grandmother it couldn't wait. "Okay, send her in."

His office door swung open almost before he finished his sentence. This intruder evidently did not take instruction well, and that alone revved up the throbbing in his temple. But since this was his nana's caregiver, he swallowed his exasperation and invited her to take a seat.

Jay was unaccustomed to women like the one now facing him, clad in a red-and-black-checkered blouse hanging over a pair of black jeans. Unlike the chic, slender, expensively dressed ladies who usually filled his world, this girl looked like she'd just jumped off a hayride. Ginger curls framed her plump cheeks, reminding him of a redheaded Kelly Clarkson, a singer he'd noticed the few times he'd watched *The Voice* with his nana. There was an attractiveness about her, he had to admit, but only if you were planning a date to McDonald's, followed by a pilgrimage to the local Walmart.

"So, Miss…Quinn, is it? You said you had some information about my grandmother?"

"It's Ms. Quinn, actually. And it is about your nana, though indirectly. I'm the new recreational aide at SALAD. And honestly, whoever designed their programming lacked even one ounce of creativity. I'm sure it bores your nana as much as the other visitors there. I want to introduce a slew of unique activities, but it's going to take more than their budget will allow. Word is that you are one of SALAD's most generous donors, and I thought if I came here directly and explained some of my plans, you might be willing to help."

Jay stifled a laugh. "I appreciate your initiative, but I'm afraid I only deal with the big-picture items, like getting a new wing built or organizing large fundraisers. I don't involve myself in the everyday minutia of running the place." He noted her eyes, light green. Practically hypnotic, especially when flashing with indignation like right now. You almost never see women with green eyes, he mused.

"Perhaps it's that 'minutia' you *should* involve yourself with. What is it you do here, anyway?"

He pulled back, surprised by the affront. This little firecracker didn't pull any punches, did she? It was hard to take umbrage, though, when his attacker looked like she'd just walked off the set of *Hee-Haw*.

"I protect the well-being of the elderly. Make sure they're not being taken advantage of so they can enjoy the best quality of life in their old age."

Carra shook her head, and her cheeks grew red. "Maybe it's time you started looking a little more closely at their everyday lives, get your neatly manicured hands dirty."

Jay snuck a peek at his fingernails, wondering what they had done to incite her fury.

"Look, I know the SALAD Center is a pet project of yours and it's where your nana spends her days. But these seniors didn't work hard all their lives to waste their golden years piecing together puzzles and playing cards. Yet, it's the best programming Judith Ferester has to offer. Do you think that's adequate or does it make a mockery of your fundraising efforts? Is that what you want for your grandmother, to waste her days twiddling her thumbs?"

He leaned forward, shaking his head, concern replacing amusement.

"And that's only part of the problem. I deliver lunch and dinner trays to homebound seniors before I start my shift. There's one woman who's a hoarder. Her home is filled with dust balls the size of Oklahoma and boxes stretching up to the ceiling that could topple over at any moment and crush her. Her fridge is history, so the trays I bring her go bad in the heat. Will your extra wing keep her food chilled? I don't think so. But I'm heading over there Saturday with some friends and hopefully an appliance repair person to see if we can help."

Jay tried to respond, but Carra didn't give him the opportunity to get a word in edgewise.

"Then there's this woman in a wheelchair who can barely make it through the day, she's so lonely for the dogs Social Services convinced her to give away. I've asked SALAD's transport department to add her to their daily route, but I'm not sure that's the answer. What if once she arrives, the programming bores her to tears? How will checkers fill the void in her heart?"

At this point, Jay didn't even bother to interrupt her emotional outburst, figuring that eventually she'd have to pause to take a breath.

"Finally, there's this obese man who babysits his grandkids, but he plays them stories on Audible because I don't think he can read. Will your thirty-thousand-foot overview help implement a literacy program at SALAD? Because that's what I intend to do, with or without your help."

Overwhelmed by her passionate argument, Jay was dazed. Women did not talk to him like this. Ones like Adriana tried to control him, but they never scolded him. Yet, when Carra stood to leave, her body still shaking, he wanted to make sure she understood his inaction wasn't out of heartlessness but a lack of time.

"Please, sit back down for a moment," he said, indicating the chair. "From what I understand, you're not supposed to engage with the clients. So how do you know all this?"

"I don't engage with them," she answered sharply. "But when I drop off their food, if they're using walkers or wheelchairs, I feel bound to leave the trays in the kitchen. The cleaning? That's on my time, not SALAD's. Is it illegal for me to volunteer my own time to help people? I think not. So, back to my question, are you comfortable with the status quo of these people's daily minutia, as you described it?"

"No...I...I...I guess not," he said, unsure of where those words came from; they were definitely not the ones he'd intended. The one thing he did know was that her fervent intensity was eliciting more from him than just outrage over programming and worry over his nana.

"You'll help then?" She shot him a look that reminded him of when he was six, a Little Leaguer whose indoor batting practice broke his nana's favorite vase.

"Well...I...I suppose I could join you on your morning rounds and see the situation for myself. And when I have less on my plate, I'd love to hear your plans for improving the center. Would that be fair?"

What the hell. Jay Prentiss prosecuted elder abusers. He stared down weaselly relatives trying to swindle impaired parents and grandparents out of their life savings. Jay Prentiss did not ask farm girls who'd hustled their way into his office if what he was proposing was fair. He must be suffering from an aneurysm.

Carra looked slightly taken aback, as if his acquiescence genuinely surprised her. He silently scored her reaction as a tiny victory for the good guys. Because he was a good guy, no matter what she might think. He had to find a way to prove it to her, though he hadn't the foggiest idea why that had suddenly become so important to him.

She looked him squarely in the eye. "Will you come tomorrow morning? My route starts at eight o'clock at the distribution center. You can follow along in your...whatever. Tesla? Mercedes?"

It was the first time he'd heard those brands spoken of with a sneer instead of with reverence. Or jealousy. Carra Quinn was certainly an odd duck. Or was she a breath of fresh air? The jury was out.

"Lexus, actually," he said with a touch of embarrassment. Again, what the hell? Was he supposed to apologize for working twelve-hour days, seven days a week?

"Why don't I meet you there and tag along?" he suggested. "That way, you can share your insights into each of the seniors before we arrive. I promise I won't say a word while we're there. Just observe."

She pursed her lips for a moment. "I guess that would be okay. It's important that you understand, and if I can make that happen it's worth a little chauffeuring. I drive a white Honda Civic. The license plate is *Car-Away*. So I'll see you at 8:00 AM tomorrow?"

"Yeah, I'll walk Solomon a little earlier than usual."

Carra bristled. "Is that the giant bloodhound in the lobby?"

"It is."

"He's a little off-putting to visitors. Some of your clients might be frightened of dogs."

Jay scoffed. "Solomon scare someone? He wouldn't hurt a fly. And he barely raises his head off that doggie bed unless there's food to steal."

"All I'm saying is some of us aren't comfortable with giant, erratic canines running loose in legal offices. But you do what you want, it's your lawsuit waiting to happen. See you tomorrow."

And with that, she sashayed out of his office, flaunting her indignation like a brightly colored scarf.

Jay gazed at the door long after it closed behind her. Who speaks to complete strangers that way? Who doesn't love bloodhounds? Who in the world was Carra Quinn? For reasons that eluded him, he couldn't wait to find out.

Chapter Ten

After the encounter with Jay, I sprinted back to my car to decompress. I hated when fury got the best of me or I spewed words without thinking. Having seen his temper in action, I'd come in more guarded than usual, despite my attention drifting to those chiseled features and adorable dimples. He was even better looking up close. I prayed my anger had masked my fascination.

Had I come off as bitchy? Did I really care what he thought?

That enormous hound in the reception area had compounded my nervousness. My last encounter with a dog that size hadn't ended well. I still had the scars on my arms and legs as a souvenir. Dogs had no business in the workplace, especially offices frequented by the public, and I felt justified in telling him so.

What if he reported me to Judith? Upsetting a big donor like Jay Prentiss would surely mean the end of my employment and my salary, meager as it was.

Granted, it wouldn't exactly be the worst thing in the world to spend the morning with him. When he wasn't ranting about insignificant issues, there was something calming about Jay. His aura made me feel protected, secure. Maybe it was that he was older and more established than the men in my past.

Just thinking about the others made my throat constrict. Relationships were suffocating. Could that be why I felt safe with Jay? The knowledge I wasn't his type nixing any chance of a romance blooming between us?

I snarfed down my lunch—a two-dollar energy bar—and headed over to the center. I had a new activity planned, and the best part was it left Judith nothing to complain about. The notebooks and pens I had stacked in my trunk—all donated by yours truly—meant the program wouldn't cost SALAD a penny.

~ * ~

The recreation room was packed as usual. I lugged in the stack of notebooks and the boxes of pens weighing down my handbag. After dumping everything onto the front table, I pocketed the cordless mic and set off to confront Froy. He had sequestered himself in a corner, immersed in paperwork, and conveniently ignoring the hubbub around him.

"Hey, how are you doing?" I asked when he finally lifted his head and acknowledged my presence.

"Not well, I got a severe chewing out yesterday from Judith, all thanks to you. She—"

"Is she here today?"

"No, she's off at some planning meeting. But I promised—"

I turned and walked toward the front of the room, cutting him off mid-sentence. I was going off the grid and it was easier to beg for forgiveness than ask for permission. When Jay's money started rolling in, Judith wouldn't dare say a word.

I switched on the mic, wincing for a moment from the feedback until I walked a few steps from the speaker. At least the noise got their attention. "Ladies and gentlemen, good afternoon!"

Seniors bobbed their heads up from gin games and poker hands. Murmurs ceased. I figured they were curious. Would the crazy new girl top her hula-hoop performance with something equally bizarre? I had everyone's attention, even Froy's, though consternation brewed in his eyes. It was go time.

"I have an exciting new project in store for the more adventurous of you. Many here may not have heard I'm an aspiring author. I majored in English at Emerson with a concentration in creative writing, and I'm currently pitching my manuscript to agents and publishers." That part was true. No need to mention the mounting yet neglected requests for revision.

"I had a wonderful conversation with Georgia Martin yesterday." I sought out her face and smiled. "She explained that many of you have life stories you're eager to share with your children and grandchildren. That's why I'm going to start a memoir-writing class right here in a corner of the recreation room. We'll meet daily, and tomorrow we'll start by discussing some writing techniques. Anyone wishing to participate please raise your hands, so I can set up the correct number of chairs."

I'd expected five or ten to respond. When twenty-five people's hands shot up, my heart skipped a beat. Ding, ding, ding, we found a winner!

"Okay, please keep those hands up. I'll hand out pads and pens so you can take notes, and if I run short today, don't worry, I'll bring more tomorrow. Please remember to put your names on the front in case your pad is misplaced. Class starts at 1:00 PM sharp. Hainfroy, can you please help me distribute the materials?"

Froy looked shocked that I'd dared to involve him. He shook his head, pointed to his watch as if to signal he was late for some big, important meeting, then scrambled off. Self-preservation at its finest. How long did I have before he'd report me to Judith? Silently, I prayed Jay's donation would reach her desk before the axe fell.

I handed out the materials myself, thrilled at the comments thrown my way: "What a wonderful idea, Carra!" "I can't wait to start!" "Do you think my life would interest anyone? I haven't done anything that momentous."

That last question was the one I was best prepared to answer. I maneuvered to the front of the room and again switched on the mic. "Excuse me for interrupting, but a lovely lady has just asked: 'What if I haven't done anything great? Should I still write a memoir?' That's a question you might be asking yourself, to which I answer, has everything in your life been smooth sailing? Or have you had to overcome a few obstacles here and there? Because your solutions may inspire others."

Conversations hummed, so I continued my semi-spontaneous sermon as I walked from table to table, directing my remarks to skeptical-looking individuals. "Have you known love in your life? Wouldn't the origins of those deep feelings enthrall others? What did you dream about in your youth? How did you make those dreams come true? And if they haven't yet materialized, are you still trying?

"Everyone has a story worth telling. Everyone has a history worth sharing. I want to help you put yours on paper."

Georgia stood unsteadily and clapped. One by one, others joined in her applause, and my face grew warm. I wasn't a theater major; I rarely coveted the spotlight. But witnessing the sadness of those on my meal delivery route sparked a desire to reinvigorate seniors like these, fan a flame of excitement lacking in their lives. Their reaction proved I had struck a collective nerve.

Amidst the cheers and applause, I saw Helen Sutherland, clad in another vintage designer knit suit, sitting alone as usual. She waved, then left the room, knitting bag in hand. I don't think she knew I was still watching because as she passed a vacated table, she swiped a gin scoresheet and stuck it in her bag.

Strange. But not so odd as to keep me from enjoying the room's enthusiastic response.

Nothing could stop me now—as long as I kept Froy and Judith

at bay, persuaded Jay to drum up some funds, covered the rent, and convinced Bea not to dislodge seniors from their residences. Other than that, I was home free.

Chapter Eleven

Solomon was not amused when Jay attempted to rouse him for an earlier-than-usual walk so he could accompany Carra on her rounds. He raised his head, sniffed indignantly, then rolled onto his side. Time to pull out the big guns, which in this case, was a handful of Beggin Strips. A sucker for the scent of bacon, Solomon sprang to life and permitted Jay to put on his collar and leash while he chomped on the treat.

They walked two blocks along the river instead of their usual three, again inciting a disparaging look from Solomon who, like his owner, was a stickler for routine. Afterward, Jay poured the hound his morning kibble and rushed to wash and find something appropriate to wear. Versace seemed an inconsiderate choice when visiting people on social security receiving subsidized meals. He could always change into a suit when he returned to pick up Solomon.

At the back of his closet hung a pair of worn Levi's, the one piece of informal clothing he'd refused to discard after college because of the memories they held. He topped it with a white Ralph Lauren shirt, but left the top button open.

Though it clashed with his attempt at a relaxed appearance, Jay splashed on the rich citrus and cypress notes of Eau d'Hadrien, certain that someone like Carra wouldn't recognize the scent, which ran close to $450 an ounce. A three-month anniversary gift from Adriana. He realized he hadn't given his supposed girlfriend a second thought since their tiff over the ties.

Jay pushed his guilt aside and stared into the mirror at what he hoped reflected a modestly dressed volunteer. Would Carra agree, he wondered, then caught himself. What was he thinking? She was a kid, brought up God knows where. What did she really understand about his world? Or was he inferring too much from one red-and-black-checkered shirt? Still, first impressions and all that...

I guess I'll learn more about the real Carra today. The thought evoked a tiny smile that he also caught in the mirror and quickly wiped off his face.

SALAD's distribution center was a ten-minute drive from his condo, and once Jay arrived he noted that the building's exterior perfectly matched the dreariness of yet another overcast day. He located Carra's white Civic and leaned against it, attempting to look nonchalant while trying to figure out what to do with his hands. He stuck them into his pockets and waited.

When she emerged, arms laden with red and blue trays, she gave him a nod, and he debated whether he should bolt up the ramp and offer to lighten her load. But by the time he decided, she was halfway to the car, so he made himself useful by popping open the trunk.

"Good morning, Ms. Quinn. How are you this lovely day?" He wanted to kick himself as soon as the words left his lips. Instead of sounding cool, he'd come across like a chimneysweep out of *Mary Poppins*, greeting the gentry as they passed.

Carra gave him the once-over and arched an eyebrow. "Nice kicks."

He glanced at his feet and sighed, realizing that while he'd dressed down his main apparel, he was still wearing a pair of Ferragamo sneakers. "They're comfortable…"

She slammed the trunk and unlocked the car doors with a click of her smart key. "You don't have to apologize for having nice things. I'm sure you worked hard for them." Was she throwing him a bone? What kind of topsy-turvy, upside-down world was this?

He wasn't sure how to respond. "I didn't grow up wealthy," was all he could come up with as they buckled their seat belts. Why was he justifying himself? This was crazy. Time to reverse course. "Tell me about the people we'll be seeing. What should I know and what should or shouldn't I say?"

She kept her eyes on the road, waiting for a break in the traffic to allow her to merge from the parking lot onto the highway. "There's really nothing to say. We're not supposed to fraternize. I figure you can carry half the trays, which will give you an excuse for being there. I'd rather you form your own impressions without me imbuing them with bias."

Imbue. Bias. She spoke well. Perhaps she was better educated than he'd originally assumed. "Fair enough." He regretted the comment's lack of wit or charm, but as he studied the way her ginger curls brushed seductively against her ivory cheeks, repartee escaped him.

Instead, he sat stone-faced and silent, occasionally stealing a peek at Carra's outfit from the corner of his eye. Khakis, topped with a short-sleeved, silky black blouse featuring a keyhole that hinted at cleavage. Black sandals matched the top. Again, far from the tailored appearance to which he was accustomed, yet utterly appropriate for this type of work. And who was he to judge, clad in worn denim pants?

"This is stop number one," said Carra, parking in front of a disheveled cottage past due for an encounter with a wrecking ball. "Be careful inside, there's a narrow, dangerous passageway separating mountains of...whatever. You'll see." She extracted two trays from the trunk, handing him one as they made their way to the front door.

She rang, and they waited, Jay standing a few steps back, fidgeting with the discomfort of being so far out of his element.

Eventually, he heard the scraping of a walker and gasped as the door cracked open, a waft of tobacco fumes assaulting him.

"Miss Carra, nice... to... see... you... again," croaked Mrs. Geraghty. "Who... is... your... handsome... friend?" She batted her eyes. He wasn't sure if she was attempting to flirt or wrestle with some form of tic.

"Mrs. Geraghty, this is Jay. He's going to be volunteering at SALAD and is shadowing me today while he learns the ropes."

Carra carefully navigated the path to the kitchen, while Jay almost tripped on a wayward kitten as he followed. He had never been in a hoarder's home before. The mold combined with the lingering stench of stale smoke almost made him gag, but vomiting would have required taking his focus off the floor and possibly slipping on cat droppings and God knows what else.

"Is... he... single?"

"I haven't the foggiest idea." Carra looked back over her shoulder. "Jay, are you single?"

"Uh, err, yes, Mrs. Geraghty, I am. What did you have in mind?" He shot her his most ingratiating smile which she returned, revealing a mouthful of rotting teeth.

Carra smirked, then went to the counter, where she pushed aside some used trays to make space. "Mrs. Geraghty, I'm going to throw these empty ones in the trash, if that's okay with you."

"No, I'll... do... that," said Mrs. Geraghty, her voice slightly panicked. Carra froze for a moment, then shoved the offending trays to the side.

The older woman coughed a few times, the hacking reminding Jay of clients he'd known with emphysema. "You should have that cough checked out, Mrs. Geraghty. Can we arrange for a doctor's appointment?"

"Oh... no... no... that's... very... kind... of... you... but... I... can't... afford... the... co-pay."

"We've overstayed our welcome," Carra interjected. "I'll see you tomorrow, Mrs. Geraghty."

Jay lingered a minute longer to reach into his wallet and handed her a business card. "If you need a ride to the doctor, or help with the co-pay, please call me. Promise you will."

Carra watched but remained silent.

"You... are... a... very... nice... boy. Carra... you... should... marry... this... one. He... smells... so... good."

"I'll take it under advisement. You have a nice day. Come on Jay, they're expecting us at the next stop."

Carra worked her way through the artificial alley, holding out both hands to ward off rogue boxes that might magically reach out and pull her into their badlands of debris.

Once outside, she bent over, put her palms on her thighs and hyperventilated, making Jay wonder if she was suffering from an asthma attack.

"You okay?" he asked.

She continued to concentrate on the cracked stone slabs that led from Mrs. Geraghty's door to the driveway, her breathing labored. "It's so sad, that's all."

"Then why did you rush me out when I was trying to help?"

She uncurled herself, smoothed her shirt, and headed toward the car. "We're not supposed to linger, remember? What if while helping, in our capacity as SALAD volunteers, we caused an accident? Can you imagine the liability?"

"Um, yeah. As a lawyer, I kinda can. But I get your point."

They got back in the car, and she shifted into reverse. "You do smell good, by the way. What cologne is that?"

He felt himself flush. "Um... I don't remember offhand. I'll check and get back to you." He remembered how she had mocked expensive cars. No way was he going to provoke her ire by admitting to overpriced cologne. "Thinking of buying it for your dad for Christmas?"

Her expression grew bitter. "I would, but he's dead."

"I'm so sorry." *Idiot. What a dumb thing to say.*

"I'm over it. It was many years ago. He left me enough to get through college, God bless him."

"My dad's gone too. Both parents, actually. Is your mom still alive?"

"I'm sorry about your parents, but could we please change the subject?"

Ugh. He'd hit another nerve. *Great going, Jay.* "Where are we headed next?"

"Mrs. Scott's house. Don't mention the dog paraphernalia. She still misses the two Goldens Social Services convinced her to give away. She's the one I'm trying to arrange transportation for. Being around people might help."

"Sounds like you also spent time talking to the clients."

She shot him a sideways glance and pulled into the driveway of the next house which, to Jay's relief, looked in far better shape. "It would be rude to remain silent as I drop off their trays, don't you think? I made the mistake of commenting how beautiful the dogs looked in the pictures scattered everywhere, and it left her devastated. I spent the night worrying she might complain to Judith."

"Judith can be kind of a ballbuster, can't she?"

Carra flashed a smile of solidarity, triggering a wave of giddiness to cascade over Jay. He'd finally broken through her brusque exterior. He rarely sought the approval of others but here, now, it felt surprisingly rewarding.

The home's timbered exterior reminded him of photos he'd seen of England's Cotswolds when he was a kid, reading about places he longed to visit once he saved enough money to travel. Reality had a way of mocking such dreams; work left him too busy to leave Rock Canyon, and without someone he loved by his side, the prospect of such trips rang hollow.

He fantasized for a moment about Adriana on holiday in Italy, but it devolved into images of her lecturing engineers about the best way to straighten the Leaning Tower of Pisa or reprimanding the Romans about the Coliseum's gaping holes: "They don't have to be ruins; it's your negligence that makes them so."

"What's so funny?" asked Carra.

Jay's focus snapped back to the lady beside him with the auburn locks and light green eyes, two trays stacked in her hands. *Those eyes... I could get lost in those eyes.* "I was thinking about someone I knew from the past who... lived in a house like this."

"You like Tudors? I also prefer homes like these, bursting with character. Especially Queen Anne Victorians. I think I must have been British in a former life."

"Then you must have loved—"

The door opened, interrupting him as he was about to remind her of the style of his office building. He cursed the homeowner's timing. It was one of the few personal admissions Carra had made all morning. He wanted to hear more.

The woman who answered sat in a wheelchair and smiled brightly at Carra, then at Jay. "You brought reinforcements, I see."

Her accent furthered the illusion that they were off somewhere in the British countryside. What would it be like to sit together in front of a roaring fire, clad in soft Aran cable knit sweaters, cuddling and sipping vintage port?

Carra took the trays to the kitchen. "Mrs. Scott, meet Jay, he's a trainee. Did SALAD contact you about transportation to the center?"

Janet looked at the floor. "No, I didn't hear from them."

Carra shook her head. "I specifically told them to add you to their route and to bring you in starting today. I'll be teaching a memoir-writing class, and I thought you might enjoy it."

Janet looked up. "Oh, that sounds wonderful. I would have loved that."

Jay felt compelled to speak, despite Carra's warnings. "I am going to give you my card. If no one comes by in the next hour, call me and I'll arrange for a wheelchair-accessible van." He ignored his companion's frown and deflected her admonishment before it left her lips. "I'm doing this as a private citizen, not as a representative of SALAD."

"Oh, young man, that's so kind of you." The tears that brimmed in Janet's eyes tugged at his heart.

"It's the least I can do. There is no reason mobility issues should limit your enjoyment of life. I'll speak to the administration at SALAD myself about getting you on their schedule."

Carra started for the door, but Janet scooted to her side. "I can't wait to attend your class and write stories about Carson and Fallon. Who knows? I might become the next W. Bruce Cameron!"

Carra bent over and put her arms around Janet, hugging her as best as the awkward position would allow. "It's my pleasure. I'll finally get some use out of my English degree. If it brings you comfort, every hour of study will have been worth it."

Halfway between the house and her car, Carra turned to Jay. "I appreciate what you did in there. When I asked you to come with me, it was so you'd see the need to fund some of my new programs. I never dreamt you'd take such a personal interest."

"I didn't expect to. What I've seen is tearing my heart apart." Jay fended off an involuntary shudder. "You were right when you said a 30,000-foot overview didn't tell the whole story. I now realize how blind I've been. My nana has me to watch out for her, but where are these people's families?"

She resumed the stroll to her Civic. "I wish I knew. I haven't asked, that would be prying. Against the rules. But maybe when they pour their hearts out in their memoirs, we'll learn more."

On the drive to their third stop, Jay broached the topic he'd been curious about since they left Janet's house. "You said you studied English."

"Yes, at Emerson. With a concentration in creative writing. Graduated this past May."

"So what prompted you to apply to SALAD?"

Carra focused on the road and waited a beat or two before answering. "Um, why wouldn't I? Giving back and all that."

He noted an edge in her voice. "Seems like an unusual choice, that's all."

She gestured to the house ahead with a lift of her head. "You might as well stay in the car for the next two stops. They don't come to the door. We're expected to leave the food on the porch."

Jay studied Carra as she walked to the houses, knocked on the doors, then left the trays. There was something so different about her. Women usually threw themselves at him. She remained aloof, even strident, except for the few moments he'd broken through her armor. She may have been chunkier than his usual dates, but her curves were... well, alluring.

Carra carried herself with confidence and expressed deep passions, whereas his girlfriends had always been reserved, deferential. She was... He searched for the word as she approached the car...refreshing.

They drove in silence for a bit, Jay grappling with thoughts of her, when the vibration of his cellphone jarred him back into the present. "Excuse me, I've got to take this," he said, figuring it was a client without checking the Caller ID.

"Hey, have a blast."

He swiped, then realized who was calling too late to change course. "Prentiss."

"Darling, it's been nearly two days. Aren't you curious how the dinner with the senator went?"

"I'm afraid this isn't a good time."

"It went swimmingly," Adriana continued. "In fact, I convinced Senator Mitsky and his wife to join the two of us for dinner in the city on a Saturday night in late October. It's a ways off, so I'm hoping we don't already have a prior engagement you never mentioned. Should I call Meggie and have her put it on your calendar?"

Jay had to admit scoring a dinner date with the senator was a coup. It could lead to significant inroads in his bid for political office.

"Sure, why not?" With Adriana speaking into his right ear and Carra sitting to his left, he suddenly felt crushed between two indomitable forces. "I have to go now. Thanks for the good work." *Click.*

Carra chuckled. Now it was his turn to ask, "What's so funny?"

She glanced over before returning her eyes to the road, a wry smile playing on her lips. "Nothing. Everything is going *swimmingly*."

He sighed. "I'm sorry. I didn't realize she was quite that loud."

"It's not a problem, *darling* and certainly none of my business. Sorry for eavesdropping."

She pulled into the driveway of their last stop alongside a badly parked red Malibu and turned off the ignition. "This is Simon Garrison's home, and it's where I need your help. I think he may be illiterate but I'm not positive, and I don't want to embarrass him by asking. He plays audiobooks to his grandkids instead of reading to them. I'm hoping a second pair of eyes will confirm it so I can help him."

"You figured all this out without stopping to chat? That's incredible." The sheepish expression on her face proved she found SALAD's restrictions as absurd as he did. The elderly needed companionship, not a short shrift.

"I might have shared a word or two with him."

"Yeah. It's not so easy to stay removed, is it?"

A wave of shared intimacy filled the car until the jangle of her cellphone ended the sweetness of the moment.

~ * ~

The call couldn't have come at a worse time. After spending the morning alternating between chiding Jay and maintaining my distance to mask how drawn I was to his looks, we'd finally stumbled onto some common ground, a mutual desire to help the needier of the seniors. Every sniff of that stupid cologne made me want to draw close and suck in more of its enticing scent. Every glance at those jeans made him appear so much more accessible than that pricey suit he'd worn the day I met him.

Then my sister had to phone to remind me of a late afternoon confab back at Rock Canyon Realty. I shooed her off before Jay could hear. The last thing I needed was for him to know I was a real estate agent.

Not that his phone conversation had been any better, some girl referring to him as "darling." At least I'd made him blush when I called him out regarding his paramour. But her existence meant any rapport we might share would be situational. We might work together toward a common goal. Hell, we might even strike up an unexpected friendship. But more than that? Men like him never clamored for women like me. "Swimmingly" wasn't even in my vocabulary.

I longed to skip the meeting and instead soak in a warm bath and scrub off some of the pheromones Jay had coaxed out of my body, secretions absent since I'd broken up with my ex back at college. But that was a whole other story, one I didn't want to dredge up, especially with Jay in my car.

"Anything important?" he asked after I hung up.

"No. At least nothing to do with SALAD. Let's go." I opened the trunk and took out my final two trays. He trailed me as I approached the front door. To my dismay, no one answered the bell or my subsequent knocks.

"Doesn't look like anyone's home," he said.

"It seems odd though. That red Chevy wasn't here yesterday. I figure he has visitors, so why not answer?"

"Not really our business, right? I guess leave the trays by the door and let's go."

I frowned, unable to ignore a churning in my stomach. Something didn't seem right, but if I said more Jay might mock my feminine intuition, equating it with unwarranted hysteria. Men always couched thoughts in the obvious, while women understood that life abounded with disasters foreshadowed by the rising hair at the back of their necks and a twitch in their gut.

I set down the trays, and we walked back to the car. "It's a shame, I wanted your opinion."

"There can always be a next time. We can stop by on Saturday after Michaela Geraghty's clean-up."

My heart fluttered. "You're really going to give up a weekend to do that?"

"Absolutely. And I'll bring a repair person to check the fridge."

I drew back, seeing him in a whole new light. Initially I thought he'd offered to tag along as lip service, a painless way to kill a morning and shut me up. Had I'd gotten him all wrong?

"On the drive back, I want to hear all about your proposed changes for the center and their estimated costs. I can endorse what Judith won't, since she's closed off to new ideas, changes of routine, and any unexpected assaults on her budget."

I threw him a serious nod, but in my head I was running a victory lap. Because I hadn't allowed his dimples to distract me, the funding was practically a done deal. I just needed his signature on the check. And along the way, I'd won an ally. Because what's that expression? *The enemy of my enemy is my friend.*

Not lover, Carra, I reminded myself. Friend.

Chapter Twelve

Despite my misgivings about Simon Garrison, I chalked up the morning as a success. After dropping Jay at the distribution center to collect his car, I drove back to the apartment for an inexpensive ramen lunch. Not the healthiest of choices.

Even with my salary from SALAD and my stepmother's support, unexpected purchases like notebooks and excess cleaning supplies were causing my bank balance to teeter on the edge of overdrawn. If I didn't want to hit up seniors for home listings, I'd have to pick up some freelance work and quickly.

To that end, I scrolled through my emails, which were sadly devoid of any response to my ongoing job search. So I used the hour to apply to a few other ads, but my heart wasn't in it, and I suspected I knew the reason why.

My mind drifted back to the car ride. Jay's faded jeans mere inches from my khakis. His cologne filling the car with a scent of sweet possibility. He'd paid attention as I detailed my plans for the center, including some I'd made up on the fly, like an Easter egg hunt adapted for the wheelchair-bound and a visiting lecture series. Somehow we'd grown from wary strangers into a humanitarian rescue team.

Back at SALAD, I rejoiced to find Janet seated in the memoir-writing circle they'd set up exactly as I requested, thanks to the few dollars I'd slipped the maintenance workers. "That young man of yours sent an accessible van for me," she gushed. "I have to thank him. Where is he?"

"Gone for the day, I'm afraid, but I'll convey the message the next time I see him," I said.

"No need. I have his card. Though I'd hoped to tell him in person."

Janet was all smiles, delighted to be socializing for a change. I'd have to call Jay later, let him know how happy he made her. A convenient excuse to speak to him again. But as friends. Just as friends.

Froy busied himself with the remaining thirty guests who had chosen not to join my writing group. He actively avoided making eye contact. Then I noticed why. Judith had returned from wherever she'd been the day before and was skeptically eyeing the new seating arrangement. I gritted my teeth as she approached my pupils, who were trickling in, notebooks and pens in hand.

Georgia Martin outstretched her arm and caught Judith's sweater a few feet before she reached my side. "Mrs. Ferester, thank you. Carra here, she's the first person at SALAD who's ever listened to me. I asked for help writing a memoir and wouldn't you know, a few days later we've got an entire class dedicated to it. She's bringing life and energy back to the center. I've already told three of my friends, and they want to come too."

I couldn't have orchestrated a better intervention if I'd tried. Judith looked as if she'd swallowed her tongue. When she finally regained her composure, she patted Georgia on the shoulder and grabbed what glory remained for herself. "We're so glad you're enjoying the new programming. Carra is…full of surprises." She regarded me coldly. Then she smiled down at Georgia. "If you have additional ideas, Mrs. Martin, my door is always open. You know that." Then to me, "Carra, a word please?"

I gave Georgia a grateful nod and followed Judith to the side of the room, out of earshot of my students. Before she uttered a syllable, I staved off any potential criticism, "My degree is in English, so no schlocky teaching methods. And I paid for the pens and paper myself, so they didn't strain your budget. In fact, I have a lot of ideas that will engage the seniors without costing you one red cent."

"This may shock you, but our programming is not haphazard," Judith responded tersely. "SALAD hired professionals with advanced degrees in social, organizational, and geropsychology to thoughtfully design and institute our agenda. Seniors are…delicate. We mustn't expose them to too much stress and change. I understand you are new. I appreciate your gusto and even your frugality. But no more surprises. You must run any ideas by me before mentioning them to the guests. Is that understood?"

She marched back to her office without waiting for my assent. Visions of Nurse Ratched danced in my head along with images of Judith's wall calendar highlighting all the days she'd be out of town for conferences and training.

My class was ready, pens poised, waiting to explore and document their memories. My mouth went dry and adrenaline flooded my veins. It was public-speaking class all over again. What was I doing? I'd never taught a day in my life. But I had reviewed memoir writing on Google the night before and scribbled some notes onto an index card which I now drew out of my pocket. Clearing my throat, I called forward every ounce of enthusiasm.

"Welcome, aspiring authors, to 'Senior's Class'! Today, we're going to talk a little about our lives and what we'd like to share with our readers. It's important to remember that a memoir isn't an autobiography. It's not meant to cover your entire life, just a recurring theme—like strength or perseverance—or one defining incident or period in your life, like tackling your first job or raising your children. Tomorrow we'll cover some techniques for plotting. Sound good?"

The seniors bobbed their silver-haired and bald heads agreeably. The class was one-third men, the rest women, and they were displaying neither frailty nor apprehension. Take that, Judith. Geropsychology, my ass.

Ms. Negativity, Blanche Schmidt, had opted out of the session. No loss. Though if she were Jay's nana, it might have been fun to read tales of what he was like as a boy, a blond, curly haired moppet, no doubt demanding even in his formative years. Then I checked myself as I remembered the empathic side he had revealed that morning.

Maybe I wanted to disregard that empathy because it made him more desirable, and why pursue the quixotic? I'd been a dreamer all my life, hence the impractical college degree, the empty bank account, and the heartache after each tragic breakup. I now viewed SALAD as a potential turning point, my path to pragmatism and making a difference.

Georgia raised her hand. "I suppose if there's a theme running through my life, it's regret. There's so much I've wanted to do, but never got the opportunity."

"Like what, Georgia?"

Others looked on as she considered my question.

"I wanted…I wanted to have children, lots of children. I came from a large family. But things didn't work out. Before I knew it, time had passed me by, and it was too late."

Her words of resignation ignited a hum of fellowship that quickly spread throughout the class. My stomach plummeted. Did others in the group feel cheated by life or resentful of the past? Was my hope of resurrecting happy memories a pipe dream?

Judith's words echoed in my ears, "Seniors are…delicate. We mustn't expose them to too much stress." Yet, in my typical Carra brilliance, I'd encouraged an entire class to upheave their repressed memories and emotions. How might that come back to haunt me?

A woman wearing a black snood raised her hand. "I'm Hannah Kupferman. I have four grandchildren and wouldn't trade them for the world."

My mouth gaped at her insensitivity, especially coming so soon after Georgia's comments. Until she continued, "But it's not all wine and roses, Georgia. Three of them have gambling issues. They've broken into my house and stolen heirlooms, then pawned them to pay their debts. My regret? How I should have put my foot down when my daughter ignored those kids growing up. Instead, I listened to everyone warning me to keep my nose out of her business."

"I'm so sorry," I whispered, unsure if my apology was directed to Georgia, Hannah, or myself for suggesting the class.

One by one, the other students voiced their laments. Risks not taken, friendships abandoned over stupid arguments, vacations postponed at the behest of bosses who later fired them, cheating them out of their pensions. Janet spoke of Carson and Fallon, her relinquished pups. A man named Gavin bemoaned his abandonment by a wife unable to cope with his cancer diagnosis. Finally, I had to clap my hands and raise my voice to interrupt the torrent of misery.

"So this is the point. Your memoir can't only be about regret." I had no idea if that was true, but I was winging it, grasping for a life preserver. "It has to be uplifting. It must rivet readers by putting them in your shoes and then teaching them what to do differently if they encounter the same situation. Let's meet again tomorrow, same time and place, and we'll discuss this concept further before delving into the rules of writing."

Class over, the room filled with the scraping of walkers, the clicks of canes, and the motors of wheelchairs. I prayed they'd disperse quickly, before Judith witnessed the gnashing of teeth and rending of garments and then tossed me out onto the sidewalk. For the next few hours, I steered clear of controversy, handing out cold drinks, commenting on the books the ladies were reading, interceding when disagreements got out of hand.

Helen sat removed from the others but within earshot of the class circle. I wandered over as she busily knit her sweater.

"Carra, I'm guessing that was probably not how you envisioned today going." An understatement. "How are you coping, dear?"

"I wanted to ask you the same thing, Helen. Why not spend time with the others? Join the writing group? I'm sure by tomorrow their outlooks will reverse, become less bleak."

"Oh no, I avoid the rearview mirror whenever possible. There's too much ahead to look forward to."

I wondered how much the future really held for her, or if she was sending me a veiled message that the class was a mistake, an exercise in regurgitating misery. "But memories are important, don't you think?"

She chuckled. "Of course. But it's more important to heed the present because that's what it is, a gift. Nothing lasts long in this life, which is why every moment matters. You can't take anything or anyone for granted."

I thought for a moment on the wisdom of her comment. Perhaps the answer was to pinpoint the seniors' regrets and help reverse them. "Aside from the community service work you suggested yesterday, what kind of programming would you prefer?"

She set her knitting on her lap and patted my thigh maternally. "Don't worry about me, dear. I'm fine on my own, keeping myself occupied, steering clear of the others with their adolescent bickering and squabbles." Then she put her finger to her lips. "Let's keep that to ourselves, okay?"

"Your secret is safe with me. But if there's ever anything I can do for you, will you promise to let me know?"

She held up three fingers. "Scout's honor."

~ * ~

I was fraught by the time I entered the conference room at Rock Canyon Realty and in no mood to become further *Bea-leaguered*. Nikki was waiting, spinning in her black leather chair like a three-year-old, a cat's-got-the-canary smile dancing on her lips.

I plopped down across from my sister, grateful for my stepmother's absence. "You look happy. You con some poor, lame sucker out of his home?"

Nikki scowled. "First off, it's limited mobility, not lame. Second, no, but I am in the chatting stage with three injured men living in homes that are no longer practical. I'll casually suggest a few ranches tomorrow. But the big news is that I am in active flirtation mode with Dr. Hottie, the director."

Now it was my turn to scowl. "He's not married?"

"I didn't ask. But I also didn't notice a wedding ring. Don't worry, Ms. Morals. I will make absolutely sure he's unattached before planning my move."

My mind darted back to Jay and that phone call with "Darling." If only I were thinner and dressed like Nikki, an inch shy of indecent exposure, I too could snag the object of my affection. I imagined her in a candy-striper outfit, handing out books and occasionally dropping them as an excuse to bend over and display her heart-shaped ass.

"Earth to Carra. How was your day?"

My sigh ushered in a weary confession. "I'm trying, but everything I do goes wrong. Judith runs the place, and she hates me. She's micromanaging my every move. There's Hainfroy, and he—"

"Hainfroy? What kind of name is that?"

"Some hipster artist pseudonym he adopted to look cool without appearing to care. Not the point. His art may be good, but his leadership skills are non-existent. He just pours juice and snitches to Judith whenever I try anything new. I'm sneaking around them both to upgrade SALAD's programs—so the seniors love me and let me list their homes—but it's hard to do with management's unyielding attitude and measly budget."

It sounded convincing, right? Especially the bit I threw in about listing the homes. Nikki and Bea would never understand that helping the elderly enjoy their golden years was reward enough.

"So I went to Jay—"

"Jay, who's Jay?" asked Bea, who'd discreetly slipped in, lugging her ubiquitous bundle of files. She plonked herself down at the head of the boardroom table, primed to pounce.

"No one. The grandson of someone at the center. He does some fundraising for them."

"Not Jay Prentiss?"

"Yeah, he's the one."

"Oh my. Jay Prentiss is one of the most eligible bachelors in all of Rock Canyon. You work that angle, honey. Marrying him will not only set you up for life, it'll grant you instant access to the senior market. You may become one of the rare writers who ends up rich."

She's heard of Jay. Just what I need, multi-level nagging. "First off, he's not my type. I don't go for demanding control freaks. And second, he has a girlfriend."

Undeterred, Bea continued, "Girlfriends aren't wives. And the fact she's his girlfriend and not yet his wife, means she's expendable."

I was awestruck. Had my stepmother no scruples? "Bea, this is not a fairy tale. I'm not Cinderella, and Jay is no prince. Before you interrupted, I was discussing how I planned to revamp SALAD's programming—"

"I heard a little something about that. Stop trying to reinvent the wheel. Spend your time getting to know the members and convincing them to sell their homes and move into assisted living. Or a condo, at the very least."

"You heard a little something about that? From whom, exactly?"

Bea smirked. "Oh, I have little birdies everywhere. They're telling me you're getting too involved in the wrong things."

The thought of Bea having spies at SALAD did not thrill me in the least.

"That's Carra," said Nikki. "Always throwing herself into things headfirst. Total immersion and upheaval." She gave me a hard look. "Like when you started sewing Barbie's outfits when we were little. All that fabric. The sewing machine you had to have. Then you complained the patterns were too girly and clichéd, so you attempted to design the 'Carra Collection.' When that got too overwhelming, you gave up and moved onto stamp collecting. You're so damn impulsive, then so quick to abandon your all-consuming passion."

I twisted my lips. "Was that necessary to bring up right now?"

"I bet you've already spent a ton on this new project," Nikki continued. "And you've been there less than a week."

"That is not true." She wasn't wrong, though I'd die before admitting it. There were the cleaning supplies I'd bought for Michaela Geraghty and this electronic C-Pen reader I found on Amazon for Simon Garrison. It would let him gather his grandkids around, book on lap, the pen reading the words aloud as he scanned each sentence. Not only would it provide a more interactive experience than the audiobooks, but it might also teach him literacy. But that cost $250 I didn't possess.

The crack about abandoning my passions? That hurt. True, once I explored something to its fullest I tended to move on, but to imply I'd quickly bore of SALAD's programming and participants? That really stung.

"Any leads on potential homes for sale, Carra?" Bea asked, breaking into my ruminations.

I thought about Janet Scott's Tudor and Simon Garrison's Cape, both in good shape, and Michaela Geraghty's fixer upper. All warranted a mention that would score points with my stepmother and keep my salary flowing. "Nothing yet, sorry."

Bea harrumphed. "How about you, Nikki? Anything to rescue me from mobile home hell?"

"I am on the trail of a few potential sales. I should know tomorrow."

"Good, keep me informed. Now, excuse me, I've got a home to show." She gathered her papers and made a quick exit.

I made kissing sounds at my sister, the kiss-ass. She rolled her eyes and stuck out her tongue. "Mom met me for lunch today at the rehab center's cafeteria. She wants to see you, Carra. All she could talk about is how much she misses you and how sorry she is about everything."

Every one of my muscles seized simultaneously, transforming me into one giant cramp of rage. "I told you no. Why do you keep bringing this up?"

"Don't you have any compassion? There's a reason she left, and she needs to explain it to you herself. She desperately wants to carve out a place in your life."

"She walked out on a husband and two kids!" Nikki gestured for me to keep it down, but I didn't care who heard. "Flat-out abandoned us. There's no explanation that will justify that. None."

"She regrets all of it. Doesn't everyone deserve a second chance?"

"Some people, maybe. Not her. Not now, not ever. If you have any respect for my feelings, do not mention her to me again."

Enough was enough. First the ominous feeling about Simon and that red Malibu, then the class going south, and now a proposed reunion with my birth mother being shoved down my throat, like it was my job to assuage her guilt. Time to go home, pour a stiff drink, draw a warm bath, and torture myself with fantasies of another woman's dimpled "darling."

Chapter Thirteen

That night, the nightmare returned, the same one that with slight variations, had haunted me over the years. I was with my family in the Midwest for an art festival my mother had dragged us to, seeking inspiration to finally finish any of her paintings. The St. Louis Union Station Hotel was like a castle, and I was enthralled. It was everything a princess-loving six-year-old could dream of.

After finishing dinner at a nearby restaurant and then tucking Nikki and me in for the evening, the usual fighting began. But this night, it seemed louder, more upsetting. Cries of "I can't do it," and "You don't understand me, you never have," woke me, and in a groggy state, I walked out of my bedroom in time to watch my mother, eyes red and cheeks tear-stained, grab her coat and bag and what I now know was a half-finished bottle of liquor then head for the door.

"Mommy, I can't sleep. Can you please read me a bedtime story?" I asked, but she never looked at me and didn't answer, just ran from the hotel room, slamming the door behind her. She didn't return for the rest of the night, and no matter how much my father held me and tried to console me, I couldn't stop crying for hours.

On this night, the dream replayed but with a new twist. It was years later, the middle of a frigid winter, and I'd been hired as the doorperson for that same hotel. I was wearing a heavy woolen maroon coat with golden epaulets and looked as regal as the building itself. All day and night long, I opened doors for guests hurrying in and out, wishing them a good day, all the while thinking how happy Kiki would be that I could send home the rent money for the month. Life was good. I was happy.

Then my mother came tearing through the lobby, drunk and disheveled, and without a look or a word—or a coat— pushed by me, through the door, then into the blizzard enveloping the street outside.

"Mom! Mom, wait!" I yelled as I ran out after her through the blinding snow, desperately looking in all directions...but she was gone. Doleful, I sulked back to my post, a shell of the happy person I'd been moments earlier, just trying to push through the day.

That's when the parade began, a long line consisting of every boy I'd ever dated in high school and every man I'd gone out with in college, each strolling through the lobby. One by one they approached, among them Colin and Derrick and Josh, all dressed in suits and tuxedos like they were on their way to a formal event. Each stopped by my side and attempted to hug or kiss me, but each time, I just turned away, opening the door, wishing them well, and ushering them out into the snow.

Surprisingly, Jay Prentiss brought up the rear, his blue eyes twinkling and his dimples beckoning. "Carra," he said, "You don't have to stay in St. Louis. Come home with me where it's warm."

It was a tempting offer but when I opened the door to leave with him, a gust of glacial air lifted and propelled him into the white abyss. "Jay...Jay..." I called, the words echoing around me...and then I woke up, covered in a sweat as cold as the city I'd just dreamt about.

~ * ~

No matter which way he contorted his body, Jay couldn't get comfortable. Not that the bed wasn't conducive to a good night's sleep, thanks to his Aireloom mattress and TOGAS's pillows of Austrian white goose down. And it wasn't that he had lost a case or taken on a particularly difficult client. It was Carra's face—the way it lit up when she smiled or turned the world sour when she frowned—that prevented him from falling into a deep slumber.

The memory of that face followed him the entire ride home. It shadowed him as he changed clothes and tugged Solomon into his Lexus and as he showed up at work a dizzying four hours late. It distracted him as he reviewed his files and returned voicemails. Even when Adriana called again, the image of Carra's visage waited patiently until she could reclaim his full attention.

The truth was, she'd gotten under his skin in a way he hadn't experienced before. Something about her reminded him of his younger days, before the loss of his parents, when he was carefree, even jokey at times. Before he'd adopted the mantle of man-of-the-house, responsible for Nana, who had devoted herself to his caregiving. And before he became convinced of the keys to success: earning enough money and grasping enough power to control whatever life might throw his way. Especially the unexpected calamities that could shatter a child's entire world in mere seconds.

Jay didn't know which fascinated him more: Carra's passion and determination or her willingness to swallow her ego to achieve her goals. Her coming to his office, asking a stranger for money could not have been easy. People around him were always posturing for position, hell-bent on winning for their own glory, while Carra appeared willing to sacrifice herself for the good of others.

What he *did* know was that she'd never fit into his life and that's what kept him from pursuing her further. She'd stick up her nose at his expensive tastes; status held no place in her world. His political ambitions would make her bristle. She wasn't the type who'd enjoy accompanying him to boring dinners with local business leaders.

Meanwhile, Adriana thrived on the networking required to bolster a burgeoning political career. While not perfect, she was clearly the better choice. So why wasn't it her face disturbing his slumber?

Still awake at 3:00 AM, Jay opened his laptop and googled "Carra Quinn." Her Facebook page was private, but he could still see her profile picture, and her smile made his skin tingle. His page was under a phony name, Borden Sargento, a nod to his love of cheese. He'd also set it to private, using the account only to converse with his college buddies. Even then, he sanitized every entry, lest some hacker leak his posts and put him in a compromising position.

He checked other social media. Carra had no Twitter account, no Instagram presence, and on LinkedIn, only a brief resume listing her accomplishments as a budding author. A few short story writing awards, but no links to the actual pieces. *Damn.*

Still wide awake, he researched appliance repair services and emailed a few requests for Saturday morning availability. Then he checked to make sure his weekend calendar was clear. There was one entry, his usual Saturday night dinner with Adriana, but that wasn't until seven. The hoarding clean-up should finish long before. He wondered how he'd view his girlfriend after spending a day around Carra. A relief or a letdown? Only time would tell.

~ * ~

Even after half a pot of chamomile tea to dull the memory of the nightmare, relaxation evaded me. Instead, concern over the grief my class had dredged up flooded me with angst. Naturally, masochist that I was, the only person to whom I wanted to pour out my heart was Jay. He'd witnessed a little of my admittedly limited experience with the SALADians—a term I'd coined, since writers *were* the rulers of the kingdom of words—and once exposed, he seemed to care deeply.

Then I considered how Jay might react if it turned out his nana wasn't naysayer Blanche Schmidt, but someone traumatized by my lecture. Probably exactly the way he'd attacked Judith over a scoresheet and an abundance of carbs. I quickly nixed thoughts of confessing.

I'll take a more upbeat approach tomorrow, I decided. The one suggested by Helen. Treasure the moment. No dwelling on the past but use its lessons to make today better. Everything would be fine.

I grabbed my cellphone and typed a flurry of new program ideas into the notes section. Some had hefty price tags, others did not. When I saw Jay on Saturday, I'd propose the more expensive ones. He'd be most vulnerable then, still basking in a self-congratulatory glow after selflessly helping Michaela de-hoard her house. It never hurt to be a little devious in one's fundraising efforts.

As sleep finally transformed determination into drowsiness, my last half-conscious thought was of Jay's plump lips, at first arguing over my padded budget, then succumbing to temptation and pressing them urgently against mine.

Chapter Fourteen

Morning deliveries went smoothly, with Michaela and Janet both singing Jay's praises. But when I arrived at Simon's door, the unsettling vibe from the previous day grew stronger. The red Malibu remained parked at a careless angle in the driveway, and no one answered my knocks, though I swore I saw the living room curtains sway as if someone was peeking from inside.

I left the tray by the front door as I had the day before and made a show of tramping to my car and driving off. Then I made a U-turn and positioned myself across the street and about a yard south—close enough to surveil, but not obvious to those I was surveilling. Setting my phone's alarm for twelve-thirty, the absolute latest I could leave to make it back to the center for my shift, I waited with cell in hand, the camera app primed for action.

My efforts paid off five minutes later when the door opened and a skinny, skeevy man in his thirties with unkempt hair and a horseshoe mustache first looked left, then right, before finally pulling the tray inside. A shiver swept up my spine as I zoomed in and captured him on video. With an hour to spare and a dozen unpleasant scenarios percolating, I stretched and braced myself for the long haul, determined to document proof of any other odd happenings at the Garrison home.

Twenty minutes later, a pair of men in business suits pulled up in a BMW. I lowered my window to overhear any distant conversation they might share. One jumped out and pounded on Garrison's door. One knock, then two, then one again—a code repeated twice. My cell recorded everything. The skeevy, mustached, biker-looking dude opened the door wide enough to accept an envelope and, in turn, handed the man a bag. The visitor hustled back to his car, and the two drove off.

Over the next half-hour, I witnessed four iterations of the same pattern, the visitors running the gamut from teenagers to provocatively dressed, strung-out women. It was clear Mr. Meth, as I'd nicknamed him, was using Garrison's house to conduct questionable commerce. The thought of what might have become of Garrison and his grandchildren turned my stomach. I switched from the camera app to Google and frantically searched for Jay's office number.

"Prentiss Elder Law," chimed a cheerful female.

"Mr. Prentiss, please."

"I'm sorry, he's in a meeting. I'd be happy to take a message and have him return the call when he's finished."

"It's important. A matter of life and death, really. Could you please interrupt and let him know Carra Quinn is on the line?"

There was a moment of silence. "Ms. Quinn, I don't see you on our list of clients—"

"I'm not a client," I said, trying to swallow my exasperation. "I work with his nana at SALAD."

"Ah yes, I remember. You were here the other day."

"That's right. Could you please get him on the line?"

"Is his grandmother okay?"

"As far as I know she's fine, but—"

"Then I'll have him call you back. What's the best number where he can reach you?"

I glared at the phone, stunned by this assistant's obtuseness. "It's 845-555-2715. But—"

"I promise, I will give him the message the second the meeting ends. Thank you, Ms. Quinn." *Click.*

I was at a loss. Should I continue observing Garrison's home and risk losing my job? No, that wouldn't help Simon and it wouldn't help me either. Should I call the police? I had my proof…or did I? I could report suspicious goings-on, but would that charge include people exchanging bags for envelopes when I didn't know the contents of either? And who knew if Garrison and the kids were even inside? They might be vacationing or visiting family.

There was no way of determining whether or not Simon was in danger until I found a safe way inside. Thanks to Jay's admin, that was evidently not happening until after my SALAD shift at the earliest. Then the door opened, and Mr. Meth walked out, scanned the area, spotted my car, and started toward me. I pressed the ignition and hit the gas.

~ * ~

Swallowing my fears, at least for the moment, I made my way to the center. My class sat primed and ready, their notepads and pens in hand. I held up one finger to signal I needed a moment before we started and approached Froy, who was preoccupying himself with a seemingly endless flow of Hawaiian Punch. "Mind if I have a sip? I didn't get lunch."

My co-worker passed judgment with a *tsk*, then acquiesced. I downed two cups of the sickly-sweet liquid and prepared myself to address my eager cadre of students when my cell buzzed. The Caller ID made my heart jump. "Carra, it's Jay. Meggie gave me the message. What's so urgent?"

"One sec." I held up my finger once again, then walked to the back of the room, out of earshot of anyone who might become easily alarmed. "Remember the last house we visited yesterday? Where no one answered and I remarked how odd that was?"

"I remember."

"It happened again today, so I parked across the street and observed. I think some guy is running a meth ring out of that house. People kept stopping by and knocking, always with the same sequence, and he'd answer then they'd exchange envelopes for packages."

A moment passed. "Jay, did you hear me?"

"Unique sequence?"

"One knock, then two, then one again. They did it twice, like a secret code."

"It sounds kind of unlikely, Carra. Meth rings don't suddenly spring up one day out of nowhere. Are you sure of what you saw?"

I blinked, incredulous that he'd be so quick to dismiss my perceptions. "I have the whole thing on video. I can email it or text it to you. Let's see what you think."

"Email it to Jay at Prentiss Law dot com. Let me look it over, and I'll call you back."

"Fine. Think we can reconnect at four?"

"Sounds like a plan."

I forwarded the files, trying to ignore the way his voice made my pulse race. At least someone else would see what I saw. Someone who might have a better idea of how to rescue Simon if he needed rescuing. A wave of relief washed over me.

My class murmured and shuffled their feet restlessly as I finally made my way to the front of the room. "Sorry for the delay. Has anyone given any thought to what we discussed, and how we can learn from our regrets to improve our lives today? Turn them into teachable moments for our readers?"

I saw Helen out of the corner of my eye, knitting and smiling, happy I had taken her suggestion and run with it. But the blank expressions on my students' faces told me more explanation was in order.

"Georgia, can I pick on you? You said yesterday how much you regretted putting things off to start your family. Can you pinpoint one moment when you could have turned that around?"

She crinkled her brow, searching her memories. Then a sly smile inched across her lips. "I guess when he wasn't looking, I should have pricked pins in his Trojans."

A collective guffaw erupted from the crowd. With one cheeky comment, Georgia had broken the ice, and everyone seemed more at ease. Students thrust up their hands, eager to match her insight and irreverence. I called on my friend, Janet.

"I wish I'd hidden my dogs when Social Services asked me to give them away 'for my own good.' Asked the neighbors to board them for a day or two."

"I should have donned my cloak of invisibility and sat in on Harvard's classes when they didn't admit me," said Bryan Redmond, who the day before had lamented his lack of a college education.

"Or you could have studied harder in high school," suggested Greta, his wife, eliciting another big laugh.

Their good humor provided another teachable moment. "There's nothing to say you can't write your memoirs tongue-in-cheek. Use comedy to soften the edges. But let's go a step further. Georgia, forgive me if I'm being insensitive, but what were some things in life you did accomplish that might have been more difficult with children around?"

She paused for a moment. "My husband and I spent quality time together. If we had both been working two or three jobs to pay the bills for a larger family, we never would have seen each other. Strangers would have raised our kids."

"Good point. Janet, I realize it's a difficult subject, but can you think of any positives to the dogs being rehomed?"

Janet looked at her lap, then lifted her eyes. "They were active babies, and once circumstances confined me to this chair, I wasn't able to keep up. They were adopted by a family with three kids and lots of land. They're probably better off now, even if I do miss them." She sniffed but appeared more at ease.

I felt my phone buzz. "Let's spend the rest of the hour documenting some downturns we've experienced and see if we can reframe them with a positive spin. We'll pick this up tomorrow. Sound good?"

The students nodded in tandem. I darted to the bathroom to check my messages.

The note from Jay was short and sweet: *Looks troubling, but I need to see for myself. Can we do rounds again tomorrow, observe Garrison's home, and figure something out?*

I shot a text back: *Pick you up at the distribution center again at 8:00 AM.* As serious as the situation was— with a man's life possibly at stake—a tiny part of me quivered with excitement. I was going to spend another morning with Jay.

Chapter Fifteen

Jay strummed on his steering wheel as he awaited Carra's arrival. Activity at the distribution center appeared brisk even from his vantage point, parked outside the rear entrance. He'd arrived fifteen minutes early, unable to control his eagerness to see Carra again. Then reprimanded himself for letting his emotions get out of control.

The video Carra sent disturbed him. He'd almost phoned a detective he knew to urge an investigation but opted for caution. If things weren't amiss, he could cause trouble for an innocent person and strain a longstanding friendship over a misunderstanding. Best to be sure, and if that meant spending another morning with Carra, all the better.

She showed up a few minutes before eight wearing tailored black pants, a pink silky shirt, and a pink-and-black checkered blazer. He wondered why she'd dressed so professionally. Was it part of her plan to rescue Simon Garrison? Or—and this was purely his ego talking—was it to impress the lawyer accompanying her on this mission?

She saw him and waved before retrieving the day's trays. He met her as she exited the center and offered to share the burden. Together they loaded the food into her trunk.

"Any ideas on how we should handle this?" she asked as they drove out of the parking lot.

"Let's first determine if what you witnessed yesterday happens again today. If the car is gone and Simon answers the door, then there's nothing to worry about."

She glanced at him askance. "That would be best, but in my gut, I think the man's in trouble and will need our help. Do you mind staying in the car while I make my first four deliveries? It'll speed things up. I'd like to leave as much time as possible to spend outside Simon's place."

She returned her gaze to the road, and he used the opportunity to sneak another peek at her outfit. While attractive, it seemed to stifle her, smothering her freewheeling spirit. This was Carra the serious, and while he was grateful for a glimpse into another aspect of her personality, he longed for carefree Carra, willful yet playful. Perhaps when this drama subsided she'd reappear.

The first four stops flew by without incident, affording Jay an excellent view of her confident gait and laughter as she greeted each client. Despite his efforts to reign in his pulse, it galloped like Secretariat three furlongs from the finish line.

She slipped back into the front seat. "Almost zero hour, you ready?"

"Ready as I'll ever be."

She restarted the engine. "You'll video everything with your phone, right?"

"I'm on it." He retrieved his cell and glanced at his messages. The name Meggie appeared three times. What could be so important at this hour? He turned the phone face down and kept it on silent, whatever his admin wanted would have to wait.

Carra edged her Honda into Garrison's driveway, to the left and at a forty-five-degree angle to the red Malibu, which looked as if it hadn't moved since Jay's previous visit. "If we're lucky, he'll remember the car from yesterday and come out to confront me," she said. "Maybe you could use that opportunity to rush inside and find Simon."

"Or I could bypass the breaking-and-entering charge and just ask the guy if he's seen the homeowner."

She sighed and grabbed the trays while he focused his cell on the front door and waited. Would she attempt the secret knock, he wondered? No, that would give them away. They were there to deliver food, not single-handedly bring down a meth ring. If a meth ring even existed to bring down.

No one came to the door. She knocked again. "Mr. Garrison, your food is here." She waited a minute and then yelled, "No problem, I'll leave it on the porch for you."

Her mouth tightened as she walked toward the car. He turned off the camera and set his phone on his lap.

"Jay, I'm sure there's someone inside. Let's not budge from the driveway. If he feels our presence may scare off his clients, he might come out and ask us to move." She winked.

"That's called trespassing."

"If no one's inside, there will be no one to complain, right?"

Carra had a point. They sat and waited.

After fifteen minutes a BMW arrived, but thanks to Carra's intentional bottleneck, the driver had to leave his car's trunk jutting into the street. She peered at its occupants through the rearview mirror.

"That's the duo I saw yesterday. Think you can video them without either noticing?"

"I can try." He turned on the camera and held it at an angle so it was half hidden by the dashboard, tilted toward the windshield.

Carra pretended to be rifling through her purse as one man hurried past, throwing them both a nasty look en route to the front door. One knock, two knocks, one knock, repeated twice, just as she'd described it. A mustached biker-type peeked out.

"Is that your Mr. Meth?" Jay asked.

"That's him. Looking as skeevy and strung out as he did yesterday."

The envelope for bag exchange followed. It didn't look like Mr. Meth even noticed them in the driveway before he shut the door and the two zoomed off.

She turned and looked him square in the eye. "Believe me now?"

"I do. But I'm not sure what we can do about it. We can't exactly force our way in and confront him. What if he's armed? We didn't see what was in the bag. It might have been sugar, for all we know. I could call a friend at the station, ask if what we've seen would constitute sufficient grounds to issue a search warrant—"

"How long would it take them to issue a warrant and bring it over here?"

"I'm not sure—a few hours? A few days? I don't normally handle this type of situation."

She grimaced. "We don't have that kind of time. What if Mr. Garrison's inside, at death's door? We need to coax out Mr. Meth so we can get in there and look around. It has to be his idea." She squeezed her eyes shut as if willing the answer to appear.

"Good luck with that. In the meantime—"

Her eyes popped open, and she revved up the car again. "Good thing I have decent insurance. Let's hope this works."

"Let's hope what wo—"

With no warning, she shifted into reverse and pressed down on the gas, smashing into the driver's side of the Malibu. They both lurched forward from the impact, accompanied by the sound of crunching metal.

"Carra, are you crazy?" he screamed, harsher than he intended. His body quivered from the jolt as memories of a far worse crash came flooding back.

"Oh no." Her tone was robotic. "I have hit another car. We must file an accident report." She turned to him. "We're at 18 Putnam Court in Rock Canyon. Would you be a doll and call the police? I want to run up and make the homeowner aware that they're coming."

The brilliance of her idea forced its way through his clouded brain and pacified his agitation. "Sure, let me do that right now." He started dialing and cracked open his door to hear whatever transpired next, in case she required his help.

Mr. Meth must have heard the crash because he bounded past her toward the site of the accident before she could reach Garrison's front door.

"Are you blind? Hasn't anyone taught you to drive?" He spat out the words at triple speed, like someone coked out of his gourd.

She put out her hands, urging him to calm down and keep a safe distance. "I'm so sorry. You parked at such an awkward angle, and I guess I wasn't paying attention. My insurance will cover all of this. My friend is on the phone right now, calling the police so we can file a—"

The man cringed. "No police. We can settle this ourselves."

"I'm afraid he's already called. I want to do everything by the book, get you the full repair cost for your vehicle. All we can do now is wait until they show up. There's a station house nearby so I'm sure it won't take—"

"No police!" He sprinted back into the house and reemerged with the car keys for his massacred Malibu. "Move your car up, move your car up, I gotta get out of here."

"But what if—"

"Move the car!" His eyes were wild and panicked.

Jay wondered if the Malibu would even start, considering the damage to the driver's side. Carra strolled back to the Honda at half-speed and took her time restarting the ignition. Mr. Meth was practically jumping out of his skin, waiting for the chance to get into his vehicle.

She inched forward, and he jerked open the driver's door, which looked like it might fall off at any moment. Banging it closed, he started the engine, which apparently survived the impact. As he threw the car into reverse, he lowered his window and shouted, "I'll get you, SALAD lady. Watch your back." Then he sped off.

Unfazed by the threat, Carra jumped out of the Honda and ran to Garrison's front door. Jay raced to keep up. "You can't go in there, that's breaking and entering."

"Even if the door's ajar, and I peer inside to speak to the car's owner to get his insurance information? And he pushes by me and runs out? Not only is that explanation plausible, it sounds completely legit." She turned the knob. Unbelievably, Mr. Meth had been in such a hurry to escape he hadn't locked the door behind him.

"If we're wrong about this..." Jay started, but Carra was already out of earshot, hunting from room to room. When he reached the dining alcove, he changed his tune.

The table featured a cornucopia of illegal wares, including baggies filled with white powder and an unsettling array of firearms. Then he heard the moaning. A strangled call for help. It was coming from the back room. Carra, ten steps ahead, had already flung open the door. He followed her through the master bedroom into the ensuite bath where an enormous man sat on the floor beside the toilet, chained by his ankle to the bathroom's radiator.

He looked up, pale and jittery, one eye blackened, and blood crusted where he must have repeatedly rubbed ankle flesh against metal to break free. "Philip figured if he kept me here at least I'd have use of the facilities," he explained, almost apologetically.

Carra was frantic. "Jay, we've got to find some way to get him out of here. This chain is so thick. Mr. Garrison, do you have any tools anywhere? A bolt cutter or something?"

Jay did a double take, surprised she knew the name of the appropriate tool, underestimating her once again.

"The police will be here soon," he said. "They'll likely have some way of releasing him. They'll call a locksmith…or a SWAT team."

"Heavy artillery? That's hardly necessary. I've been here three days; another few hours won't make much difference." Simon cracked a bittersweet smile.

"What happened, Mr. Garrison?" asked Carra. "Who is this Philip person, and how was he able to get in here and put you in this position?"

He sighed heavily. "Philip is my son-in-law. He took the kids home the other day and then came back and knocked at the door. Forced me into the bathroom at gunpoint. Said he needed a safe, quiet place to set up shop, and if I behaved he'd let me live. I thought he'd gotten clean but the drugs… I guess they make you do crazy stuff."

The hair on Jay's arms went stiff. He'd heard of cases like this before, where strung-out children hijacked their parents' or grandparents' houses, but the issue had never touched this close to home. He'd read that sometimes the junkies killed the homeowner, but thanks to Carra, they'd rescued Garrison in time.

"You look a little dehydrated sir, and I'm sure the doctors will want to admit you for observation. Otherwise, you're in excellent hands with this lovely lady. I'll wait up front for the police. We can tell them we heard moans and believed someone needed our immediate help. Since you're the homeowner, and I doubt you plan to lodge any complaints over our illegal entry, we should be in the clear. Carra, did you happen to get the license plate of the Malibu?"

"It's on the video I emailed yesterday, but the car should be easy enough to identify. It's the red one probably missing its driver's side door."

Jay knelt to address Garrison. "Do you have a place to stay? I wouldn't remain here until the police apprehend your son-in-law. It isn't safe."

"I have an army buddy who lives out of town and off the grid. I'll leave today. In the meantime, I can't thank you enough." He extended a hand and shook Jay's with all the vigor he could muster in his weakened state. "Philip fed me scraps and wasn't interested in reordering my prescriptions. You both probably saved my life."

Jay gestured toward Carra with a lift of his head. "This is the lady you need to thank. She had a bad feeling about that car in your driveway. I should have given her intuition more credit, then we would have liberated you sooner."

She blushed and gave Garrison a hug.

Jay stepped from the bathroom and reached the front door in time to watch the police pull up alongside her vehicle, which now sported a cracked bumper marred by red scratches of paint. The sight made him smile. He might have book smarts up the wazoo, but Carra Quinn's courage and quick thinking saved the day.

He mused over what he'd learned that morning. He prided himself on being a man of logic who based his actions on analysis and planning. But she had just taught him impulsivity did have a place in this world, just as she deserved a place in his heart. The question was, how realistic was a long-term relationship between them? Would her wild, untethered antics bring havoc to his staid and tightly structured world?

Chapter Sixteen

The panic attack didn't hit until I pulled my mangled Civic into SALAD's parking lot. Only then did I transform from Carra the Calm into a sweaty, quivering, rattled wreck. I prayed none of the seniors would stroll by, catch me hyperventilating, and summon an ambulance. The ensuing flurry of gossip and speculation would make it hard to corral their attention.

I'd kept my cool throughout the Garrison ordeal—almost like an observer, watching from afar—but now, fifteen minutes before the start of my shift, an avalanche of emotions threatened to bury me alive. I sucked in deep wafts of oxygen to tamp down my angst so I could face my memoir class without collapsing into tremors and tears.

Once the paramedics wheeled Simon away, I took off, leaving Jay to deal with the police officers' questions. They warned I might have to identify the perp in a lineup, but I wasn't sure why. Couldn't Simon adequately ID his own son-in-law? Truth was, I wanted to remain as far away from the memory of that abuse as possible.

Jay had been wonderful. Once he recovered from his initial rage over my premeditated crash, he even offered to have my car repaired at his expense. I'd have to deal with that sometime next week. Get a loaner. If I didn't have to get State Farm involved, all the better, since the insurance was under Bea's name, and I wanted to sidestep any uncomfortable explanations.

Thoughts of Jay pacified my anxiety. He was a rock, something solid to cling to when rising waters threatened to submerge everything nearby. Meanwhile, I was a kite, flailing in the storm. I'd only had the guts to back into that Malibu because if it had all gone wrong, he would have rescued me. Of that, I was certain.

A few minutes before the start of my shift, I finally felt grounded enough to enter the building. I had a lot on my plate: put the final touches on the rollout for the Scrabble Tournament of Champions, convince

Judith that a Fall Formal would brighten everyone's spirits, and explain the tenets of good fiction writing to my eager class of memoirists. All while trying to banish distracting thoughts of Jay from my mind.

~ * ~

After dealing with the police, Jay went to call an Uber so he could retrieve his Lexus and get on with his day. That's when he remembered that hours before, he'd left his phone on silent mode. Switching it back, a steady stream of beeps alerted him to five messages from Meggie. Rather than replay them, he hit speed-dial.

She answered on the first ring. "Where have you been? We have an emergency here."

"Hello to you too, Meggie. What's so vital it couldn't wait till lunchtime?"

"Remember Ms. Dibble? She called, half out of her mind. Something about her mother and her sister and the house. She was too distraught to speak coherently. She and her mother plan to arrive at the office by two."

~ * ~

Solomon made no attempt to conceal his displeasure over changes to his routine. He flopped onto his office doggie bed with the canine equivalent of a harrumph when Jay finally made it in at 1:56 PM. Meggie, sporting a hot-pink minidress and a new septum piercing, greeted him with a pile of messages.

Jay pointed to the silver barbell adorning her nostrils. "Exactly what is that?"

"Stylish, that's what it is."

He didn't have time for this. "Either take it out or push it up so it's invisible. This is a business office, not a nightclub."

He could tell she was on the verge of her usual retort, a combination of assertions regarding labor laws, freedom of speech, and the need to attract a more youthful clientele. Nothing he was in the mood to debate right now. He stomped into the conference room to wait for his clients, slamming the door behind him.

When Meggie ushered in Gemi Dibble and her mother moments later, Jay was alarmed by the change in the younger woman's appearance. No makeup, tousled hair peeking out from under her hijab, her expression dour. Beside her, her mother stood quivering and confused, her housecoat wrinkled and stained.

"Mr. Prentiss, this is my mother, Diann." Gemi's eyes glistened. "She is now homeless, thanks to my sister, Siti."

"Take a seat, please, and we'll work this out." He was already off his game, never comfortable around weepy women, much less disoriented ones. Diann's eyes were unfocused, something he'd seen many times as an elder attorney. It was a prime symptom of dementia. "Can we get either of you something to drink?"

Gemi waved her off, and Meggie took her leave.

He braced himself for the worst, especially since he'd never done anything to precipitate Siti's departure, despite Gemi's earlier conclusions.

"During her visit and without my knowledge, Siti manipulated my mother into signing over the deed to her house. Then she sold it from underneath her." There was a hitch in the younger woman's voice, as she appeared to battle back tears. "The new owners and their real estate agent stopped by to warn that they'd set the closing for next Friday. They expect my mother to be out by the day before, so they can do the walkthrough in an empty house. Otherwise, they'll get the sheriff involved, and he'll forcibly remove her. Throw her furniture onto the street. Can you help us, Mr. Prentiss? I live in a one-bedroom apartment. There isn't room for my mother and all her things."

Jay fought the impulse to clench his hands into quivering fists. It never paid to display emotion in front of clients. At least now he understood why Siti left for Vegas without his intervention; she needed to skip town to avoid the fallout from her real estate scam. "Do you have a copy of the deed? And the contract of sale?"

"Siti scanned and emailed copies of the documents from Las Vegas, assuring me my mother agreed to everything. I have them here." She pulled some folded papers from her purse and pushed them across the table.

He took a quick look. The deed transfer was notarized by a Sandra Nichols and it looked official. He'd have to study it in more depth later.

"There is some good news. The home hasn't closed yet so we might be able to void the sale. If not, in New York it's a lot more difficult to evict a tenant than people think, so we have time on our side. Could your sister have forged the signature or was your mother at the notary's office for the deed transfer?"

"Mama, did you hear Mr. Prentiss? Did you go to the notary?"

Diann looked dazed. "What is a notary? Why are we here?"

Ms. Dibble turned back to Jay. "This is what it's like, trying to get through to her these days. Half the time she doesn't even know my name. How could a notary in good conscience approve something like this?"

Jay shook his head. "We'll definitely track down Sandra Nichols. Explore what other documents she's authenticated and whether any of them smack of...impropriety. If we can discredit her work, that would strengthen our case. The harder part might be recovering the money these buyers paid your sister. Which real estate agent came to your home?"

"Someone from Rock Canyon Realty. I don't remember her name...Marlo something. Could it be on the sales contract?"

Jay skimmed the document again. "I don't see it here, but it won't be difficult to track down. Please don't repeat this, but I'm not the biggest fan of real estate agents. That company in particular. It's shark-ridden, even after that debacle with the Realtor Retaliator murders a few years back. The owner is Deborah Lee Decker. Let me have a word with her and see what I can find out."

"I'd be so appreciative, Mr. Prentiss. Truth is, the best thing for my mother might be to go into assisted living, somewhere with a memory center. Then those nice buyers can move into the house they purchased. But I'll need the proceeds of the sale to pay the fees, so if you could force Siti to return ownership of the home to my mother, maybe we won't have to reverse the rest of the transaction."

That would be the easiest solution for the family. Unfortunately, it would be the most difficult for Jay. "Do you have a way for us to contact the purchasers, Ms. Dibble? I don't see that information on the contract."

"Yes, they gave me their number so I'd alert them when they could schedule their walkthrough."

The pad and pen Gemi had used during her last visit still rested on the table. Jay pushed them toward her. "Please copy down that number, along with anything else you know about the sale. Then go home and try to relax. I'll see what I can find out, and I'll also reach out to the real estate agent, explain the situation, and see if I can buy you more time."

She scrawled the requested information. "If you can work this out, I'll be forever grateful, Mr. Prentiss. Everyone in my community will hear what you've done. Lots more business will come your way."

He smiled. "Honestly, I hope your friends will only need my services to write their wills and help plan their estates. I don't want them running into this kind of situation."

She gathered up her mother and led her past reception toward the stairs. Jay was about to press the intercom and ask Meggie to get Deborah Lee Decker on the line when his cellphone rang. For a split second, he pictured Carra's face and hoped it might be her calling to update him about Simon Garrison. Then he'd mention the Dibble situation, and they'd commiserate over this barrage of bad luck.

His heart fell a little when the Caller ID read Adriana. "Hey, things are a little crazy, can I call—"

"I won't keep you long. I wanted to let you know I'll be leaving town tomorrow for a few days. A client wants to organize a press conference, and there's a lot of prep work involved. So can we move Saturday's dinner to tonight?"

"Sure, I guess so." He wondered if his indifference spilled into his delivery. Not that anything was wrong with Adriana. She was the same beautiful, resourceful woman he'd dated for the past half-year. But something had changed, something inside him and the way he viewed her, viewed women in general, that had diminished his former enthusiasm for their relationship.

If he'd sounded apathetic, she didn't seem to notice as she barreled forward. "How about Poisson? The owner is a friend. I can get us a table."

Even three years after opening, Poisson was still Rock Canyon's "in" spot, serving the best seafood around. It was also the town's most romantic restaurant. He hesitated, suspicious of whatever Adriana might have up her silken sleeve. "I'm not sure I'm up for anything that fancy."

"Oh, don't be silly. Great food, amazing ambiance; it'll be fun. I'll set it up for eight o'clock. Do you want to pick me up or…?"

"I'm not sure how late I'll have to work tonight, then I've got to drop Solomon back home and feed him, so let me meet you there."

"Got it. See you then."

Jay balked as he slipped the phone back into his pocket. Something about this was fishy, pardon the pun. Elegant restaurant, six months together—had his refusal to accompany her to the fundraiser the other night roused her from complacency, raised the urgency of redefining their relationship into something with a title, like fiancée?

This did not bode well but if a confrontation was imminent, better sooner than later. Carra hadn't mentioned a boyfriend, but that didn't mean she was unattached. Saturday's de-hoarding date was just around the corner. The perfect opportunity to do some fishing around. Another aquatic pun. She would bring out the humorous side of him yet.

~ * ~

My students' enthusiasm transitioned my harrowing morning into a rewarding afternoon. They ate up my suggestions about which fiction techniques would bring their stories to life and make their memoirs pop. Even Blanche, who had reconsidered her earlier boycott, appeared genuinely absorbed as I discussed how to create enough suspense to keep readers turning pages.

"We can write it like a mystery," she marveled, "keep them

guessing what's going to happen next, even though our kids already know how it all turned out."

"They may know the 'you' of today, but not the 'you' that flourished before they were born," I explained. "That's what will keep them glued to your narrative."

It was a lightbulb moment for many, and they scribbled furiously. I basked in pride, realizing I'd turned the class from hours of maudlin regret into pages of riveting prose.

After we wrapped up, Blanche hobbled over and handed me a folded note. "This is my home address. I was wondering if you might stop by later today for a snack. I need to discuss something with you."

The invitation shocked me, especially since she was usually such a disinterested sourpuss, but part of me was intrigued, having earmarked her as Jay's nana. Here was a chance to nose around, check out any photos that revealed what he looked like as a kid, get the inside scoop on what he was like growing up. I wasn't sure about the center's policy regarding visiting SALADians at home, but then again, it wasn't like I hadn't already broken a slew of rules on my deliveries. Anyway, who were they to tell me how to spend my personal time?

"Sure, that works. Around six?"

"Then it's a date." Blanche nodded, as if mentally checking off a box on her to-do list.

I gave her a thumbs up for what I imagined would be a very enlightening visit.

Chapter Seventeen

Jay appreciated Rock Canyon Realty's headquarters—a grand Queen Anne Victorian of pastel pinks and purples—since the choice of office architecture mirrored his own. He was less fond of the gaggle of real estate agents plotting inside, each with their own agenda and individual interpretation of what passed for ethical behavior.

Beyond the reception desk, he noticed rows of cubicles that were mostly unoccupied. He knew the agency had taken a hit recently. But it was hard to say if all those desks were empty because agents had abandoned RCR, or if they were merely off in the field overcharging buyers for substandard homes.

A petite blonde waved from behind glass walls that separated her large office at the rear of the bullpen. Her voice boomed over the intercom, "Judy, you can send in that gentleman. He has an appointment." Startled, Judy looked up from her computer. She pointed a finger at Deborah Lee Decker's office and returned her gaze to the monitor.

"Mr. Prentiss, I haven't seen you since the Chamber's annual meeting last year. To what do I owe the honor of this visit?" The owner placed her elbows on the desk, chin resting on interlaced fingers.

"Deborah Lee, one of my clients has been the victim of real estate fraud, and I'm afraid it might involve your agency." Her pasted-on smile lost its tackiness as he leaned back in the chair across from her, hands clasped on his lap.

Deborah Lee's jaw fell, exaggerating her affront. "That's impossible, Jay. My agents are as honest as the day is long."

"Only on Winter Solstice at the North Pole," he said with a chuckle, but then grew serious. "However, it's August, we're in Rock Canyon, and your agents are notorious for playing fast and easy with the truth. So come on, Ms. Decker, let's work together and do something good for someone."

The agency owner's mouth twisted, as if contemplating her next step. "Tell me what this is all about. It's possible someone may have made a tiny, innocent mistake."

"Anyone can make an error. Even one of your angels. It's the upcoming sale of 75 Devendorf Drive. Your agency represents the buyers."

Deborah Lee turned to her computer and typed the address into the MLS. "Ah yes. Marlo Bowden's deal. We're set to close next Friday."

Jay tilted forward. "Here's the thing, Deborah Lee. The home belongs to Diann Dibble and—"

"No. It belongs to a Siti Dibble. I have a copy of the deed right here."

"Siti is Diann's daughter. She flitted into town, convinced her addled mother to sign over the deed, then sold the home without her knowledge. Diann is not competent to sign any contract. She'll be out on the street if this deal goes through. Surely you don't want that kind of publicity for the agency, especially now."

Deborah Lee steepled her fingers and patted the tips together. The move reminded Jay of Ernst Stavro Blofeld in the Bond movies, sans his white Persian cat.

"Marlo Bowden found the home on a For Sale by Owner site, brought in a ready, willing, and able set of buyers, and initiated a meeting of the minds. As a buyer's broker, Marlo is not privy to what goes on in the heads of the sellers or what family drama may have precipitated their decision to sell the home. She handled the sale professionally, and as the procuring cause, she's entitled to the commission, which the seller offered out at three percent."

Jay felt the blood rush to his face. "This is not about commission. It's about looking out for an old, befuddled woman about to be evicted from her home with no place to go."

Deborah Lee stood, signaling they'd reached an impasse. "I wish I could help, Jay, I really do, but see it from our side. Mr. and Mrs. Eisenberg entered into the contract in good faith. They've already sold their home, packed up their belongings, and arranged for movers. I can't simply tell them the deal is off."

"Fine," Jay spat. "I'll find another way to handle this. Deborah Lee, I'll say one thing for you, you're consistent."

She smiled. "And you are a good man, always looking to do right by your clients. I admire that. How is that condo working for you at Riverfront Towers? I could net you a tidy profit if you'd consider selling."

Jay shook his head in disbelief then headed for the exit.

~ * ~

A long, frustrating day at work ushered in what promised to be a long, frustrating dinner at Poisson. Jay squeezed past the packed bar to a darkly lit table at the back, where Adriana was already waiting. Dressed in a strapless, blue-and-black poppy print dress, her hair drawn into a tight bun, she looked stunning as always. He felt a stirring in his nether regions.

"I'm afraid I might not be particularly good company. The last twelve hours have been a bit trying," he said as he pulled out the chair perpendicular to hers.

She smiled adoringly. "Tell me about it. I'm a good listener."

As the wine steward poured their aperitifs, he recited the *Reader's Digest* version, starting with the morning rescue but conveniently leaving out any description of Carra, other than "a volunteer who alerted me to the situation and then damaged a car to rescue the hostage inside." But as he recalled the event and her involvement, his nether regions stirred again, and a ribbon of longing rose in his chest.

"How brave of you. Do you think he'd repeat the story for the papers?"

Jay scowled. "I wouldn't dream of asking. It's personal, and I'm sure quite embarrassing for him."

"True… but it's also great publicity for you and your firm. Not to mention your run for state assembly. If we shine a light on accomplishments like these—"

"It's out of the question Aidie. I am not exploiting someone else's misfortune for my financial or political gain."

She emitted a lilting laugh. "Then you'd better resign yourself to a position as city dogcatcher, unless someone savvier beats you out."

The waiter brought their orders: scallops for her, stuffed shrimp for him. He played with his food, debating whether to recount the Dibble fiasco. She'd probably want to condense it into a press release. Then again, it might delay her big reveal, the real reason she'd moved up dinner.

"I had another incident come up today. Lovely woman, Indonesian I think, came in with her mother. Her sister had flown in from Vegas, lived with the mother for a while—who appears to be battling dementia—and convinced her to sign over the deed to her house. Then she sold it without a mention before flying back home. She's playing the slots, waiting for the check, while her mother gets kicked onto the sidewalk."

Adriana idly speared a scallop. "Sounds like a loser of a case. Daughter sold the house fair and square. The other sister should take in the mother, and you should move on to something more high profile. Not many Indonesians in Rock Canyon. Even if you could overturn the sale, it wouldn't win you many votes."

Jay moved a shrimp around his plate without eating it. Adriana's response was the one he had expected. Cold, calculated, and without empathy.

He'd once believed the two of them were cut from the same cloth, but no longer. True, he could appear rigid at work, divorced from emotion like every good lawyer, but he'd never allow himself to turn as coarse as the burlap woman beside him. He changed the subject and cut to the chase.

"This is a very fancy restaurant, Aidie. Are we celebrating something? This upcoming press conference of yours, the one you're jetting off to tomorrow to prepare for?"

"It is a big event, and if I pull it off it should earn me a promotion," she said. "But no, this is unrelated. Ironically, considering everything you just mentioned, I wanted to discuss real estate."

He gulped. "What about it?"

"My lease is up at the end of next month. With all the time we've been spending together, and the fact you gave me a key and all—"

"That key was for you to let Solomon out if work prevented me from getting home on the weekends."

"Yes, of course, darling, but I use it to let myself in for other things too." She gave him a wink, causing a chill to zigzag up his spine. "Anyway, it's insane, my paying all this money for rent to a stranger when I could cut your bills in half by moving in with you. It makes perfect sense. Especially since I spend so much time there anyway. So, what do you think?" She flashed her most winning smile, coupled with a few seductive bats of her fake eyelashes.

"What do I think?" He echoed the question softly, staring down at his uneaten food while scavenging through his brain for the right words.

"I could pack as soon as I get back from Chicago. If you're worried about where my things would fit, I can put a lot of them into storage. You don't have nearly enough closet space for my entire wardrobe, even with that second bedroom, but if things work out, we can always sell and buy—"

"It's too soon."

"What's too soon? Us moving to someplace bigger?"

"No. You moving in at all. We've only been together a few

months—"

"Six months. Going on seven. If you're not sure by now…" She narrowed her eyes, perhaps reconsidering the ultimatum she intended to issue.

"The truth is, I've been thinking we should take a break. I'm… I sense we're on different timetables. Let's give it a rest for a few months, and if we find we miss each other, we can always resume our relationship then." There. He'd done it. He felt like Atlas in Gaia, shrugging the weight of the world off his shoulders.

To her credit, if the suggestion perturbed Adriana, she didn't let it show. Instead, like any good publicist, she silently stabbed at her seafood. mulling over his words until she prepared an appropriate response. "Fair enough. You need time to be sure. Understandable. I'll renew my lease but only month-to-month. I'll call you in a few weeks to see where your head is at. In the meantime, I assume I'm free to see other men?"

If she thought she'd pulled a trump card from her deck of manipulation, she was wrong. He adopted a somber expression to disguise his delight. "I guess I have no choice. It would be wrong to have my cake and eat it too. We should both look around. That way, if we come back together, it'll be without regret, knowing we're really the perfect match."

She forced a smile, clearly unhappy with his answer, but Jay was already past caring. He looked over her shoulder at the couple seated to their left. The woman was auburn-haired and chunky and reminded him of Carra. The thought of her left him lighthearted and eager for Saturday to arrive.

Chapter Eighteen

With more than an ounce of apprehension, I knocked on Blanche's door, a small ranch off Paley Court, in the snazzier section of town. The lawn was well manicured, the rose bushes evenly spaced apart, precisely what you'd expect from the grandmother of an exacting, anal-retentive lawyer. I wondered if this was where Jay had spent his summers or if his grandparents moved here after he'd left for college and law school.

The doorbell, with its grand church chime, overwhelmed the modest home, like a lion's roar from a kitten's mouth. Several locks unlatched before the door edged open. True to her pessimistic nature, Blanche protected her domain as if a home invasion were imminent.

"Ah, Carra, it's you... Come in, come in." Blanche eked out an awkward smile, exercising *zygomaticus major* muscles long out of use.

She ushered me through the living room with its lime-green couch and gold shag carpeting and into the dining room where she'd set up late afternoon tea. I looked past the rainbow cookies, chipped bone china cups, and severe furniture, instead surveying the sideboard for any signs of young Jay. Nothing, except an oddly placed combination of drugstore cosmetics, makeup brushes, and a light-up portable mirror, all better suited for a bedroom vanity.

"Sit, sit. I hope you like marzipan, even if it is store-bought. I didn't have time to bake."

"Oh, Mrs. Schmidt, it's very sweet of you, but you needn't have gone to so much trouble." I tried in vain to make myself comfortable, but it was difficult to nestle into a prototype of the electric chair. "You made it sound like you needed to discuss something important."

I waited for the words I suspected would soon follow: "I have a grandson you'd be perfect for."

She poured two cups of tea, pushed one toward me, and pointed to the sugar cubes and creamer. "You'll probably think this is silly, but…"

"I'm sure it won't be silly at all." I pictured the introduction she'd propose, two strangers meeting at the local coffee house, the surprise on Jay's face when he realized the blind date his nana had arranged was with a girl he'd already met. One he'd probably written off as stocky and plebeian, but now appeared viable when viewed through the lens of Nana-sanctioned romance. What of "Darling," that woman on the phone, I wondered. Was Blanche aware she was in the picture?

"You always look so pretty. I was hoping… Could you teach me to put on makeup the way you do?"

I swallowed my prepared response, "Oh, I rarely agree to blind dates," as I struggled to regroup. "Um, sure. But what's wrong with the makeup you're wearing?"

Blanche focused on her cup and saucer, its red floral design matching the flush in her cheeks. "It's not working."

"But you look great," I said, trying to keep the conversation upbeat.

"He isn't noticing me."

Aha. Now we were getting somewhere; the mention of her love life immediately upgraded our relationship to a first-name basis. "Who isn't noticing you, Blanche?"

She looked up meekly. "Edward. Edward Gold. He's the handsome one, the pianist. Have you spoken to him or heard him play?"

"I think so." I vaguely recalled seeing a tall gentleman sitting at the center's keyboard. He wasn't in the writing class, so I hadn't met him personally.

"I've never had the guts to go up to a man and tell him I liked him. When we're in the same room, he looks right through me. He likes Adina Cohen, that stuck-up bitch. All because of those stupid chocolate chip cookies she brings in…she's going to give everyone diabetes, that's what she's going to do."

Wow, it was exactly as Froy described, high school redux. Just a tad like what Bea had urged me to do to Jay's girlfriend, meddle in a relationship that lacked a wedding ring. Still, if this would help solidify my relationship with Blanche's grandson…

"Blanche, why don't we do this? I'll do your makeup, and if you like it, I'll show you how to replicate what I've done. Then, with your permission, we can go into your closet and put together a knock-em-dead outfit. That way, you'll look stunning on Monday when I ask Edward Gold if he'd like to join our writing class. How does that sound?"

I'd never seen a face transform so quickly from glum to hopeful, like Cinderella after her fairy godmother transformed the pumpkin into a carriage. This visit might not have uncovered any insight into Jay, or whether Blanche was his nana, but if she was, I'd earn brownie points for my efforts.

Speaking of brownies, I considered my fledgling cosmetics skills and what I'd seen so far of Blanche's wardrobe and added, "Wouldn't hurt to bake a little something yourself. In the words of author Sarah Ockler: 'I've never met a problem a proper cupcake couldn't fix.'"

Chapter Nineteen

Saturday couldn't come fast enough. I loaded brooms, mops, dust pans, and buckets into my still-mangled Honda, along with enough Mr. Clean to sanitize Andrew Dice Clay's jokes. Kiki carried three sets of masks and gloves, as close to hazmat gear as I felt comfortable bringing without insulting Mrs. Geraghty. The one thing I didn't feel prepared for was facing Jay again. I wasn't sure how I felt about him.

More interested than before? Sure. But now that Blanche's lack of matchmaking had squashed my blind date hopes, what was the point of setting my sights on a man with a "Darling" in his life?

Deciding what to wear had been a major topic of discussion at breakfast. How to dress provocatively but still functionally? It's not like I could carry boxes to the curb in five-inch stilettos, even if I owned a pair, which I did not.

I searched my closet for some older yet stylish clothes that I wouldn't mind getting trashed and settled on a red tank top over a pair of black chinos, black sneakers, and a thin, gold ankle bracelet. I wore my hair back in a ponytail, more for comfort than appeal, but Kiki kept prattling on about how it accentuated my cheekbones. Whatever. This was as good as it was going to get. And he *did* have a girlfriend.

When we arrived at Michaela's house at ten, Jay's Lexus and the appliance repair truck were already parked across the street. My heart jumped when I saw his dimples, like tiny parentheses on either side of his growing smile. He stepped from his car, sporting the faded jeans from the other day, topped by a SALAD T-shirt he must have picked up at some fundraising event. Emblazoned with the words *SALAD: Senior Hunger ReLeaf,* the thin, white shirt did nothing to hide the contours of the muscles that bulged underneath. I was grateful he made his way toward our car since the sight of him left my knees one tendon short of buckling.

Kiki popped the trunk and unloaded cleaning supplies while I stood slack-jawed, trying to conjure up a coherent greeting. Jay rescued me, scuttling wordlessly to Kiki's side and volunteering his help. The repairman lifted his toolbox to assure me he was on the case. I grabbed the bucket crammed with cleaning solutions and sponges, while Jay carried a bouquet of mops and brooms, and Kiki brought up the rear with gloves and masks. Together, we marched to Michaela's front door, a disaster-relief crew determined to transform a hoarder's hell into a sparkling showplace.

"I've been looking forward to this," Jay shared. "Getting rid of the garbage, putting everything in its place. I honestly don't know how she can survive in there."

When Michaela finally answered the door, she appeared more startled than welcoming. That should have been a red flag that things would not progress as planned. I reminded her of the conversation we'd had the morning before.

"Oh... that's right... *cough*... the icebox... come in."

Shrouded in a fog of stale smoke, Michaela and her walker led the way, snaking through the Rockies of refuse to the kitchen. I stole a peek at Jay, who scowled at each pile he passed.

The repairman, Vic, pushed some old SALAD trays from the counter to clear a place for his toolbox. Noting Michaela's look of consternation, I gestured for her to follow me into the dining room, which was also piled high with boxes, the table implied rather than visible. We set down our supplies in whatever open spaces we could find.

"Mrs. Geraghty, I thought you and I should start in here while Vic gets to work in the kitchen. We're planning to be here all day. Won't it be great having the fridge working again? And to have the house cleared of all this clutter?"

Her eyes did not share my burst of enthusiasm. "I... don't... understand."

Jay and Kiki squeezed through the dining room doorway as I donned my rubber gloves and outlined the plan. "Don't you remember? We agreed to help you clear out the house, so you'll have more room to walk around and find everything you need." I gestured for Jay to join me, oversized Hefty bag in hand, and then I reached into the closest box, pulling out a filthy doll with a broken porcelain face. "We can start with this. You don't need this anymore, do you?"

"Noooo! What... are... you... doing?" Michaela's shriek prefaced a stream of coughing and hacking.

I was so surprised by her reaction, I dropped the doll on the floor, then almost destabilized a column of boxes reaching to retrieve it.

Jay instantly braced the cardboard pillar as I regained my

balance. "Mrs. Geraghty, I'm Jay. We were here the other day when you thanked us for offering to help. Don't you recall? We're trying to make this home more livable for you."

Panicked as a cornered animal, Michaela reached out and grabbed the doll, comforting it as she would a small child. "These... are... my... things. I... don't... want... them... touched."

Kiki stepped forward. "Mrs. Geraghty, we can't get the floors washed and the house dusted if we don't move some of these boxes out of the way. That seems logical, right? If you don't want us throwing anything out, do you have room in the basement where we can store these things while we clean up?"

"I... don't... want... anything... moved. I... need... everything... where it... is." Michaela lifted her walker and banged it against the floor for emphasis.

"But if we don't move—"

A bolt of electricity jolted my body as Jay squeezed my shoulder, cutting short a harangue designed to convince Mrs. Geraghty of her incoherent thinking. He pulled me out of Michaela's earshot and whispered, "It's her house, Carra. Believe me, no one wants to put it in order more than I do, but she has the right to have it anyway she wants. It's not our business. Let me see how Vic is doing with the fridge, then we'll get out of here. The three of us can go to brunch and lick our wounds. My treat."

"I wish—"

"You have the best of intentions, but there are emotional issues going on here that are way beyond either of our expertise. The last thing we want is to create additional anxiety for this troubled woman. Hang out, I'll be right back."

I mourned a little as he walked into the kitchen, already missing the way his warm breath had caressed my ear. It was such a shame. We could have done so much good here. Perhaps at a later date, I'd suggest a psychologist who specialized in hoarding issues and a decluttering expert, like on the cable shows.

He detoured briefly to speak with Kiki, who then headed back to the car, gloves and mask in hand. Michaela stood her ground, still clutching her doll and staring suspiciously to make sure I kept my mitts off her belongings.

When Jay returned, his expression was serious. "Mrs. Geraghty, I'm afraid your refrigerator is so old they can't fix it. I sent Vic home. But I promised you it would be in working order, and I'd like to make good on that promise. How about I arrange for a brand new, state-of-the-art, refrigerator-freezer to be delivered, professionally installed, and this old one carted away?"

Michaela's lip quivered. "That's... very... kind... but... no. It's... my... fridge. I'm... used... to... it... and... I... want... to... keep... it."

I wanted to yell, "But it doesn't work!" at the top of my lungs but Jay, sensing my frustration, again squeezed my shoulders.

"Mrs. Geraghty, that's your choice, of course." He reached into his jeans pocket and pulled a card from his wallet. "Here's my number, in case you've misplaced it. This offer has no time limit. You call whenever you decide you want a new fridge. Fair enough?"

She glanced at the card then looked back up with a befuddled expression.

I pointed to my ears and shouted, "Can you hear me, Mrs. Geraghty? Are your hearing aids working okay?" Maybe that was the problem all along. She just couldn't understand what we were saying.

"No... I... hear... you... fine. Please... leave. Now."

There was nothing left to do but gather whatever supplies Kiki hadn't removed and navigate our way back through the maze of clutter and out the front door.

"Think we should call someone?" I asked as we neared the Honda.

"Someone?"

"Family. Caretakers. A doctor. She's not right in the head."

Jay brandished a self-satisfied smirk. "Who was it that said getting involved with the clients, other than to deliver their meals, was against the rules?"

I rolled my eyes. "I did, but—"

"But nothing. It's over. How do you feel about eating at Eggs Over E Street? They make a mean mimosa, and you look like you have a few sorrows you need to drown."

~ * ~

We managed to grab the last open table before the late brunch crowd rushed in. Kiki and I sat on one side, Jay opposite me on the other. *Nice view.*

True to his word, he ordered a pitcher of mimosas. Kiki requested her own pitcher of diet soda, assuming the role of designated driver. "It's the least I can do after Jay offered to replace that woman's fridge." The twinkle in her eye told me she liked and trusted him. A good sign since she wasn't the easiest person to win over.

The waiter poured generous portions of the champagne-and-orange-juice elixir, then handed us menus. I had a hankering for artichokes and spinach, so I ordered the Eggs Sardou. Jay and Kiki both went for chocolate chip pancakes.

"Over it yet?" Another smirk from Jay McSmirkington.

"I'll live. I hope she can though, with no refrigeration and nowhere to walk. One day a cardboard tower is going to collapse and knock her right into a coma." To drive home my point, I stared past those golden frames, right into his baby blues, and forced back a fantasy of twirling those honey locks with my pointer finger. "Let's talk about something else."

"Okay, let's," he agreed. "Funny thing happened to me the other day at work. I'd love to hear your thoughts. Are you both game?"

"We're not attorneys, but okay, shoot." Kiki relaxed into her seat, no doubt enjoying today's episode of the *Jay and Carra Pretend They're Not Flirting* show.

He recounted a story about a woman and her two daughters, one of whom had swindled her mother out of her home, but the house hadn't yet closed. He said he was at a loss to help her and feared the mother would soon be left homeless or cramped into a tiny apartment with her one decent daughter. The fact that he asked for our help, that he felt close enough to share confidential information, left me breathless.

I sat with my Eggs Sardou, silently mulling his dilemma as he moved onto other topics, including bloodhounds, which enthralled Kiki since her family had once owned one. It wasn't until I was sopping up the yolk with a slice of Italian bread that I realized I knew exactly how to help him. The trick was figuring out how to convey it without divulging a secret of my own.

Part of my real estate training included a class called, "Ten Ways the Deal Can Fall Apart," and it contained the answer to his problem. But how to tell him without revealing I had any connection to real estate? If he suspected I might be at SALAD to convince the seniors to sell their homes, he'd never talk to me again. He was too protective of his nana to feel empathy for my situation.

Then it hit me, a solution so ridiculously simple it left me giddy.

"You think cleaning drool from the ceiling is funny?" he asked when he noticed my growing grin.

"No, I just realized the Dibble problem is solvable. I researched the real estate business last year for a short story. Do you, by any chance, have contacts in environmental law?"

His nose twitched and crinkled with curiosity. "I lease office space to an environmental law firm on the second floor of my building."

"Think they would do you a favor, for a good cause?"

"What are you getting at?"

I told him. Then all three of us smiled.

~ * ~

Monday morning, after my rounds—which included discovering Michaela had pinned a threatening note on her door, instructing me to leave her tray on the porch without speaking to her or there'd be consequences—I paid a visit to Prentiss Elder Law. Jay's scantily clad admin eyed me warily but informed her boss that Carra Quinn was back. Together, he and I climbed the stairs to Global Consciousness Environmental Law. Their receptionist set us up in a private office and exited with a verbal disclaimer: "Do whatever you need to, but I know nothing."

Jay stood by my side as I dialed the 702 number he provided and put the phone on speaker. Since he was handling Gemi's lawsuit, we wanted to keep his call involvement untraceable. It was ten o'clock on the East Coast but seven in Las Vegas. A sleepy voice answered, "Huh? What?" but I didn't feel sorry about yanking a fraudster out of a deep slumber.

"This is K.C. Dougherty at Global Consciousness in Rock Canyon," I said, borrowing the name of an associate at the firm. "I am looking for Siti Dibble."

"This is Siti."

"Are you the owner of 75 Devendorf Drive?"

"What is this about?"

"My clients, Damon and Raya Eisenberg, were scheduled to close on the property next week, but there's an issue."

"What kind of issue?"

"The buyers realized they hadn't inspected the septic system before signing the contracts. They asked the woman living there, a Diann Dibble, who I gather is a relative of yours, if they could conduct the test before closing to ensure everything is in working order. She agreed. But when we did some digging, we discovered the system is failing."

"How much will that cost to fix?"

"It can run as high as $8,000 but—"

"So fix it," barked Siti, anger replacing her sleepiness. "Take it out of the proceeds at closing. I'm good with that."

I winked at Jay. It was as if she were following verbatim the script I'd written, and now it was time for Operation Double Trouble. "If only it were that simple. We searched for another area to relocate the leech field, and that's when we discovered an abandoned underground oil tank." This was where I was winging it. I wasn't sure how deeply they buried such tanks or their proximity to an acceptable leech field, but if I didn't know, I figured neither did she.

"That's impossible. There's an oil tank in the garage."

"Yes, now. Originally, an underground oil tank serviced the house until someone buried and replaced it with the above-ground variety." I looked at Jay, who shrugged. Apparently, my improvised answer sounded convincing, at least to him.

"All right, so put the leech field somewhere else, I guess." Now she was getting really irritated.

"State law requires underground oil tanks to be emptied, cleaned, and purged of all vapors before burial because the tanks can corrode and leak. Unfortunately, many residents skipped that process, the former owners of 75 Devendorf Drive among them. When we tested around your tank, we found that oil had seeped out and contaminated the surrounding soil. According to EPA guidelines, you must remediate."

"Sounds like a racket to me." Siti obviously viewed the world through her own lens of corruption.

"I'd be happy to mail you a copy of the guidelines if you like."

"How much is this remediation going to cost me?"

"It depends how extensive the leak is and how far the oil has spread. Conservatively, anywhere from $30,000 to $50,000, which is your responsibility unless you carry oil tank leakage insurance. Do you happen to have your policy number handy?" I had to bite my lip to keep from convulsing into laughter.

"As a matter of fact, I don't. Can't you just fix everything now and take it out of the sale proceeds later?"

"Unfortunately, you must complete remediation before transferring title, which means all expenses must be paid in advance of the sale."

There was silence. I glanced up at Jay and he down at me. With my fingers, I counted three, two, one.

"I'm afraid there's been a mistake." Siti's response was right on cue. "I'm not the owner. The owner is Diann Dibble, the woman who permitted you to run the test. Check with her or my sister, Gemi. They'll show you the deed."

"We'll do that, but if we find you are the owner, we will have to start proceedings to have the work done then put a lien on your assets to cover the costs. Have a good day, Ms. Dibble."

I hung up and high-fived Jay. Then we let Gemi know the good news: she could expect a fax containing an amended deed as soon as her sister could locate another notary.

"I don't know how I can thank you," said Jay. "That was pure genius and an excellent performance to boot."

My cell buzzed, and I held up a finger. "Let me deal with this, then we can discuss suitable compensation." I strolled to the other side of the office for some privacy. "This is Carra."

"Carra, it's Blanche."

"Oh, hello, it's so good to hear from you."

"I wanted to tell you I'm wearing the outfit we picked out, and I am all ready for 'Project Go for the Gold.'"

"Perfect." I laughed, remembering how pleased we were when we came up with the name.

"I even made butterscotch and walnut blondies."

"Sounds delicious."

"I wanted to make sure you'll be at the center today to invite Edward to the writing group."

"Oh, I'll be there. I'm looking forward to it. See you later."

After disconnecting the call, I turned my attention back to Jay, whose cheer now seemed somewhat subdued, his effusiveness reduced from boil to simmer. I chalked it up to the interruption giving him time to reflect and return to his usual staid self. I figured I'd plow ahead, regardless.

"As for your offer, there is one thing you can do. Judith turned down my proposal for a Harvest Moon Dance at the center, but I know the seniors would love it. I've got some time before my shift starts. Can we brainstorm some way to hold it anyway?"

Chapter Twenty

After throwing around a few ideas, seeing Carra to her car, and picking up some Starbucks, Jay returned to his office, where the familiar scent of rose, bergamot, and orange assailed his nostrils. "What did Adriana want?"

Meggie fidgeted in her seat. "She wasn't here today, Mr. Prentiss."

"I can smell her perfume."

"No, it's mine. A gift from my new boyfriend."

He made no effort to hide his incredulity as he walked past her desk. "Really? Well, if he'll spring for A La Rose at $500 a bottle, I'd say he's a keeper."

Whatever. Even if his ex-girlfriend pumped Meggie for intel, there was little the admin could share that would cause damage. They were through. If he had been tentative before, this morning put any lingering doubts to rest. Adriana advised him to ditch the Dibble case and leave the poor mother to her own devices. Carra listened to the problem, thought it through, and quickly devised a brilliant solution— just as she had with Simon Garrison's dilemma. No flies on that girl.

It was her cellphone call that concerned him. He nursed his coffee as he reviewed the conversation he overheard: *'It's so good to hear from you... perfect... sounds delicious... I'll be there. I'm looking forward to it.'* Carra had a dinner date. And it wasn't with him.

He was in over his head, awash in emotions with which he was unfamiliar. The thought of her sitting with another man at a fancy restaurant sank his stomach like an anvil in a bottomless sea. And he was powerless to stop it.

Since the accident when he was eight, Jay had avoided the panic of chaos at all costs. He'd mired his life in structure and routine, battling impulsivity, analyzing situations to anticipate all potential outcomes — strategies that might have left him appearing calculated and somber, but which had served him well. Now Carra had landed like a cyclone, sucking him into her vortex. The ironic thing was, he liked it. He liked the thrill of surprise, the pathways she uncovered by straying from his carefully constructed grid. She'd served up a tidbit of unpredictability, and he'd become addicted to its exotic flavor and was unwilling to share that dish with whatever Tom, Dick, or Harry had been part of her life up to now.

The question was how to proceed. She didn't know he was available. Hell, on the last phone call she'd overheard Adriana called him "darling." Yet, if she knew he was available, it might make him look desperate if he chased her. No, she had to be the pursuer. There was only one way to accomplish that: become so devastatingly helpful to her cause he'd be impossible to resist. And her cause *du jour* was a dance for the seniors at SALAD. He picked up the phone and started making calls.

~ * ~

I grabbed a quick fast-food lunch at a drive-thru and sped over to the center, fingers crossed that my matchmaking advice would pay off for Blanche. It wasn't as if *my* love life was going gangbusters. Far from it. I hadn't dated in months, and now some woman who was no doubt slimmer, more sophisticated, and definitely more disciplined, had claimed the object of my affection.

There was still the chance that Blanche, once she was happily involved with Edward, might take pity on me and suggest a date with her grandson—who may or may not be Jay Prentiss.

A woman stood waiting outside the center's front door as I ambled up the walkway. Long brown hair, V-neck Boho maxi dress in a blue Indian pattern—she was clearly an artist. There was something so familiar about her. A knot formed in my stomach. When I drew close enough to see the expression in her eyes, I started to shake, more from rage than fear. Pivoting, I ran, the woman calling my name while in full pursuit. I jumped into my Honda and locked the doors before she could catch me.

That didn't stop her from banging on the window and shouting, "We need to talk, Carraway. You can't avoid me forever!"

Wanna make a bet? I pressed the ignition and lurched forward, eager to drive away her image and the memories it dredged up. Lying on a gurney in the hospital's hallway, nine years old, an Akita-sized bite decorating my upper arm and another on my thigh. Talk of rabies injections. Calling for my mother only to be told by my dad she wasn't coming. Not then, maybe not ever. It was the last time I'd seen her, other than in my nightmares, until today. Hopefully this would be the last time for good.

Who lets a young child near an unleashed guard dog in the park? Who doesn't pay attention when that dog attacks? Who runs instead of calling for help? If that person was your mother, would any excuse suffice? Not for me, no matter how many times Nikki might plead for me to reconsider. I still woke up covered in sweat from harrowing visions of dogs charging out of nowhere, leaping into the air, and knocking me to the ground. If my sister wanted to be bighearted and forgive our mother, that was her decision. I preferred to keep my ties severed into eternity.

I parked half a mile away and, still shaking with fury, I placed a call to my sister.

"What is it, Carra?" she answered after a few rings. "I'm just about to get into the pool with one of the rehab patients."

"Nik, where the hell do you get off telling Daisy where I work? She practically assaulted me outside the center just now."

The phone went silent for a moment.

"I would never do that, Carra. You made your feelings on this quite clear. I might not agree with your decision, but I respect it."

I remained unconvinced. "How did she find me then?"

"No idea. She may have been spying on me to see if I'd lead her to you. After she saw us together, she shadowed you instead. That's the only thing I can think of unless your address and workplace is somewhere online?"

"No. I'm careful about that. She couldn't have found me via the internet."

"Daisy never mentioned a surprise confrontation, Carra. You must believe me. I've got to go now, but we'll talk later. Go list a house."

It sounded like Nikki was on the level but that didn't solve my immediate problem: how to continue to avoid Daisy. Maybe I could ask Jay how I could get a restraining order. He still owed me a favor, and it was another great excuse to get in touch.

I waited a good ten minutes before driving back, then approached the center from the rear. It meant walking past Judith's office when I was already late, risking a second reprimand, but I had no other option. Sparring with her would be preferable to another skirmish with Daisy.

To my relief, Judith was AWOL, but Froy was quick to look up from juice duty. He glanced at his watch and stared imploringly in my direction. I detoured from my awaiting students to swing by his side and murmur, "Tell you what, if you want to take off early today, I'll stay and clean up."

Froy gave me one sharp nod before continuing to pour. His

acquiescence taught me that his silence was a commodity easily purchased by absorbing part of his workload. Good to know.

I spotted Blanche chatting with some others from my class. She did look more glamorous than usual, her hair permed and dyed a lighter silver, her rouge and lipstick more cherry than pink. She wore a dark blue dress and stockings in lieu of her usual polyester pants suit and low heels instead of orthopedics. A plate of blondies sat on her lap and, strategically, an empty chair by her side.

"Good afternoon everyone, you're all looking wonderful today." I shot Blanche a meaningful glance before continuing to address the group. "I hope you had an amazing weekend. We're going to start today with a writing sprint. It's not for your memoirs but simply to get the creative juices flowing. Your prompt is, 'When I was younger...' Think about that, and we'll quietly write for ten minutes. Afterward, if you'd like, you can read what you've written to the rest of the group."

To my surprise, no one objected or raised questions. They opened their notebooks and started jotting down thoughts, buying me time to help Blanche with her quest for romance. A well-preserved and elegant man matching her elaborate description sat reading a newspaper on a couch across the room. He had more hair than most, a lock or two roguishly hanging over one eye.

I strolled to his side. "You're Edward Gold, right?"

He tilted his head from the tabloid and raised a brow. "I am."

I sat beside him without permission, recalling my early teens when I'd wait for rock and rollers outside their hotel entrances or slip notes through their limousine windows. The good old days, before my dad's cancer diagnosis. "I hear you play piano. A few of the ladies told me you're very good."

He laughed, and his face flushed. "Thanks for the compliment. I have my moments." Blanche had good taste. Everything about Edward oozed charm.

"We haven't met. I'm Carra Quinn, the new recreational aide. I'm planning some special events for the center, and I'd love to add a karaoke night if you'd ever consider playing the backing tracks."

He beamed. "I'm not sure about karaoke but if you get that old clunker tuned, I'd love to host a sing-along. We could serve mocktails like at a piano bar, but instead we'd call it the SALAD Bar."

"That would be amazing. I'm curious... Did you ever play in a band when you were younger?"

"More than one. Those were heady times." He winked, and I felt myself falling in love.

"I bet you have quite a history. Why haven't you joined my

memoir class, start memorializing some of those stories? There's no pressure. I provide the pad and pen and some pointers on how to make the story flow. If, when, and how much you write are all up to you."

"I got around some, it's true. But I'm not sure anyone would be interested in what this bad boy did in his youth." He chuckled, but I could see the wheels were turning.

"Then you can keep it for yourself or your family as a permanent reminder of past adventures. Have you thought about joining another band?"

Edward shook his head wistfully. "Ms. Quinn, next June, I will be seventy-six years old. There's no band sitting around, waiting for me to take over their guitars or keyboards."

"That's where you'd be mistaken." I reached into my purse and pulled out a handful of pages I'd printed off the web, having anticipated such an objection. "These are all online ads from seniors looking for musicians to replace members who've left their bands. What do you like to play best? Rock? Jazz? Pop?"

His eyes glazed over, the memories taking hold. "I played a lot of sixties and seventies stuff. Zeppelin, Ozzie, Steve Miller, Pink Floyd, you name it. Even a little Fleetwood Mac, Elton, Billy. That list of yours really includes old fogies like me still playing?"

I handed him the pages. He pushed his reading glasses back onto the bridge of his nose and skimmed my research. A smile inched across his face. "This is fantastic. Thank you, Carra."

"It's my pleasure. So, would you consider joining us? Try it out, just for today. I have an empty seat with your name on it."

"Why not?" A youthful vibe crept into his voice. "I can read the newspaper any day."

I sat him next to Blanche, who was so tongue-tied all she could do was nod. But by the time I'd returned with a pad and pen for him, he was munching on a blondie and chatting with his blushing seatmate. Carra Quinn, Senior Matchmaker, I thought with satisfaction as I called the class back to order. This day might end on a cheerful note after all.

Chapter Twenty-One

Two weeks passed without a word from Carra, though to Jay, it felt like years. He understood there really wasn't any reason for them to speak—they'd already discussed preliminary ideas for the dance, and each had volunteered to research various aspects and convene again "sometime soon." It was the vagueness of the timing that bothered him; he preferred control over his schedule whenever possible.

For fourteen days, he'd tried but failed to vanquish the thought of her from his mind. He'd kept busy with cases that reminded him of her wavy locks and voluptuous body, like helping Gemi handle her mother's move into assisted living and checking on Simon's case to see if the police had apprehended his son-in-law.

Jay fished for SALAD intel when he visited his nana, asking how things were going at the center, but his grandmother only said "fine" and changed the topic. Adriana phoned occasionally to ask how he was faring, keeping the lines of communication open, the hope alive—on her end, anyway. He'd mentally archived that relationship, eager to open the file on a new one.

After yet another morning at his desk, leafing through briefs without being able to concentrate, Jay decided to abandon their "sometime soon" strategy. Surely enough time had passed to make any call seem casual.

He glared at the phone, willing heavenly inspiration to shine down and propel him into action. But the cell lay there, unaware, uncooperative, deriding his indecision. He scorned people who hesitated or choked when the pressure was on. Now he'd become one of them.

How hard was it to call a woman and ask her out to lunch? He had an excuse—he'd found the perfect venue for their Harvest Moon Dance. All that remained was sharing the details with the red-headed firecracker who'd captured his heart.

He was unsure of where to take her. Maybe that was the

problem—not a fear of rejection but inexperience with the process. Yes, that was it. He didn't treat clients to lunch often…they always met in his office or at their homes. Feeling more secure, he hit the intercom.

"Can I help you, Mr. Prentiss?"

"Meggie, can you suggest a few low-key restaurants for a business lunch? Someplace that's not too noisy?"

Silence. "Um, any food preference?"

She had him there. He didn't have a clue what Carra liked. Better play it safe. "Something middle-of-the-road. Salads, burgers, pasta…but upscale. Not a diner."

Another pause. "Brady's might work. It's like an Irish pub, lots of booths, so some privacy. Food's good. Also, Perry Winkle's, over on Miller. If you don't mind the whole place bathed in different shades of blue."

"Which do you prefer?" It made sense to get a woman's perspective.

"If it were me, I'd eat at Perry Winkle's. But I'm not a businessman—"

"That sounds fine. I trust your judgement. Please book me a table for two at noon."

"Sure thing."

Perfect. Once a reservation existed, he had no choice but to ask Carra out. Otherwise, he'd inconvenienced both Meggie and whoever at the restaurant was taking down reservations. He reached for his cell and punched in the number.

The sound of a car engine accompanied Carra's voice when she answered with a surprised, "Hello?" He must have caught her on her SALAD delivery rounds.

"Carra, it's Jay. Jay Prentiss. Am I calling at a bad time?"

"No, I dropped off Michaela's tray, and I still have four more to go. They substituted another house for Simon's on my route since he's still in hiding. What's up?"

She sounded cheery. That was encouraging.

"I was wondering…" *No, that sounded too tenuous.* "I've put together some logistics for the events we discussed. Are you free today for lunch? I wanted to run them by you, see what you thought." *Good. That sounded reasonable. Professional, impersonal. Not at all "date-like."*

"It's hard to turn down the lure of 'logistics,'" she teased. He imagined her fingers air-quoting the word, mocking his formality. "I have to be at SALAD by one for my shift though."

"So would noon work? I hear Perry Winkle's over on Miller has decent food."

"As long as it's decent."

Another jab. He ached to kiss the tongue out of her cheek.

"Miller is a quick four-block drive from the center," she said. "I guess I'll see you then."

He set down the cell and sagged into his chair. One hurdle down but what to say over lunch? Locations, prices, available dates–that part was simple. But what about the small talk that would inevitably follow?

Banter bewildered him. Women usually chased him, which burdened them with keeping the conversation lively. Now it fell on his shoulders, but would they buckle under the weight, leaving him hemming and hawing, grasping for words? He googled the word "charm," then admonished himself. If he couldn't be himself, why bother? Why was this girl, at least ten years his junior, tying him up in knots? Ridiculous. And yet…

He donned his ear pods, googled "How to Flirt," and spent the next hour watching instructional YouTube videos.

~ * ~

Jay's call blindsided me. Over the past two weeks, I'd almost banished him from my consciousness. Emphasis on the word almost. But at night, those dimples would invade my dreams and leave me sweaty and bothered. And here he was, asking me to lunch. Did that mean "Darling" was out of the picture or was Jay a player, looking to have his cupcake and eat it too?

I'd kept busy since I'd seen him last, including going to a few copywriting interviews that didn't pan out and receiving a letter of complaint from Michaela, who requested someone more respectful be assigned to her deliveries. When Judith questioned me, I explained I had offered to help declutter her home and get her fridge fixed. I saw no need to recount the entire disaster. To my surprise, Judith did not fire me. She merely cautioned me again about fraternizing with the clients and advised Michaela they were short on substitutes but promised I would steer clear.

I must have left Judith's office sulking because Helen noticed and invited me to sit beside her.

"I've added so many activities, but you're always sitting alone outside Judith's office. Why is that?" I asked.

"It's where all the action is," she teased. "Like today. Why the sad face?"

I gave her the short version, sans any reference to Jay or Kiki. "Judith may not have sent me packing, but this incident can't have helped my long-term prospects of remaining at SALAD post-probation."

"Don't be so hard on yourself, dear. You were following your heart, doing what you thought was right."

"Thank you, Helen. I appreciate that. You are one of my favorite people here. But you seem so lonely. I wish I saw you interacting more with the others."

"As I explained before, I really prefer to be on my own, dear." She set down her knitting to give me her full attention. "I'm here because my family worries I'm losing my marbles, which I'm not, and they want some eyes on me during the day. So, to save them from worrying and hovering, I come to SALAD. Everyone's happier that way."

"If you have to be here anyway, wouldn't it be fun to have a friend or two?"

"I've had enough of seventh grade. No need to live through it again. But it will please you to know, I've eavesdropped a little on your memoir class. It got me thinking about someone I miss from my past."

My ears perked up. "A lost love, perhaps?"

Helen's eyes turned melancholy. "Something like that. I married young, and after we had my daughter, my husband fell down an elevator shaft at work, and we lost him."

"I'm so sorry."

She patted my knee. "That's all right, it was a long time ago. Anyway, I got a job as a secretary and lived the life of a single mother. Saw my girl all the way through school, her marriage, and the birth of Jonathan, my grandson. Shortly after he was born, I met Troy through work. Love is different when you're in your forties. It's not that giddy, high-flying craziness. It's a deeper, more secure, grounded sort of love."

I giggled, unable to disguise my amusement. "Helen and Troy? Really?"

"You're not the first to point that out. If you're going to joke about us honeymooning in Greece, it's been done, *ad nauseum*. Unfortunately, we never got that far."

"Oh no. What happened?"

She shrugged. "Something came up that took me away from that job and out of state. Life goes on, you'll find that out as you grow older. But I've started thinking about Troy again. Even looked him up on the internet. So, I have benefitted from your class a bit, if it makes you feel better. Please don't repeat what I've told you. It's kind of personal."

I winked. "My lips are sealed."

Helen's seventh grade analogy wasn't far off the mark. Blanche, now aglow from the attentions of her new beau, had christened me the Henry Higgins of the geriatric set. Her friends would grab my arm and invite me to dinner, only to ambush me once I arrived with tales of their unrequited crushes. Marguerite lusted after Jason, but he belonged to Claudette. Mildred was in love with Irving, but he coveted Deidre. Phyllis wanted Gail to notice her, but Gail only had eyes for Theresa. It wasn't high school; it was the script for *The Old and the Resuscitated*.

I did for them what I'd done for Blanche. Helped them with makeup tips, coordinated their wardrobe. I even helped them shop online for trendier, more flattering outfits. Each of them consulted with me regarding what sugar-laden treats to bake to win over their man, which forced Judith to confiscate cookies and pies from the recreation room when glucose levels soared out of control.

I eased my conscience by telling myself that if the widowers these women clamored after were genuinely happy with their current lady friends, none of my efforts would make a difference. But deep down, I worried I was butting in where I didn't belong.

Occasionally, the women felt beholden enough to reciprocate, setting me up on blind dates with their grandsons. I'd endured three such dates over the past few weeks, with three gawky, immature recent grads, all short on sophistication and even shorter on employment. Two out of the three expected me to treat for dinner, because unlike them, I had a paying job. If Jay hadn't impressed me before, compared to these dudes he was a god among mortals.

A few of the visits resulted in more than matchmaking and makeovers. Janet invited me over to look through photos of her rehomed dogs. The love with which she turned the pages of her photo album, describing their adventures together, left my heart aching.

Bryan Redmond and I sat together in his living room, reviewing catalogs to determine which local college might be the most welcoming. Despite my reassurances, his greatest fear was that the younger students would mock him for his advanced age. And Edward asked me to sit in on his rehearsal with his new band, Geritol Overdose. All men over seventy who had welcomed him as their keyboardist with open arms. And boy could they rock, even in their advanced years.

So the call from Jay intrigued me, not only because I missed him, but I also had some donations I wanted to solicit to help Janet, Bryan, and the others. Jay had been so willing to cover Michaela's appliance costs, perhaps he had some residual generosity burning a hole in his pocket. Lunch would be a great opportunity to ask.

I arrived at Perry Winkle's a few minutes late—it never paid to look too eager.

The place looked like the set of *Blue's Clues*. Everywhere you turned, a different hue of blue. As the hostess walked me to the table, *Blue Eyes* by Elton John ended, immediately followed by Linda

Ronstadt's *Blue Bayou*. Monitors hanging from the ceiling played episodes of *NYPD Blue*.

Jay was already waiting at our table, rolling his eyes to reflect a level of disbelief that matched my own. "I'm sorry...my admin recommended this place. I didn't realize it would be so..."

"Hokey?" I volunteered.

"I was going to say 'colorful.'"

"Azure, it will be just fine."

"Sort of sapphires up the taste buds," he countered.

"Think I can order some mashed potatoes and navy?" I said, unwilling to surrender and let him have the last pun.

Jay hesitated then frowned. "Can't think of anything else, so I guess you win."

I raised my chin in victory and accepted a menu from our server. Her name tag read Scarlet.

"Scarlet?" asked Jay. "How did you manage to get hired here with that name?"

"Affirmative action." She left the menus and headed for the kitchen. It was a practiced retort no doubt repeated several times a day to wise-ass customers like us.

"I guess I'll try the *indigoulash*," I told Scarlet when she returned for our orders, Bob Dylan's "Tangled Up in Blue" playing in the background.

"The *coBaltimore* crab cakes for me," said Jay, cringing in jest.

I enjoyed seeing this side of him, relaxed and enjoying the jokes.

Once Scarlet left I think we both felt a little awkward, so I decided to break the silence. It was either that or sing along to "Blue Suede Shoes." "So, what have you come up with for SALAD?"

He opened his briefcase and pulled out a folder. "When you said Judith nixed using the center for the dance, I came up with some alternate locations. I think the community room at St. Augustine's works best. They need the money, and the facility has a built-in sound system."

I looked over his paperwork. It revealed copious research. A clue to his perfectionistic nature or a desire to impress?

"A fair number of the SALADians—that's my nickname for them—aren't Christian. So I'm afraid a mention of St. Augustine might put them off before they even arrive." I thumbed through his other suggestions. "This one—the hall at the Lion's Club might work."

"Not too feline? Not apt to insult the more canine of the group?" Jay asked dryly.

I looked up. "*Rip-roaringly* funny."

"That was my *mane* objective."

"Jokes aside, it looks like it would cost us around $500. Plus whatever music and refreshments might run. Think anyone would object to paying a small cover charge?"

Jay tilted his head in an adorable way that let me imagine what he must have looked like when he was a toddler. What a shame I'd never know him at that age.

"I don't mind sponsoring the event myself," he said as he reached for a roll and some butter.

"Really? Are you sure? It could run over a thousand, all in. Even if we record some music onto an iPod and only serve juice—"

"I was thinking more of a live band. Make it really special."

Wow. I was about to protest that he was being far too generous when a willowy, raven-haired model-type in a tailored jacket and miniskirt stopped at our table. She'd wrapped her hair into a chignon, which only served to expose an expression of strained constipation. Jay must have noticed my surprise because he glanced up, and abruptly, the mood at the table changed.

"Adriana." He pushed his chair back and stood, no doubt a throwback to manners ingrained at an early age. "Carra, this is my... friend, Adriana. Adriana, this is Carra."

"What a surprise finding you here, Jay." She pasted on a fake smile as she signaled for him to retake his seat, then slowly deigned to glance in my direction. "And Carra. I've never heard of that name before. Sounds exotic."

"It's short for Carraway." I tried to match her snippiness, but the words came out more as a squeak.

"How seedy." She shook her head with self-satisfaction, as if with that chestnut, she'd landed the *coup de grâce*. "Jay, I'm sorry to interrupt but seeing you here saves me a phone call. Did I leave my umbrella at your place? I can't find it anywhere."

His back went rigid. "I believe nothing of yours remained at the apartment after we ended things."

"I don't consider a hiatus an ending, darling. Remember, we have that dinner with Senator Mitsky and his wife coming up. Anyway, would you mind if I used my key to poke around later, make sure I left nothing in the drawers or closet?"

What a bitch. I get it. You two were involved.

"I think this would be an excellent time for you to return that key. Please cancel with the senator. I won't be able to make it."

"Don't be too hasty, Jay. Dinners with Mitsky don't come along every week. Take some time and think about it. As for the key, I don't believe I have it on me." Adjusting her purse, she cranked up the treacle and said, "I must run but it's been so lovely to meet you...Carra, wasn't it? I'll be in touch, Jay." Off she flitted, with Neil Diamond's "Song Sung Blue" accompanying her exit.

I could tell Jay was in a tough position. If he explained himself, it would look like he was apologizing, an admission that he hoped our relationship would blossom. However, if he ignored the whole thing, he might seem callous, or disinterested in my feelings about Adriana's existence.

I decided to let him off the hook. "'Darling,' I presume?"

"Yup." He pressed his lips together and looked down at his half-buttered roll.

Scarlet showed up right on cue with my goulash and Jay's crab cakes, then hurried off to avoid further name mockery.

Time to march forward and leave "Darling" in the dust. "I'll have to get going soon. How about we concentrate on the dance?" I stabbed a morsel of beef and brought it to my lips. The food turned out to be much better than the décor and soundtrack had led me to believe.

He uncreased his brow, relieved by the topic change. "So, Carraway, huh? Like in *The Great Gatsby*?"

I almost choked on my stew. He was the first to get it right. My mother always said someday a man would, and that's how I'd know he was the one for me.

I struggled to regain my composure. "My sister's name is Nikki. My mom was Daisy. She loved that whole roaring twenties theme. Very fanciful, my mom. Spent her life chasing after dreams, with no real grasp on reality."

"So, I guess the name Jay fits into your mom's vision, huh?"

"Should I refer to you as Mr. Gatsby from now on?"

He popped another bite of crab cake into his mouth. "I'd prefer not. I don't particularly like how his life turned out."

"True dat. But speaking of Gatsby and his grand parties, we should meet a few more times and plan this dance properly. Pick a date, work out all the details. Why not ask your nana for some suggestions? By the way, I'm curious. Since there's no Mrs. Prentiss at the center, who exactly is she?"

"Ah, can't give that away. Wouldn't want her to get special treatment."

He stared at his plate, suddenly fascinated by his side of tomato gazpacho.

Odd... From the first moment I'd seen him, complaining about gin games and carb-heavy meals, I understood he very much expected special treatment for his grandmother. He was hiding something. The question was, what? Judging by the attention his gazpacho was receiving, I wouldn't get answers today. I placed a mental marker next to the word nana and returned to the subject of the dance.

"So...when can we meet next? I'd love to hold the dance by the end of the month, before the evenings get too chilly. I've got seniors hot to trot, so what about scheduling it for a Friday night, immediately after the center closes? That way, we can pick them all up from one place. We must provide transport home though. Many of these folks are too old to drive, and I don't want them taking a public bus late at night. By the way, I might have the perfect band for you. The keyboardist is a SALADian."

"Sounds good. How about meeting this Thursday night after your shift? An early dinner? Somewhere...less blue?"

I fished my phone from my purse and pretended to check my calendar. "That'll work. While I've got you, there are one or two things I was hoping you might help me with."

~ * ~

As Carra rattled off a list of ways to improve the lives of her elderly flock, with his financial help, of course, Jay basked in her passion and the creativity of her suggestions. If he wanted to capture her heart, helping her cause was the way in.

Even better, he'd subtly asked her out for Thursday. A prime dating night, at least from what he'd gathered after overhearing Meggie blather with her friends. He wondered if Carra would like Poisson, or if a casual venue would be more suitable. Meggie had mentioned Brady's. He'd check it out personally before suggesting it to avoid another Perry Winkle debacle.

The thought of Meggie filled him with fury. Adriana hadn't happened by today's restaurant accidentally. First the reception area smelling of his ex's signature scent and now this. His admin had to be feeding her information. But why?

Jay tried to vanquish his rage and concentrate instead on the bounce of Carra's curls as she emphasized a point. Finally, she stopped listing her demands long enough to swig her soda.

"I don't suppose you have any friends looking for a job as an administrative assistant. Or you, perhaps?" he asked. It was worth a shot.

"Me? No, I'm learning that I'm not the stuck-in-front-of-a-computer, nine-to-five type. Why? Something wrong with yours?"

"Just wondering, that's all."

She put down her glass, glanced at her watch, and reached for her purse. "Wow, this hour *blue* by fast. It's almost one, and I've got to get going. Can I cover my half of the meal?"

He drew back in surprise. Another first. He couldn't remember the last time any woman he dated offered to pay for anything. "Tell you what. Save it to buy something special for the seniors."

"That's sweet. Well, thanks for lunch and for all your research. *Teal* we meet again." She hurried off to the tune of Crystal Gayle crooning, "Don't It Make My Brown Eyes Blue."

Had to get in the last pun, he mused, noting she looked as good from the back as she did from the front.

Jay ordered a cappuccino and reviewed his messages, deciding to let his irritation with Meggie subside before returning to the office. Stumbling upon this palace intrigue now meant he could pump her for information later. If Adriana planned to use his admin as a conduit to access his plans, well, two could play at that game. When he looked up, to his surprise, a woman had taken Carra's seat.

"I'm so sorry to disturb you, but I need a favor, and you may be the one person who can help me."

Perfect. Another addition to his overburdened caseload. But she was here, her eyes filled with desperation, and he wasn't one to be rude. "Please, start at the beginning. I'd be happy to listen. Tell me what I can do."

Chapter Twenty-Two

On my drive to the center, I reviewed the surprises revealed over lunch. Jay had a sense of humor and a quick wit. I didn't see that coming. He was also more generous than I had previously imagined, willing to spend whatever it took to make my Harvest Moon Dance the senior event of the season.

But the big news of the day was that he asked me out for Thursday night. And he understood what Carraway stood for. That was huge. Kiki and I had a lot to talk about tonight.

Oh, but Adriana. "Darling." Make that "Darling" with the lost umbrella she somehow misplaced in his apartment, the one to which she had her own key. Jay said they were finished. She'd countered with that hiatus crack. If it were only a break, he wouldn't jeopardize their relationship by saying it was over in front of her, right? In his mind, it *had* to be history. Or was I missing something? Another topic to analyze with Kiki, down to his last uttered syllable.

I was itching to spread the word about the dance, giving my rutting seniors an excuse to make a move on their intended targets and ask them out before their regular squeezes caught wind of the event. Blanche, Marguerite, Mildred, and Phyllis might have scored, but now Evelyn, Brenda, and Greer were all pimping out their grandsons in exchange for cosmetic tips and advice on the best baked goods to lure a widower from his current hussy. A Harvest Moon Dance could save me a lot of time and energy.

Today, some of my students had agreed to read from their memoirs. Most had written at least twenty-five pages, which was a good start. The only one who had written nothing was yours truly. I'd pulled out my Revise and Resubmit requests and studied the suggestions but couldn't propel myself into action. How ridiculous, considering I'd spent months getting those original eighty-thousand words onto paper. Deep down, I knew the editors' suggestions were solid advice that would make the novel publishable. Yet, something was stopping me, an elusive demon with no face and no name. Maybe Kiki and Nikki were right. Perhaps I did have a fear of success.

I certainly had no compunction about my students succeeding. I boosted their confidence at every turn. The number willing to read today was a testament to their level of assurance. What was worrisome, I noted as I entered the rec room, was that Judith had chosen this day to observe.

Up until now, she'd left the memoir-writing class alone. Not that she approved—mainly because it was something new, initiated by an underling—but it didn't tax the budget, and it kept the seniors occupied and happy. Her persnickety attitude shut down creativity, however, and I took comfort that she sat at the back of the room, out of eyeshot of most of the nearsighted participants.

Since having my pupils read their work constituted a special event, I'd purchased a cordless, Bluetooth microphone and mini amp so the readers wouldn't have to shout to be heard. Kiki razzed me about the eighty-dollar price tag ("It would be nice if you put that money toward the electric bill.") but I justified the expense as vital to the success of the program and my continued employment.

What I hadn't counted on was the curiosity of the rest of the seniors. They'd drafted a reluctant Froy into arranging the remaining rec room chairs around the perimeter of the reading circle. The bigger audience put more pressure on my authors, but if they minded, they didn't show it. I switched on the equipment and prayed to the gods of open mic for this experiment to go well.

As the person who'd suggested the class, it seemed fitting that Georgia kick off the afternoon. She cleared her throat and advised the crowd she'd be reading from the third chapter, not from the beginning. Then she held the pages a few inches from her thick lenses and began: "I'll always remember that Sunday and that talk. We were in our early thirties, living in a tiny apartment. We'd come home from church, and I was preparing dinner while Louis watched the Jets play the Bills on the black-and-white Panasonic we kept on the kitchen table.

"'I spent the day with Myra,' I said during a commercial, looking down at the carrots I was chopping so he wouldn't see the dampness in my eyes. 'She complains about the twins, but God has blessed her with two healthy babies.'

"'I'd complain too if I had to spend all day working at a factory like Gerald does, just to see every penny going toward diapers and formula,' he said. 'At night, he can't catch a break because when one baby stops bawling, the other starts. It's not the picnic you're picturing, Georgia.'

"'True, but it's a picnic I'd like us to share, ants and all.'

"'We've had this argument a thousand times,' he grumbled. 'You've seen three doctors, and they all agree, your insides ain't hospitable to carrying babies. I'm okay with that, I'll love you no matter what. We'll adopt, I promise. But we've got to be smart about it, Georgie. Sock away the savings. Buy a three-bedroom in the suburbs. Newark ain't the best place to raise kids. If we're gonna do it, let's do it right.'

"'Okay,' I said, swallowing my misgivings. 'We'll wait.'

"I didn't think much more about that conversation until ten years later, when I was sitting by Louis's hospital bed. High blood pressure had brought on a massive heart attack. Doctors said he probably wasn't gonna make it, but I told them to keep that to themselves. No point in upsetting the man when his days were numbered.

"'Georgie,' he said, grasping my hand like a lifeline, 'When I get out of here, let's go right to whoever we gotta see to adopt a kid. I was wrong about the waiting. There ain't no perfect time. As long as we give 'em love, it don't matter how small the apartment or how empty my wallet. They'll be all right.'

"I squeezed his palm. 'You're going to be a wonderful papa,' I told him.

"'Can't wait to find out,' he replied.

"'That night, he had a second attack. He was dead by morning. I'll never know if we would have made good parents, because we were too busy being expert procrastinators. So busy worrying and analyzing, we let life pass us by. That will always be my greatest regret."

She looked up, her hands shaking, either from delayed stage fright or the power of her own sentiments set down in print. No one knew quite how to react. The silence in the room was deafening.

Helen, my greatest supporter, rose from her seat, put her hands together, and yelled, "Bravo!" One by one, the others followed suit, and the room soon filled with applause. The standing ovation prompted Georgia to lift her glasses and pat away tears. Judith broke through the circle and scurried to her side.

"Are you all right, Ms. Martin? I want to apologize for whatever Carra asked you to do that has upset you so."

I balled my fists, so angry at her for throwing me under the bus without a moment's hesitation.

It took Georgia a minute to gather herself and respond. "Mrs. Ferester, why would you say such a thing? This lovely girl, Carra Quinn, gave me an opportunity to reflect upon my life. Because of her and this class, I've been able to come to terms with my choices and with my past. She even introduced me to the people at the Foster Grandparents program last week. If you don't see me around here as much, it's because I'm going to have my own child to take out and spoil a few times a week. I would have never thought of it if it weren't for her."

Judith furrowed her brow, as if Georgia were speaking in Martian. Or maybe it was the potential loss of income that concerned her as SALADians found alternate ways to keep themselves busy.

"I'm in a band now because of Carra," Edward yelled above the fray. "I'd given up on that part of my life, but she reminded me of what I loved when I was younger and assured me that talent never dies. That girl is a treasure, the queen of second chances. Never let her go."

The Queen of Second Chances. It had a nice ring to it, especially since I came from royalty, my stepmother being the Queen Bea of mobile homes and all. Sovereignty must run in the family.

"The band's called Geritol Overdose, and they're fantastic. Come see them!" Blanche added at the top of her lungs. I guess you're never too old to be a groupie either…

"She saved me from being housebound and lonely," Janet called out. "Next week, we're going to a shelter for senior rescue dogs, because that's about the activity level I can handle considering this stupid wheelchair. Without her, I'd still be depressed and staring at my four walls. But now I can look forward to another fur baby or two."

The room vibrated with private conversation and public protest. My face grew hot from all the attention, especially because I hadn't wanted Judith to find out about all my extracurriculars. If she called me out, I wondered if it would be fair to mention Jay had also been complicit. That might take some of the wind out of her sails. Thank goodness she knew nothing about our upcoming dance. The very mention of it would probably make her explode.

I watched with trepidation as she seemed to process the mushrooming insurrection. She shot an inquiring look at Froy, who shrugged and returned to his eternal pouring of juice, a fountain in human form. As the temperature in the room skyrocketed, she wisely chose the path of least resistance, the one that would avoid further client dissatisfaction. Signaling for the clamor to subside, she borrowed the mic from Georgia's lapel and addressed the growing unrest.

"I didn't mean to suggest Carra was in the wrong, but remember, my job is to keep you all calm, healthy, and happy. When I see one of our most beloved seniors in tears, wouldn't you want me to check, make sure she's okay?"

Amazing how Judith didn't trip over the lies spilling from her lips.

"We appreciate your concern," said Edward. "But we're fine.

Better than fine. Are you adequately reassured? Can we finish our reading in peace?"

Judith went crimson. She was apparently not used to being chided the way she chided others, but she wouldn't dare disagree with any of her patrons. She handed the mic back to Georgia, signaled for the class to carry on, and hurriedly retreated to her office.

After I attached the mic to the next reader's lapel, I turned to throw Helen a nod of thanks for starting the applause. To my dismay, she and her knitting had already departed.

~ * ~

When Jay wanted clarity, he knew exactly where to turn. So it was no surprise when he arrived unexpectedly at his nana's house the day after his luncheon with Carra. An early dinner together at Brady's would also give him a chance to check out the place before his Thursday night date.

Once ensconced in a private booth with red cushions on oak benches, she looked him right in the eye. "What's troubling you, Jay?"

"What makes you think anything is bothering me, Nan? Can't I treat my beautiful grandmother to a midweek dinner?"

"You can and you should, but I know you, and I know something is wrong. Let's have it. Are you having issues with Adriana or with work?"

He recoiled slightly. "Neither actually." He passed her the breadbasket, and she selected a pumpernickel roll. "Work's been going well recently. Helped a woman recover a house that her daughter tried to sell without her knowledge." A vision of Carra on the phone convincing Siti that her leaking oil tank was a money pit made him smile.

"That's admirable. What about Adriana, then?"

He felt the smile fade as he grabbed some cornbread from the basket. "I've grown interested in someone else, but I'm not sure it's appropriate."

Nana drew her eyebrows together. "Why? Is she underage?"

"No, she's about ten years younger than me, I guess."

"Is she lewd? A drunk? A drug addict?"

He was quick to defend Carra. "Oh no, nothing like that. It's just… she's different from the girls I usually date."

Nana snorted. "Thank goodness for that. Means she won't have a stick halfway up her ass."

Jay was dumbstruck. "Who's the lewd one now?"

She pulled her glasses down and stared over the rims. "You keep dating this prototype of the quintessential ice queen. They probably look great on paper, with a perfect pedigree and the right Ivy League schooling, but they have no personality. No zip. All so blah. This last one was the worst of the bunch."

"Then it should delight you to hear I've ended it with Adriana. Told her we were through."

"She must have been thrilled."

"I don't think she quite believes me. The new girl and I were at lunch the other day, and Adriana hunted us down and made a big point of saying we were on hiatus."

"She'll get the idea, eventually. Tell me about the new girl."

"You've probably met her, Nan. She works at SALAD. Carra Quinn?"

Nana chuckled as she took the menu offered by the server. "I guess you've saved me some time then."

"What do you mean?"

"The new 'in' thing at SALAD these days is for the widows to set Carra up with their grandsons. I might have mentioned you to her earlier, but you were involved with Adriana so—"

Jay grew rigid at the idea of Carra being in such demand. He remembered the phone call he'd overheard. At the time, he assumed she might have one suitor, but his nana made it sound like fixing up Carra was a new Olympic sport. If that were the case, he planned to be the lone contestant going for the gold. "Has she gone out with any of them?"

"Three from what I've overheard. None of which sounded like they went too successfully." She turned to the server and ordered a Cobb salad.

Jay waved him off, having lost his appetite. "Did the grandmothers say why?"

Her eyes twinkled. "If you're going out with the girl, why don't you ask her yourself?"

"I will, I will...but we're not going out yet. We're...we're talking. Getting to know each other, planning a big event together."

She tilted her head. "What kind of event? A wedding would be nice. I'd like to live long enough to see you married."

"One thing at a time. You can't repeat this, but we're planning an off-site dance for the seniors. Judith Ferester squashed the idea when Carra suggested holding one at the center."

"Judith seems to have it in for Carra and anything she suggests. She prefers keeping things simple, easy. That new girl is shaking everything up, and it unnerves Judith. Just like Carra is unnerving you."

He scoffed and downed his glass of water. "I am not unnerved. I am..."

"Smitten?"

"Something like that, I'm embarrassed to say. You know how I don't enjoy being out of control."

"Probably better than anyone." The waiter served her salad, and as she savored a lump of blue cheese, she added, "But this girl...they're calling her the Queen of Second Chances because she's helped everyone remember what was good about their lives when they were younger. Suggesting how they might recapture those feelings now or change the things they regret. It's..." Her eyes glazed over, as if dreaming about something in her past.

"Nana?"

"It's very rejuvenating. Everyone's happier, walking with a bounce in their step. Confidence is soaring, new relationships forming. She's brought magic to the center, a spell of hope."

That's my girl, Jay thought with pride as he ripped off another piece of cornbread and slathered it in butter. "It sounds like you wouldn't be against my seeing Carra... even though she isn't what most people would expect in a politician's partner?"

"Remember when you were little and used to ask all those questions about kings and queens, and we dug up my video of Prince Charles's wedding to Diana Spencer?"

Jay eyed his grandmother quizzically. "I remember. Why?"

"Everyone thought she was the perfect woman for him. They spent millions on that spectacle. But Charles and Diana were miserable and eventually, he ended up with Camilla Parker Bowles, the woman he should have married in the first place. Why did they waste so many years in misery? Because the royal family believed that Camilla, a divorcee, was unacceptable. My point is, don't judge compatibility by other people's standards. You've got a brain and a heart. Use them and make the choice that's best for you."

He never felt as close to his grandmother as he did at that moment. He took one more look around the pub and then pulled out his phone and dialed Carra's number. "Hey, it's me. Sorry to bother you, but I was wondering...about Thursday... How do you feel about fish?"

Chapter Twenty-Three

"He's taking you to Poisson? That's huge, girl."

Nikki looked genuinely impressed as we sat in the conference room at Rock Canyon Realty, waiting for Bea to show. These meetings were becoming an unwanted drag on my schedule, especially now that so much of my free time involved visiting seniors' homes. Still, Bea was paying part of my salary, however meager, and I owed her at least this much.

"Maybe he wants to show off how much he can afford," I said.

"Isn't he already doing that by sponsoring the entire dance? Nah, this is a date, and it's major. I'm going to expect a full report on Friday."

Tiring of this line of interrogation, I changed the topic to Nikki's favorite subject, her own love life. "How are things going with the rehab center director?"

"He's not inviting me to the most romantic restaurant in town, that's how. But we have our moments. The thing is, they may exist solely in my imagination. He asks me to help a client in the pool and I'm thinking, 'He wants to see my butt while I swim away,' when in reality, he might just want me to help the patient."

"Has it gone anywhere beyond that? Intimate asides or questions about your personal life?"

"Sorry to make everyone wait," Bea interrupted as she burst into the room like a hailstorm, chucking her files on the desk. "Let's have everyone's updates, starting with Nikki and the rehab center."

"Mr. Grundel will be listing his house with me next week. There's no way he can hack climbing three levels any longer, not since the car crash. I'll be taking his wife out on Saturday to look at ranches." She sat back in her chair, a self-satisfied smile reminding me that by December, she'd be the solitary daughter still working on the team.

"Excellent work, Nikki. Your split from that double sale will likely bring in the five grand you needed for that car down payment. How about you, Carra? What good news do you have for me?"

"She's got a big date with Mr. Moneybags on Thursday," Nikki teased.

The dollar signs in Bea's eyes shone from clear across the room. "Tell us more, Carra."

"There's nothing to tell." I willed a lightning bolt to strike me down so I wouldn't have to endure this conversation. "I'm not even sure it's a date. It's more of a planning session for an event I'd like to organize for SALAD." There. Hopefully that would put an end to it.

"At Poisson."

Thanks, Nikki, you had to poke the bear.

"No one goes to Poisson for a planning session, Carra. Do you have an interest in this man?" asked my stepmother.

Good question. From the day I'd first gone to his office, I'd seen him and his fundraising as a means to an end. A way to improve seniors' lives instead of treating them Bea's way, as potential real estate conquests. His help made my days at SALAD tolerable, while still allowing me to look myself in the mirror at night. Not as a user, but as an agent of change. Except I had been a user, hadn't I? I'd been using him.

Now, my perception of him had softened. Handsome and generous, even if he was a straight-laced, intractable stickler for rules—like when we broke into Simon Garrison's home without a warrant to rescue him. Trespassing, indeed. Still, he was an anchor to my flights of fancy, my safe place. My stomach flip-flopped when I thought about him…until I recalled his temper. His mercurial nature reminded me of my birth mother and not in a good way. I decided a shrug to Bea's interrogative would have to suffice.

Unperturbed, she pressed on. "You must fill us in on every detail. In the meantime, any houses to list?"

I sensed I needed to throw Bea a bone. "Several seniors have invited me to their homes. Many of them are lovely. But no one has expressed the slightest interest in downsizing or moving into assisted living."

Bea narrowed her eyes, her X-ray vision cutting through my armor of deception. "Did you ask? Did you mention how much equity those houses might hold? If they bought the property back in the seventies, their investment might have quadrupled by now. But if the economy tanks, then poof, their profit disappears. Hundreds of thousands lost, all because you didn't push them to either sell or refinance. It's practically malpractice."

Bea's idea of malpractice differed from mine, but I thought of something that might satisfy both of our missions. "Some seniors have started dating. If they decide to move in together, then one of them will probably sell, and I promise I'll zoom right in for the kill."

"No need for that facetious tone, Carra." Bea's voice was thick with frustration. "You're the one with money troubles. I'm handing you the ladder to financial independence. If you fear heights, I'm sure the fast-food industry would be delighted to employ a quick-witted worker such as yourself. Though you'll probably talk the diners out of the Happy Meal and refer them to the local salad bar."

She gathered her files and left without another word.

Nikki shot me a nasty look. "Now you've done it, Carra. If she changes her mind about this gig and pulls me out of the rehab center, I'll never talk to you again."

"Yeah, it would be a shame to stop ripping paraplegics from their homes, displacing them, and creating even more stress in their lives. A real loss." I surprised myself with the venom spilling from my lips.

"At least I can make the rent. Where will you be living in November?"

Set and match.

My sister took off, leaving me alone in the conference room, asking myself the same thing. In one short meeting, I'd managed to put my job in jeopardy while infuriating both my stepmother and sister. If Bea pulled my salary, where exactly would I go?

Chapter Twenty-Four

Jay fiddled with the silverware while waiting for Carra to arrive. Poisson was as crowded as a sardine can, but a fifty-dollar bill secured them a prized spot in a dark, romantic corner. He sat facing out, affording him a perfect view of anyone who might unexpectedly approach their table. Since he'd made the reservations himself, without Meggie's knowledge, he doubted Adriana would pop in but he couldn't be sure. Meanwhile, Carra would have nowhere to look except into his eyes, which would reflect his sincere intent to pursue their relationship on a deeper level.

He wore his best dark blue Armani suit, the one with the silver pinstripes, along with a white shirt and no tie; formal but still casual.

When she entered the restaurant, he knew he'd chosen well. She'd also dressed in dark blue, a square-necked sheath dress with a matching cardigan. As the greeter guided her to his table, he stood and noticed a solitary element of classic Carra whimsy: dangling carnival prize earrings resembling tiny clear plastic bags, each filled with fake water and a tiny goldfish.

He stifled a laugh. "Nice earrings."

The greeter pulled out her chair, and both she and Jay sat down.

"When in Rome, and all that." She took a long look at his outfit. "Armani?"

"How did you know?"

She batted her eyelashes. "Suits you."

"Another night of puns?"

The server poured water into their crystal glasses and the sommelier handed them each a wine menu. Jay skimmed it quickly. "They have a nice Gavi di Gavi. Would you like to try it?"

Carra tilted her head. "Sure. Why not?" Once the sommelier took his leave, she leaned forward and murmured, "I thought we were going to review logistics. When did this become a date?"

He kept his tone even, carefully choosing his words. "When my grandmother told me how busy your evenings had become lately, I thought it might take something special to lure you away."

"Ah, your grandmother...and who exactly would that be?"

"Fishing for names again, are we?"

As her grin matched his own, a tiny red curl bobbed seductively against her cheek. "If I'm going to fish, Poisson would be the place to do it. So, spill."

"She would be someone who holds your talents in very high regard. She told me you've made a tremendous difference at SALAD."

He watched Carra's face turn crimson in the candlelight's glow. The wine steward poured a swig of Gavi for Jay to sample and after he approved, he filled their glasses. Carra took a deep gulp. She's as nervous as I am, Jay thought.

"Time to talk logistics, Ms. Quinn. I've booked the Lion's Club Hall for October 25th. It's a Friday night, and I've reserved it from six to ten. I've arranged for decorations as well as hors d'oeuvres and refreshments—nothing alcoholic. A fleet of wheelchair-accessible vans will pick the seniors up at the rec center then drop them all home afterward. Once you verify that the band you suggested is free that night, I can pay their deposit, and we should be all set. Unless you can think of anything I missed."

Carra lifted her eyebrows. "You did all that, entirely on your own?"

"I did."

She took another sip of wine. "I'm impressed. Thank you. I'll call the band tomorrow and see if they're free. I'm sure they'll offer us a discount since one of them is a member of the center. Jay, this dance must be costing you a fortune."

"I told you, don't worry about the money. I'm an elder attorney, I can always write it off as a marketing expense since I'll be there, shaking hands and introducing myself."

Carra's face clouded over, puzzling him. After a moment, he added, "I am invited, aren't I?"

She shook off whatever was bothering her. "Of course you are. Yes, it would be great exposure. I'm sure all those people need someone to plan their estates and draw up their wills, but deep down I don't believe you're doing any of this as a marketing ploy."

"I'm not, but I do have ulterior motives." He attempted to waggle his eyebrows but by her confused expression, he gathered he hadn't pulled it off. "I'm trying to imitate Groucho Marx."

"Oh good, I was afraid you were having a seizure." They both burst into laughter.

After they ordered dinner—two servings of Shrimp Newburg—she resurrected the conversation. "Are you going to share your nefarious scheme, or should I fear the worst and call the authorities?"

"It's nothing all that devious. I was hoping we could go out again this Saturday night. Another dinner, and a movie?

"With no logistics subterfuge? Wouldn't that be like, an actual date?"

He nodded. "It would be. I admit it."

"How would Adriana feel about that, I wonder?"

"I really don't care. As I said in the restaurant, it's over."

"She seemed to think you were on a break."

"It doesn't matter what she thinks. We're done. How about you? Will any random grandsons challenge me to a duel if they discover us out together?"

She snickered. "I'm afraid they'll be too busy playing on their Xboxes to notice."

They continued to chat about their lives—his years at law school, the writer's block that was stymying the publication of her novel—until the server brought their dinners. Their intimacy made her almost forget her apprehension over his temper.

After enjoying a shrimp or two, Carra laid out her terms for the date. "I have two conditions: first, no elder law intrusions, which means no hostages to rescue or house deals to quash."

"Deal. Though as I recall, the hostage was on your watch, not mine. What's the second condition?"

"You spend the day with me as well. Along with whatever funds you're willing to donate to the cause, I'm going to show you an afternoon you'll never forget."

~ * ~

I woke up before the alarm rang and, instead of lolling about, I showered and got ready for the day. Kiki lifted her gaze from her laptop and did a double take when I joined her for breakfast.

"You're up at eight? On a Saturday? Isn't that like 2:00 AM in Carra Land? Since when do you wear a blazer on the weekends?"

"There's no law that says I can't look nice just because it's not a weekday." I grabbed a bowl and a spoon and sat down beside her at the kitchen table, stealing some of the cereal and milk she left out. "If you must know, I'm going out with Jay today, and I probably won't have a chance to change before dinner."

"Dinner, is it? Third time this week you two are eating out. You want to talk about this?"

I shook the box of Cheerios and concentrated on the way they tinkled as they poured into my bowl, anything to drown out my roommate's ribbing.

"Fine. Don't tell me. I'm glad you're here because I need to show you something. Look at the one on top." She turned her monitor toward me, displaying a list of copywriting ads on Indeed. The top one bore the headline, "Junior Editor, *Sixty Years On*."

Intrigued, I clicked, and the more I read, the faster my heart raced:

Sixty Years On *is a Manhattan-based magazine dedicated to improving the lives of the social security set. We cover continuing education opportunities, lifestyle changes, health and fitness, travel, dining out, and legal issues affecting the community. We want fresh eyes and fresh ideas to contribute articles and edit freelance material, plus oversee layout and social media. Recent grads welcome. Send resumes and writing samples.*

I blinked and read it again.

"Sounds like you might be uniquely qualified, no?"

"Indeed...no pun intended. Is Elton John aware they're borrowing their magazine title from his discography?"

"Why are you being glib? This job is your ticket to getting out from under Bea's thumb and reframing the past few months into something positive, like qualifying you for this gig."

Something in Kiki's tone struck a nerve. "You honestly believe I've accomplished nothing since August except satisfying my stepmother? I've helped turn people's lives around. I freed one man from being kept captive in his own bathroom. Helped another woman save her home. There are marriages that might happen because I played Cupid."

"So what are you saying? SALAD is a dream come true? You're never leaving? You've spent weeks complaining about Judith's micromanagement, Froy's lethargy, and Bea's nagging. Sent out hundreds of resumes. This is the job you've been jonesing for, and the experience you've picked up with these seniors makes you the perfect candidate. What's the problem?"

My head started pounding, but it wasn't entirely Kiki's fault. Partly, it was due to my own confusion. Unbeknownst to her, I'd been vacillating over leaving the center. I'd even stopped applying for writing jobs.

Was it due to my pride over the difference I'd made at SALAD? The way the seniors depended on me and how I'd watched them grow as they turned their lives around? Or was it that once I left, Jay and I wouldn't have a project to collaborate on any longer?

All great questions, but the truth was SALAD alone couldn't pay the bills and because I hadn't sold any homes for Bea, her subsidies were about to run dry. Time was fleeting. If I wanted to keep living with Kiki and hold onto my integrity—i.e., not sell seniors' houses from under them—*Sixty Years On* was my best bet.

"There's no problem," I said as I walked toward my bedroom. "Please email me the link. I'm going to apply while it's still fresh in my mind. Thanks roomie, I owe you one."

~ * ~

Saturday, 10:00 AM. We met in the parking lot of Prentiss Elder Law since it made no sense to take two cars. Jay waved from his Lexus, and I slipped in beside him, experiencing the same excitement and terror I'd felt when I clicked "Send" on my first publisher query. He'd dressed more informally than me, wearing black jeans and a light gray cashmere sweater that showcased the blue in his eyes. I fought the temptation to lean over and kiss him hello.

"Hey, how's it going?" I fastened my seatbelt, though it did little to hold back my exuberance.

"It's going," he said. "But where are we going? I'm still in the dark about today's agenda."

"Do you have whichever credit cards link to your charity funds?"

He donned a serious look. "I do."

For a split second, I pictured him at the altar, speaking those very words. Had he been thinking the same when he uttered them? This was no time for romantic speculation. I yanked myself from fantasy back into the present. "We're starting at Best Friends Sanctuary, over on Maple. I arranged for a wheelchair-accessible taxi to pick up Janet. I told her we'd meet her there by ten-thirty to pay the driver."

Jay started the ignition. We drove in silence for a bit, serenaded by the purring of the car's engine. Occasionally, I sneaked a peek at his profile while trying to ignore the electricity generated by his body's proximity to mine. But my body had different ideas, gurgling with chemical reactions that suggested—make that insisted—that Jay Prentiss was no longer my means to an end. He may have been the prize all along.

We pulled up to the sanctuary a minute ahead of Janet's van. She traveled with a portable, non-motorized wheelchair and I jumped out to help her roll safely to the sidewalk. "Are you as excited as I am, Janet? We're going to meet your new best friend today."

"All because of your suggestions and research. I can't thank you enough." Her glow warmed my soul on this chilly morning. It seemed insane she hadn't considered the senior dog route before, but soon she'd have the companionship she craved.

Jay caught up to us and kissed Janet on the cheek before handing his credit card to the driver. She blushed. "Isn't that the icing on the cake? A dog and the attentions of such a fetching young man, all on the same day."

Now it was Jay's turn to blush as he wheeled Janet up the ramp and through the entrance doors.

There were formalities to attend to before viewing the dogs, namely an application to complete and interviews with the adoption gatekeepers. Janet dazzled with tales of her former canine companions. The descriptions of her adventures with Carson and Fallon nearly brought the staff to tears.

"I think we have the perfect fur baby for you," said Gloria, the lead consultant. "Let's set you up in one of our Meet and Greet rooms, and I'll bring him in."

She led us to a private room with beige vinyl flooring and white cinderblock walls. We waited anxiously as Janet commented how the persistent barking coming from the adjacent kennel reinforced her desire for a new pup.

My knees grew weak at the thought of encountering any dog, but I held it together for my friend's sake.

Gloria returned, a silver-muzzled black American Staffordshire Terrier on a leash by her side. I estimated his weight at around eighty pounds, a square and sturdy brute, which prompted me to retreat by several feet.

"Some people nickname them Pit Bulls but don't let their uninformed and malicious comments sway you," said Gloria, clearly detecting my concern. "It's all about the way their owners raise them."

"It isn't him, it's all dogs. One attacked me when I was younger. Janet is the one adopting the pup, so please, carry on."

Sensing I was a lost cause, Gloria turned to Janet. "Angus here is ten years young, a total lovebug. He's got a lot of life left in him, and yet he won't pull on the leash when you walk him, so he's perfect for you. He's only still here because adopters tend to overlook black dogs, especially when they're older. Isn't that right Angus?"

Upon hearing his name, the AmStaff looked up at the consultant with a combination of curiosity and devotion. Gloria led him to Janet and handed her the leash. "I'll leave you to get acquainted, but don't worry, we keep watch via video camera. He's fairly mellow, I don't think he'll give you any trouble. Whatever you do though, don't say p-l-a-y-t-i-m-e, A-n-g-u-s— he goes mad."

She threw me an empathetic smile and departed.

Janet leaned over until she was face-to-face with this formidable canine. He took one look and ran his long, slobbering tongue from the tip of her chin up to the bridge of her nose. It was love at first sight for both.

I kept my distance, still wary. Jay was more daring, kneeling beside the beast and scratching under his ears. Janet dropped the leash to give the dog more freedom, causing my heart to catapult into my throat. Rather than choose this moment to attack, Angus merely pawed Jay's arm in appreciation then submissively rolled onto his back, inviting belly rubs.

"Come here, Carra." Jay held out his hand and reached for mine.

I was unaccustomed to his dominant tone being directed my way, and the raw sexiness made my knees buckle. Yet, I held back, standing my ground.

"Carra, don't you trust me? Do you think I'd let anything bad happen to you?"

The logical side of my brain argued he'd just met the dog and was in no position to advocate on the beast's behalf. The emotional side wanted to feel his palm on mine. Angus broke the stalemate by moseying over to me and, despite my protestations, nudging my arm with his snout, prodding for attention as if mystified that anyone could resist his charms.

Holding my breath, I gingerly patted the top of his head. He welcomed my show of faith by plonking down at my feet, awaiting further adulation.

"If you can take on Judith Ferester, you can take on Mr. Mush here," said Jay. "Go on, Ms. Fearless. I dare you."

He'd finally figured out the way to my core: the lure of the taunt. My competitive nature never allowed me to turn down a dare, not even something as silly as the cinnamon challenge. I took a deep breath and knelt beside Angus. The dog remained calm and, again, rolled on his back. I rubbed his tummy, and he rewarded me with a series of thuds as his tail beat against the acrylic tile.

"There's my brave girl." Jay crawled over and grazed his lips against my cheek.

If it were anyone else, I would have admonished him for calling me "girl." But his tenderness sucked the fire from any rebuke, replacing it with a burning desire for another kiss, maybe an evening filled with them and not on the cheek…

Not the time, not the place, I warned myself. This was Janet's day.

I turned to my friend in the wheelchair who'd been observing the whole affair and asked, "What do you think? Are you going to bring him home and love him forever?"

"Funny you should say that. I was going to ask you the same thing."

Gloria returned, full of cheer. "So, what's the decision, Janet? If you want him, we can place a few quick calls to confirm your references and set you up with our Forever Friends kit. It's a leash, harness, set of bowls, a week of dog food, and an appointment with a local vet, so you can verify he's as healthy as we say."

"I've never been more certain of anything in my life. But save those supplies for someone in greater need. I have everything you mentioned at home."

"There's one thing I must caution you about Angus," said Gloria. "He hasn't had the easiest life. His last owners moved and left him abandoned in the house. For that reason, he's very clingy. Only leave for short periods; otherwise, he'll suffer separation anxiety. Is that doable?"

Janet's expression darkened, and I knew she was regretting the prospect of giving up SALAD and all the new friends she made there. I silently vowed I wouldn't allow any stupid "No Pets" rule to destroy the happiness she deserved.

"Janet, I bet you can bring Angus to the center if you have him certified as an Emotional Support Animal. Judith won't like it, but I doubt there's much she can do about it. Isn't that right Jay?"

"We can certainly set you up with a prescription letter and get Angus registered as an ESA, that part's easy," he said. "But, while there are rules in place protecting emotional support animals from being barred from homes and airplanes, I don't know of any case law covering senior centers. I wouldn't sweat it though. Considering SALAD caters to those in need, it would generate terrible publicity if Judith refused. I could make a call or two, clear away any objections."

"That would be incredible. Thank you, Jay." Janet used words to show gratitude. I planned to be more physically demonstrative later.

Once we escorted Janet and Angus home and watched him claim his rightful place on her favorite couch, I directed Jay to drive us to Computer Cavalcade.

"Electronics, eh? A digital scheme to drive Judith out of her mind?" It was hard to disregard the twinkle in his eye. "She's going to flip out over Angus. I can hear it now: 'Who's going to sweep up the hair? Wipe up the drool? Supply the food? It's not in our budget! It will disrupt the seniors!'" He did a mean Judith impression.

"Not to mention the Froy factor," I added. "The dog might interfere with his endless juice distribution. No Jay, fear thee not, the next stop won't involve anything that barks or sheds. It may lead to one senior spending less time at the center, but all for a good cause."

I scoured the aisles at Computer Cavalcade until I found the perfect laptop. Big monitor, so the classwork would be easier to see. Lots of storage for homework. A good camera and tons of battery life. All for $699, plus tax. And warranty. And Office360. And, of course, a carrying case. The final total came to $1,025.

"I promise, double promise, triple promise that this will be the last thing I ask you for," I swore to Jay at checkout. "I can't wait to present it to Bryan, the man I told you about who regretted skipping college. Online classes are the perfect answer to his fear of being derided by kids in their twenties. He wants to study psychology. Never had the time or patience to attend college when he was younger. He calls it his biggest regret. With this one purchase, you are going to change a man's life."

My prediction proved to be an understatement. Once we reached Bryan's home and he opened the box, he burst into tears. "No one has ever cared about what I wanted, or what I felt I'd lost out on in my youth. You are the first. There are no words…"

The three of us sat together on his rundown sofa, Jay and I helping him download applications and enroll in some free classes offered by Coursera. We'd already agreed that at age eighty-eight, it was the knowledge he was after, not the sheepskin. Together, we scrolled through the curriculum.

"So where to first? Intro to Psych at Yale? Social Psych at Wesleyan? Or maybe Buddhism and Modern Psychology at Princeton?" I asked.

Jay voted for Princeton. "My alma mater and all."

A Princeton man. Impressive.

"It's sort of overwhelming," said Bryan. "I want to think it over, maybe discuss this with my wife when she gets home from shopping."

"Procrastination's what got you here in the first place," said Jay. "Take one tiny step, my friend. Register for one free course. It's on demand so you can study whenever you want, with no one watching. Almost two million people have enrolled over the years. What's the worst thing that can happen? I'm sure your wife would agree."

Jay's insight floored me. Whereas I had focused on Bryan's lack of determination in his youth and his lack of a computer in the present, Jay had sensed something different: hesitancy in the man's everyday life. Whether it was from fear of success or fear of failure, something more than potential mockery had kept Bryan from attending college, and Jay intended to help him overcome that hurdle.

Bryan's hands were still trembling several minutes later as Jay's coaching prompted him to hit the "Register" button for Yale's Intro Psych course. Then together, we watched the first video and set up a schedule for him to do the readings and proceed through the fifty-eight classes that followed.

Jay asked Bryan for his phone number and plugged it into his cell, along with a reminder on his calendar. "I'm going to call you every morning at ten. That gives you lots of time to watch the video and do the readings before you head to SALAD. In two months, you'll have graduated. Sound good?"

While my gift of a computer garnered thanks, Jay's offer elicited genuine appreciation. Maybe no one had ever challenged Bryan before, or was determined enough to uncover his true issue. I may have given him hope, but Jay translated it into action and accountability. He had an innate understanding of what made people tick. We made quite the team.

It was after three o'clock when we pulled away from Bryan's apartment building, still plenty of time left before dinner. Jay hadn't mentioned where he was taking me, but Poisson would be a hard act to follow. The food had been divine, the company enchanting. All that the evening lacked was a goodnight kiss. Had he wavered over making the first move? Or perhaps he was still under the spell of the willowy Adriana.

Tonight, I hoped he was over both the fear and the filly. "Good day so far, Jay?"

"Amazing. Best money spent in a long time. What you said when we met was one-hundred-percent true. It's one thing to help from a thirty-thousand-foot vantage point; there's always a buffer. Wills and estate planning are often handled by the clients when they're younger, or their children, when the clients are less coherent. When you meet the people in person, find out what they need and how to make it happen, that's when you get your hands dirty and you make a difference."

"That marks the end of my shopping spree," I said. "Where to next?"

"I have an idea, bear with me." He turned on the radio, and Tom Petty's voice rang from the speakers. We sang along to "I Won't Back Down" as he wound through the streets of Rock Canyon, pulling up outside the Lion's Club. "I thought you might like to check out the venue for our Harvest Moon event?"

"I'd love to."

The receptionist, whose badge read, "Bootsie," guided us through the deserted building, leaving us alone in the auditorium when she heard another visitor ringing the bell. It was simple but ample for our needs. Dark blue curtains hung from the ceilings, hiding the walls and creating a more intimate vibe.

Jay pointed to the left wall. "I figured we could set up long tables with refreshments over there. Ask them to arrange several tables around the perimeter and leave the center open for dancing. The band can perform on the platform upfront. There's plenty of room for their amps. What do you think?"

"Never mind me. What does your nana think?"

"She liked the idea. She loved that we were planning this together."

"Aha! So she'll be there. When I see the two of you chatting, I'll learn her identity at last."

He smirked. "I promise I'll point her out. The three of us can toast the event's success with some punch. To repeat: what do you think?"

I pictured my inkling of an idea fleshed out into reality. "It will be marvelous, that's what I think."

"I'm not convinced," he said. "Maybe we should test it out."

"How so?"

He pulled out his cell, clicked on Spotify, and turned up the volume. The Flamingos crooning "I Only Have Eyes for You" filled the air. He slipped the phone back into his jeans pocket and held out his arms. I tried to act cool, but my smile was impossible to conceal. I glided into his embrace, put my arms around his neck, and nestled my cheek against his chest. We rocked back and forth to the music, neither one of us breaking our rhythm when the song transitioned into Foreigner's "I Want to Know What Love Is."

I pulled back my head and stared into his baby blues. "I think it'll work."

His whisper matched mine. "I think so too."

If the music was still playing, I couldn't hear it, so deeply drawn into the alternative reality we'd forged together. I tilted my head up as he lowered his lips toward mine. At that moment, the room blurred then ceased to exist.

"Oh, oh, I'm so sorry." Bootsie's exclamation snapped us out of our private world with the sharpness of a car breaking for a small child.

Bootsie bolted, and I jerked out of our embrace. The awkwardness of the moment was palpable, my throat constricting as if all the oxygen had been sucked from the room, my shivering arms betraying my Cinderella-at-midnight sense of vulnerability.

"I should go. I have a million things to do at home. Can I take a raincheck on dinner?"

"But, but—"

"Please... I can walk from here. Let's touch base next week and finalize any plans for the event. I can't thank you enough for today, for your generosity. You're the best."

I ran from the hall and started the two-mile trek home. I'd pick up my car some other time.

. With every step, I dug deep for an answer. Why had I just done to Jay what I'd done to Colin and Derrick and Josh—use any flaw, in this case a temper I'd only seen once—as an excuse to withdraw? And with every step, my subconscious motives became clearer. Just like in my nightmare, I'd showed Jay the door when he got too close, forcing him out into the cold rather than risk letting him hurt me the way my mother had. Each of those men had deserved better. I'd hoped it would be different with Jay, but in a way it was worse because our emotional connection was stronger.

Tears doused my cheeks as I passed couples walking arm in arm, mourning how yet again, I'd sabotaged my own happiness. It was an insidious pattern, and one I knew I'd have to break unless I wanted to resign myself to a bitter life alone.

I remembered Nikki's haunting words about my mother: "Until you deal with this, give her another chance, you'll never be free of how her leaving affected you." Was that it? Was my love life yet another casualty Daisy's departure had left in its wake?

If that was true, then maybe I *was* doomed to a solitary life. Because while losing a man like Jay was heartbreaking, nothing would destroy me more completely than welcoming my birth mother back into my life only to have her betray my trust once again.

Chapter Twenty-Five

Jay spent the next two weeks wondering what he'd done wrong. Fresh cases came in, old ones got settled, and he went through the motions numbly and by rote, constantly obsessing over Carra. Had he moved too quickly? Said something untoward? Given her the wrong idea about his intentions? Was he nothing to her but a blank check to pay for her senior shopping sprees?

Adriana phoned twice. He didn't take the calls, just let them go to voicemail and deleted the messages, unplayed. He ran the scenario by his nana, who assured him Carra had never mentioned another man, nor had recent gossip detailed any romantic entanglements with members' grandsons.

"Some people shrink away from the possibility of success," she told him. "They're scared the reality won't measure up to their expectations. God knows, the perfect man doesn't come around all that often. That I can guarantee you. If she doesn't recognize what a catch you are, my sweet boy, then she isn't as smart as I'd given her credit for."

Back home, he thought about his grandmother's comments and recalled the conversation he'd had with the woman at Perry Winkle's who'd mysteriously taken Carra's seat after she'd left. Her story offered a plausible reason for Carra's skittishness. He'd discuss it with his enigmatic redhead—if he ever got her alone again.

Over the next few weeks, they shared a few pre-dance planning conversations, especially about décor. All very cut and dry. The theme was to be "Dress from Your Favorite Decade." They figured it gave the seniors an excuse to wear their favorite clothes without worrying about buying anything new. Carra said she'd reached out to Edward, and his band was practicing songs ranging from the fifties to the eighties. For his part, Jay hired an event-planning firm to put all their plans into motion.

One issue remained unresolved: the barrier between them, which felt like an impenetrable gulf. How to navigate those precarious waves without either of them drowning?

Thoughts of treacherous waters reminded Jay of Gatsby and how they'd discovered his namesake floating dead in his swimming pool. That's when the answer hit Jay, the perfect way to break through. He turned to his computer and started searching the internet.

~ * ~

Two weeks passed, and I was still berating myself over the way I'd bolted from the Lion's Club. Jay had done absolutely nothing wrong. I wanted him at that moment, badly. Just like I wanted to publish a novel but couldn't implement the editors' suggested revisions. Chalk it up to self-sabotage. I was a choker.

He sounded friendly enough when he called, though a bit guarded. Perhaps he'd forgiven me. At least everything was coming together for the dance. I'd publicized the event privately but warned the seniors to keep things on the QT, lest Judith find out and somehow squash our plans. Not that she had jurisdiction over what happened outside the center, but who knew what kind of vengeful stunt she could pull?

Thankfully, once Angus announced his arrival with an excited bark, Judith became too preoccupied with the dog to inflict any damage. Much to the director's dismay, the AmStaff accompanied Janet to SALAD every afternoon. I hadn't a clue why Judith was freaking. Even though I steered clear, the other patrons adored him. If Judith had been savvier and less resistant to change, she could have marketed his presence as pet therapy.

Our Harvest Moon Dance had captured the collective imagination of the SALADians. Not only was Blanche attending with our keyboardist Edward, but thanks to the success of my makeovers, Marguerite was coming with Jason, Mildred with Irving, and Phyllis with Gail. Ah, the power of baked goods and the allure of eyeliner to alter the course of romance.

I'd also gone all out and splurged on a twenties-style black flapper ensemble—fringed dress with plunging neckline, fake pearl necklace, black gloves, and a silver, feathered head dress. The online cosplay store charged extra to have it rush-shipped, which meant I'd be a few dollars short for the rent, but this was my big event, the pinnacle moment of my nascent career at SALAD. If it were a success, I'd use it as a proof point when negotiating with Judith for more innovative activities and maybe a raise when my status changed from probation to permanent. That would definitely help me pay Kiki back for any extra she laid out for this month's rent, plus interest.

Naturally, I needed an outfit that stood out. Since the theme was clothing from previous decades and my parents had named me after a character in *The Great Gatsby*, why not show up dressed like one?

Or was all the expense and rationalization an elaborate, subconscious excuse for wearing something that might catch Jay's eye? Now that I'd come to terms with the reasons I'd initially turned away, perhaps something sexy to rekindle the ardor I'd doused?

~ * ~

The Friday of the dance finally arrived. I delivered my morning trays and doubled back home to grab some lunch. My clothing splurge ruled out any restaurant visits for the next month. It was Cheerios for breakfast, bran flakes for lunch, and if things didn't look up soon, ketchup sandwiches for dinner.

I checked my email, anything to distract from the flakes' cardboard taste. The first thing that popped up was a note from the Human Resources Director at *Sixty Years On,* the publication I'd applied to a few weeks prior. I was still torn about changing jobs, but had promised myself that for Kiki's sake, if they answered, I'd go through with the interview.

Dear Ms. Quinn:

Thank you for forwarding your application and resume in response to our search for an associate editor. We would love to have you visit our offices at 261 Madison Avenue, 39th floor, for an interview. Out of respect for our applicants' current work situations, we are conducting interviews over the weekend. Please bring two copies of your resume and your portfolio of clips to our offices at 10:00 AM on Saturday, October 26th. A prompt reply to this email will secure the interview slot. Thank you again for your interest and good luck!

Sincerely,
Marina Oaks
Director, Human Resources

My stomach somersaulted against my ribcage. An editorial interview. Finally, a job that suited my qualifications and could cover my expenses, but tomorrow morning? So soon after the dance, my biggest SALAD triumph? Despite my hesitance, I shot back my acceptance and considered the particulars.

I'd go right to sleep after the dance, then wake up bright and early tomorrow morning and trek into Manhattan. It was very doable. Unless I got hired. Then what?

How could I justify turning down the job, especially to Kiki, when the rent-hungry landlord came pounding on our door? Still, the more I thought about it, the more I wondered if my work with the elderly was more rewarding than a byline or two. I was already missing Georgia and Helen and even Blanche, and I hadn't even left yet. Maybe I'd take the position, then sneak into SALAD occasionally, visit my beloved seniors under the guise of research. I had so many of their home addresses now, thanks to the makeover campaign. Accepting the job might force me to say *adieu*, but not necessarily goodbye.

The silver lining, of course, would be telling Bea I was leaving real estate, that I'd never prey on the elderly to propel her career as she'd once hoped I would. Maybe then, when I came home for the holidays, we could celebrate without the nagging reprise of "How Many Houses Have You Sold for Me Lately?" hanging over my head like mistletoe. I yearned to tear up my real estate pocket card and forever bid farewell to the idea of displacing the elderly from their homes. A sales career might be great for some, but me? I was an artist. And a caregiver, thanks to what I'd learned about myself over the past three months.

I relegated concerns over the impending interview to the back of my mind and placed my Gatsby outfit in the trunk of my car. By changing at the Lion's Club instead of at the center, I'd avoid having to explain the costume to Judith and risk her interfering somehow. If she questioned why the seniors were dressed up, I'd tell her we'd declared today "Dress Formal for Fun."

I arrived at SALAD for my shift with a spring in my step that quickly turned into a lump in my throat as I listened to my students reading their work. If the opportunity at *Sixty Years On* panned out, this might be our final class together.

Afterward, I quietly reminded my pupils of the bus that would depart for the Lion's Club immediately after the recreation session ended. Everyone was eager for a special night out. As much as I dreaded seeing Jay again in the aftermath of our disastrous last encounter, I couldn't wait for him to witness the excitement in the seniors' eyes, how much they appreciated all he'd done for them. A sentiment I shared thousandfold. I could have kicked myself for letting two weeks pass without expressing my gratitude and addressing the issue between us.

At 4:45 PM, as my shift was winding down, Froy tapped on my shoulder and warned that Judith was waiting for me in her office. That was unusual. We normally didn't meet outside of our weekly scheduled update sessions. "Any idea what she wants?"

Froy answered with his patented shrug. I skulked over to her office, not looking forward to a scolding that might dampen my mood for the night ahead. There were seniors to delight and a relationship to repair, and I needed my wits about me.

Helen tipped her head as I approached, knitting in her usual position outside Judith's lair. "That sweater must be close to done," I said, admiring its complicated Fair Isle pattern.

She proudly displayed the garment, which was three-quarters finished. "I can't wait for Jonathan to wear it."

"Judith wants me for something, but let's have a quick chat when I'm through. I don't suppose you've reconsidered coming to the dance?"

She shook her head, as I expected. It was a shame. She was my favorite person at SALAD, and I would have loved to introduce her to Jay.

I knocked on the office door and let myself in. Judith sat behind her desk, wearing her usual acerbic expression.

"Ms. Quinn, please have a seat." *Uh oh, Ms. Quinn? Not Carra? This can't be good.* "I will get right to the point. We've had several complaints from patrons at the center about your extracurricular activities. I'm afraid we have no choice but to let you go."

WTF? I shot out of the chair, every nerve end short-circuiting. Liar. There were no complaints. Had she finally tired of my constantly usurping her authority? Or had Froy passed on a few bogus complaints to grasp at some undeserved job security? I did have this new editorial position in my back pocket, but deep down I knew SALAD was where I belonged, and Judith's accusation reinforced my determination to investigate away these supposed complaints and stay.

"That's impossible." My voice climbed two decibels above place-of-business acceptable. "Everyone likes me here. No one has said one cross word. I have the right to defend myself and present my side of the story. So, precisely who complained and what did they say?"

Judith calmly removed a letter from an envelope, slowly unfolded it, and read snippets aloud.

"We, the undersigned, would like Carra Quinn removed from the SALAD Center. She has interfered in our private lives and ruined ongoing romantic relationships. We would be happy to elaborate if necessary. If she remains, not only will you lose our business, but we will go to the newspapers. SALAD should be a haven, a safe space. Not one where we risk the destruction of our love lives to attend."

Huh? "What are you talking about?" I said. "This doesn't make any sense. It's got to be a mistake."

"Really? It's signed by Claudette Scovey, Deidre John, Theresa Coviello, and Adina Cohen. Those names sound familiar?" There was a checkmate finality to Judith's voice that told me the question was rhetorical.

Suddenly everything became clear. My oversteps had come back to bite me in the pocketbook. Each of those women had lost a lover, thanks to my recent turn as Pygmalion. I'd never considered the other side. Hell hath no fury like a widow scorned.

"If that's not enough, I understand you're planning a Harvest Moon Dance for our members. I have warned you repeatedly about interfering in their lives. If anything happens to them because of your meddling, I will sue you to the full extent of the law."

My blood pressure shot up like a puck at a high striker carnival game, the deafening imaginary bell blocking out all sense as I spewed out a career-ending diatribe.

"Let me tell you something, Judith. I have made a difference here that, despite all your good intentions, you and your constant fretting over change have not. You have no jurisdiction over what your patrons do when they leave your hallowed center halls. My guess is that when I'm gone, you'll get more complaints from seniors who miss me than those who lost their suitors. You do what you want, but it's not the smartest course of action."

Judith's posture stiffened, apparently surprised by my outburst. "I hired you because your stepmother and I came to an understanding. I never thought it was a good idea, and my instincts have proven me correct. Please collect your effects and leave the premises. We'll mail your final check to the address on your W-2."

My stepmother, huh? There was the leak, Bea's inside track to my goings-on. No wonder Judith hadn't wanted me to make waves. Or hadn't fired me when I had. The "understanding" probably involved me soliciting house listings, not implementing programming changes. Had Bea promised Judith a piece of the action from sales resulting from my sojourn here? Nothing would surprise me at this point.

But the mention of that final check was like the world's loudest alarm clock shattering my eardrums. Acing tomorrow's interview was now more vital than ever. Otherwise, without either salary, I'd be out on the street in weeks. Or worse, living with Bea, hawking condos and mobile homes.

I stomped out, eliciting a look of surprise on Helen's face as I passed. "Carra, is everything all right?"

I pivoted and sat beside her. I owed her an explanation, especially since I wouldn't be able to say a final goodbye at the dance tonight. "Judith let me go. Today is my last day."

Helen set down her knitting and gave me a hug. "Chin up, Carra. You're meant for better things than SALAD."

"But I really felt I made a difference here."

"You did, my dear, and everyone here will miss you. The truth is, this is too small a stage for your talents. You deserve so much more. I'll tell you a secret: you aren't the only one who won't be coming back after today. I'm leaving tonight on a little trip."

"Really, Helen? Where are you going?"

She smiled slyly and put a finger to her lips. "It's a secret."

"Are you going on a Troy hunt? Tracking down your long-lost boyfriend?"

"I really couldn't say," she replied. But her grin gave her away.

"Oh Helen, that's so romantic! I wish the best for you. Safe travels and all the success in the world. You know, it's never too late to find true love."

She nodded and hugged me again. "And it's never too early to find true love either, Carra Quinn. You remember that. Sometimes, happiness might seem scary because there's so much on the line if things go wrong. But don't let fear stop you from experiencing joy when you have the chance. Promise me that."

Tears welled in my eyes as I remembered how terror had pulled me from Jay the last time we met. If I was going to miss anyone from the center, it was Helen and her sage advice. "I promise I will."

"Now get moving. As I recall, you have a dance to chaperone."

"I do, Helen. I do."

Adrenaline erupted through my system like an oil strike. There was nothing I could do about my job tonight, but I had the biggest event of my career to pull off. And fences to mend with the one man who'd brought the type of joy into my life I'd promised Helen I'd pursue.

I pictured the hall decorated to the nines, the buffet table overflowing with food and refreshments, and amidst the excitement, Jay—standing strong and steady—waiting for me to arrive.

~ * ~

I attempted to forget my disturbing encounter with Judith as I followed the bus to the Lion's Club. Jay's admin Meggie was on board as chaperone, dressed as a pink-haired, tattooed Marilyn Monroe from *The Seven-Year Itch,* V-necked white dress and all. Her job was to account for everyone who had RSVP'd, and ensure they arrived safely at the venue, then back home again.

I figured Jay was probably already inside, monitoring the table arrangements and the catering staff. I slipped through the foyer and into the ladies' room before anyone spotted me. The last thing I wanted was to bring down the festive mood with my shame over being fired and having betrayed the elderly women who'd written that damning letter.

Donning the flapper costume lifted my spirits. I admired the reflection in the mirror more for the authenticity of the outfit than the way it placed previously shrouded parts of me on full display. The black fringes swung seductively as I twisted my hips, the hemline falling just above my knees. I really did look like I'd stepped out of a party at Jay Gatsby's mansion on West Egg. Hopefully my décolletage wouldn't insult the more prudish members of my flock. I took one last look, adjusting the glittering silver headdress with its single feather at the back, then emerged to make my grand reveal.

The first thing that struck me was how beautifully the event planners had decorated the room. Photo blow-ups of classic film stars like Grace Kelly, Clark Gable, and Humphrey Bogart graced the dark blue curtains covering the walls, while shiny silver cardboard stars dangled from the ceiling. A spotlight, meant to resemble a giant harvest moon, cast a romantic glow from the hall's upper left corner. Guests crowded around buffet tables brimming with food and drink before dining at one of the rounds of eight that bordered the dance floor.

Some seniors had adorned their wheelchairs with Christmas tinsel in purples, reds, and silvers. Edward, looking dapper in black tails and white tie, caught my eye and gave me an approving thumbs up from the makeshift stage while his musicians tuned their instruments. Everything was perfect, except Jay was nowhere in sight.

The loudspeaker crackled and Edward, having appointed himself emcee for the evening, greeted his fellow SALADians: "Hello, you wacky seniors and welcome to our Harvest Moon Dance. Before we begin, I'd like to thank three special people who made this evening possible.

"First, to my sweetie Blanche, for inviting me." He waved to his girlfriend amid a smattering of applause. I guessed his ex, Adina, and my other detractors present in the crowd were less than thrilled about the salute. "And to the beautiful Carra Quinn in her charming flapper dress, for dreaming up this entire event." The applause grew louder, and my face burned. "Finally, to that fine gentleman at the rear, elder attorney Jay Prentiss, our event's sponsor, who contributed the funds to make all this happen."

I strained to catch a glimpse of Jay, who pushed through the throng to stand by my side. I couldn't mask my surprise when I saw his outfit: a pink seersucker suit with matching buttoned vest, a pink-and-brown tie, and a matching pocket handkerchief. A pair of wingtip brown-and-white oxfords completed the look—Jay Gatsby in the flesh.

"Great minds think alike," he said as he took my hand and twirled me, my fringes flying as wildly as my mood.

"I think these two twenties characters should have the dance floor to themselves for our first number, don't you agree?" Edward pumped his arms, encouraging the already cheering crowd.

"Did you set this up?" I shouted to Jay over the din, my hand still clasped in his, like he was afraid I might run off again.

"You look cute when you blush," he yelled back, avoiding the question.

The band launched into a jazzy version of "Love Is the Drug," right out of the second Gatsby movie soundtrack. Ballroom dancing was not my strong suit, but Jay led like a pro and we faked it. No one really cared. They were all clapping to the rhythm, egging us on. After a minute, several other couples flooded the floor, mercifully taking off some of the pressure.

He pulled me close and whispered in my ear, "I've missed you, Carra. It took every ounce of willpower not to show up at SALAD these past two weeks and ask what I did to offend you. But to hell with that because you're here tonight, dressed as my date, so you'd better be prepared to dance the night away." Then he placed his finger under my chin, lifting it so our lips aligned.

"You did nothing wrong. I—"

He pressed his mouth hard against mine, his passion taking priority over my explanation. A kiss as incredible as I'd spent the past fourteen nights imagining. I leaned into it, longing to inhale him whole, to capture the moment so it would never end. He slid his hands along my sides and up my spine, drawing me closer. We were lovers in the age of Prohibition, daring and carefree, sneaking a tryst at an underground speakeasy. The Lion's Club hall, SALAD, Rock Canyon—all ceased to exist as we luxuriated in a world of our own making.

Someone pointed the spotlight on us, killing the moment. We pulled apart, but this time I was determined not to run. He was my lifeline, someone to ground me as my world turned upside down.

I needed a drink and told him so. We pushed through the throng of dancers to the refreshment table.

"Water, soda, or something stronger? I have a flask in my pocket."

I couldn't hide my shock. This seemed very out of character. "Are you trying to get me drunk, Mr. Prentiss?"

He grinned. "Absolutely. How about a cup of vodka-laced Kool Aid?"

"After the day I've had, that sounds perfect."

He spiked two drinks and after signaling to Meggie to keep an eye on things, pulled me into the quiet of the reception area. "What's wrong? What happened today that's got you so frazzled?"

I filled him in on the Judith disaster and my impending job interview.

He gave me a reassuring embrace. "When one door closes, a window opens, as my nana would say. Sounds like you would have left SALAD anyway, though it's their loss."

"I was going to let people here know, but it might be better not to say anything. Let them enjoy the night."

"I think that's a smart decision. We should leave them be and instead, celebrate this new job of yours." He poured some straight vodka into the remainder of my Kool-Aid.

"I haven't gotten it yet. I have to make it through the interview tomorrow."

"Come on, consider the time you've spent at SALAD. Who has a better grasp of the senior mindset than you? If you don't believe me, let's go watch them enjoy the party."

We strolled back and squeezed onto the dance floor, using the crowd as an excuse to press tightly against one another. Occasionally, someone would cut in—Blanche looking to "trip the light fantastic with the dashing young lawyer," and Bryan, fresh from psychology class, asking for a dance with "the woman who finally turned me into a scholar." But after these interruptions, sweet as they were, we came back together, clicking like magnets as we swayed to the music of Geritol Overdose.

Far too soon, the overheads grew bright, heralding the end of the evening. "A total success," raved several of the seniors as they grabbed their wraps then headed to the fleet of accessible vans Jay had arranged to transport them home. Saying goodbye, perhaps for the last time. So bittersweet. I held back my tears as we saw them off. Then we ambled back inside, hand in hand, to thank the staff and help return the hall to its pre-party condition.

"Funny, I never did see you chat with your nana. Are you finally going to tell me which of these ladies she is?"

Jay looked as if someone walloped him with a giant mallet. "Oh my God, I was so wrapped up in the excitement of seeing you, I didn't think about her all evening. Some grandson. I didn't see her here though, which is odd because she verified the date repeatedly. Let me give her a call, make sure everything's okay. Then would you consider sharing a nightcap or perhaps a little alone time back at my apartment?"

Would I ever.

He stepped away while I bustled around the room, stacking used Dixie Cups for rinsing and recycling. All the while, I considered his invitation. The thought of curling up against him in the privacy of his home gave me goosebumps. What had I been waiting for? Why had I kept my distance?

He walked over, his forehead creased with worry. "There's no answer. It's probably nothing, she might have turned in early. I think we should pop in on the way to my place, just to make sure. Is that okay with you?"

How could I say no to someone so protective of his nana? After finishing the clean-up, we strolled to his Lexus, stopping every few steps to indulge in long, luxurious, open-mouthed kisses.

"I can bring you back to pick up your car later tonight…or in the morning. Whatever you like."

I didn't protest or suggest an alternative plan. It sounded good to me.

We drove south past the center to the better part of town, with Eddie Money's "Take Me Home Tonight" filling the car's interior with romantic suggestion. Again, I broached the question that had been perplexing me for weeks. "I'm going to find out in a minute anyway, so why don't you spare me the suspense and just tell me? Who is this nana of yours?"

"She's a lovely woman. You've probably seen her at SALAD, knitting her heart out. Her name is Helen Sutherland."

The breath caught in my throat. It couldn't be. "But… she told me her grandson's name is Jonathan."

"Yes, that's my proper name. Jonathan Prentiss. Though I've gone by Jay as far back as I can remember."

Words failed me. It suddenly all made sense. The gin game he'd originally complained about, fearing his nana was being swindled out of her social security. Helen's dislike of the people at the center. The scoresheets I'd seen her pull off tables and stick in her purse as she passed through the recreation room. She wanted Jay to think she was active in group activities so he wouldn't worry. A lie I'd heard Judith perpetuate to his face. Now, the trip to visit her lost love…oh my God, he didn't know. And I was the one who had to tell him.

"Here we are, Casa Nana." The security officer waved to Jay before electronically opening the community's elegant iron gates. A minute later, we pulled into the driveway of a small townhouse close to the entrance. "I'll jump out. You can stay in the car. Unless you want to say hello."

"Jay, I'm not sure how to tell you this. Helen isn't inside."

He gave me a curious look. "What do you mean?"

"She left town. This afternoon. She told me before I left the center."

"What the hell?" He leapt out of the car, ran to the entrance, then rang the bell. When that yielded no response, he pounded furiously. Same result. Out of options, he reached into his pocket, pulled out his spare key, and unlocked the door himself.

~ * ~

Jay yanked open the door and ran inside, remembering to turn on the lights only as an afterthought. His first stop was Helen's bedroom, where he found the mattress neatly covered by a pink-and-white floral duvet and a mass of decorative pillows, but devoid of any sign of his nana. He pulled open the closet door to find it half-empty, her suitcase missing. Same with the bathroom. There were empty spaces where her toothbrush and medicines usually stood.

"I've found something," Carra called from the kitchen.

He hurried toward her voice, finding her by the breakfast table with an envelope in her outstretched hand. He grabbed it and tore it open, dreading the missive but forcing himself to read it aloud for Carra's benefit.

"My Dearest Jonathan:

"I have no doubt you will be angry with me for leaving without telling you first, but I also know that had I informed you of my desire to leave, you would have done everything in your power to prevent it. Please forgive me but try to understand.

"When you lost your parents and came to live with me..." He winced at revealing something he hadn't intended to share, "...nothing made me happier than the chance to raise you and watch you develop into the fine man you've become. The sacrifices were well worth the rewards. But now that you're grown and living your own life, I've realized, by listening to Carra's memoir class..." He looked up at Carra, making no attempt to hide an expression of blame and disgust, "...that one unvoiced regret lingered, one avenue left untraveled.

"I know you worry about my health, that according to the doctors, my occasional unsteadiness is one of the early signs of dementia, but they also say the full onset could be years off. I appreciate all you have done to make me comfortable and part of your life. Your visits are always the highlight of my week. Yet, a loneliness grips me, a longing I can only satisfy by reuniting with someone who truly understands my past and wants me to be a part of his future. I owe it to myself to explore that relationship and see if it will take root.

"I ask you to respect my wishes and not come after me but rather..." He read the rest silently, holding back his tears.

"What came next? What does she want you to do?" asked Carra impatiently.

"Pursue success at work, that kind of thing." His voice cracked as he refolded the note and stuck it into his pocket. No need to share Helen's wish that he "settle down with a nice girl like Carra" when he was too furious to even look her in the eye. Instead, he scanned the room. "Her computer is over on the desk. Let's see if we can figure out where she went."

"But her note said—"

"I don't give a damn what the note said," he snapped, walking to the desk and pulling out the chair. "She's not stable, physically or mentally. The doctors told me privately that Alzheimer's is a very real possibility. She isn't safe out there on her own. We have to find her."

"We? She always struck me as competent and in control. I respect her decision."

He turned on the computer and glared at the password screen. "You put the idea in her head, and you're going to help me find her," he snarled. How could she deny responsibility for Helen skipping town when her class was clearly the precipitating cause?

Carra shook her head and rolled her eyes. "Fine. I'll help you. Not because I think Helen is in peril, only because you're clearly shaken and need someone to talk you off the ledge."

"I don't care what the reason is. This is something you're going to see through to the end."

Her eyes narrowed. "What exactly are you implying? That I'm usually irresponsible when it comes to the seniors? That I offer reckless suggestions and then leave them to their own devices?"

"No, no. Look, I'm crazed. The woman raised me since I was eight. I can't lose her, so come on, help me figure out her password."

"Try your name. Or your nickname."

Jay typed in variations. Nothing.

"Or the name of any old pets... or SALAD?"

Again, he came up short.

"How about Troy?"

He twisted to face her. "Who's Troy?"

Carra diverted her gaze, as if she knew the response would condemn her in his eyes. "The man she's gone searching for."

He typed in "Troy." Then "Searching for Troy." And "Long Lost Love Troy." The password screen denied access, mocking him. Frustrated, he banged his fist against the oak desk.

"Here's a thought," she said, "Try 'Second Chance.'"

Carra's suggestion resonated. He typed, and his heart leaped as the display changed to Helen's home screen, featuring a photo of the two of them at his Princeton graduation, his arm around her shoulders and the look on her face making it clear she was bursting with pride. Immediately, he clicked on her browsing history, figuring that while his grandmother had smarts, her tech savvy would preclude her from erasing her cache. With Carra peering over his shoulder, he scanned the list, stopping at the Greyhound website link. One click and up popped a schedule between New York City and Cincinnati, Ohio.

"There's a 12:05 AM bus that leaves Port Authority and gets into Cincy at 4:15 PM tomorrow." He glanced at the clock on the desk. It was already after eleven. There was no way to stop her from boarding, but he could intercept her on the other side, as long as they left right now. "Come on. We'll stop off at my place to pick up Solomon and get right on the road."

"But my clothes..." She glanced down at the flapper dress peeking out from under her unbuttoned coat. "My car's still at the Lion's Club. And my job interview... it's tomorrow at ten."

He looked her square in the eye. "She knows you, likes you, and is probably more likely to listen to you than to me, especially since you put this 'reversing regret' idea into her head. So, what's more important, Carra? My grandmother's life, which your memoir class threw into jeopardy, or a writing job? Decide."

She blinked. "Your grandmother, of course. But she's not in—"

"Then let's get moving. Your car will be fine. You can call the magazine tomorrow morning and reschedule your interview—I'm sure they'll make an exception for an emergency. We can pick you up some clothes when we get there.

"I'll bring the laptop. You can search for clues while I drive. And go pick out a dress from her closet." He turned off the computer and pulled the plug from the outlet.

"Why do I need her dress? She's not my size. And how can you even be sure she's going to Cincinnati? Maybe it's a red herring she used to throw you off her scent."

"The dress is not for you, it's for Solomon. He's a tracking animal, let's let him track. The reason I'm sure she's bound for Cincinnati is that it's where I grew up. If there are any loose ends in her past, that's where we'll find them."

~ * ~

I wasn't thrilled with Jay at the moment, and that was an understatement. First, there was the matter of chasing after Helen, who had made it abundantly clear she wanted to be left alone to travel wherever the trail to Troy's heart might lead. Second, the only thing separating my scantily clad body from the late October chill was a lightweight trench coat. I had no change of clothes, no toothpaste, no makeup. Not even a hairbrush since I'd brought the tiniest of purses, one only large enough for my phone and car key.

Third, and most pressing, there was a large, smelly bloodhound in the backseat that kept slobbering on my shoulder, turning my stomach with the smell of his hot, stinky dog breath. A constant stream of drool welled on my coat's rayon epaulet. Though I'd learned to tolerate Angus and cautiously pet him when delivering Janet's food, I was by no means a "dog fancier." But unlike Solomon and his saliva, I swallowed my discontent, and for good reason.

The resurgence of Jay's hair-trigger temper didn't please me, especially since it brought back unwanted memories of my mother. Still, I reminded myself that I'd seen him remain cool and collected in contentious situations, such as when dealing with Adriana at the restaurant, and with Simon Garrison's meth-addicted son-in-law, Philip. It was clear that where his nana was concerned, ire clouded, nay obliterated, the man's usual calm demeanor. His devotion was a more endearing quality than his temper was a flaw, so I decided to cut him some slack.

At his urging, I read through Helen's emails, searching for anything that might lead us to her in a city as large as Cincinnati. If there had been correspondence between her and Troy, she'd been shrewd enough to delete it and empty her trash folder.

"I'm sorry, there's nothing here, nothing to indicate where she might head once she arrives in town." My words broke the silence in the car, which was previously punctuated only by the cadence of Solomon's panting.

"If we miss her at the depot we'll stop at all the hotels, show them her picture in case she's checking in under an assumed name. We'll find her."

I closed my eyes to prevent him from seeing my look of disbelief. I'd checked. There were close to 250 hotels between Cincinnati and its Northern Kentucky suburbs. He was transforming an elderly woman's road trip into a manhunt worthy of a *Fugitive* episode.

I closed the laptop, placed it on the floor, and gazed out the window. We were heading west on I-80, passing through Warren County, N.J. I yawned. It was nearly 2:00 AM and it had been an exhausting day. Even Solomon had finally collapsed in the back seat, his panting replaced by a constant rumble of snoring and the occasional sleep-whimper.

"Do you mind if I nod off? You can wake me up anytime you want me to take the wheel."

"You go ahead and sleep. I'm running on adrenaline, I'll be fine.

The important thing is that we make it to the terminal before she gets off the bus."

I could tell he was trying to be patient with me, but every word vibrated with annoyance. Did he really believe this was all my fault? It's not like I knew Helen Sutherland was his nana. Neither one of them had thought to share that tidbit of information. In fact, he'd refused to tell me. Whatever. If he was still irritated when I woke up, at least I'd be rested and better equipped to deal.

Chapter Twenty-Six

Every few minutes, Jay turned his gaze from the monotony of the highway to check the clock. They were making good time, and if traffic stayed light and he kept his foot glued to the accelerator, they'd beat the 1351 bus to the Cincinnati terminal because unlike them, he wasn't planning an hour stop in Pittsburgh. If they got hungry, he'd pull into a rest stop and grab them a couple of burgers, take a quick bathroom break, refuel. Fifteen minutes tops.

He snuck a quick peek at his passenger. Carra was dead to the world.

She even looks gorgeous in her sleep. He remembered how he'd barked orders earlier. *Good going, Lothario. Fastest way to a woman's heart is jumping down her throat.*

He'd practically accused her of helping his nana skip town, which was ridiculous. She hadn't even taken Carra's memoir-writing class–he'd asked. He'd never given Carra his grandmother's name, so resolved was he to keep the sadness of his past from her. He wanted to win a heart untainted by pity.

Once she knew the truth, he feared she'd never look at him the same way. So he'd been careful to never show up at the center during her shift and to never call Helen anything but Nana when Carra was around.

Then, the shameful way he'd handled her objections. How callous, to ask her to put his search above her own chance for the job of her dreams. If the magazine wouldn't reschedule her interview, would Carra have a source of income when they returned? He wanted to rewind time, take back every word. Somehow, he had to find a way to smooth things over when she awoke.

It was around 5:30 AM when he pulled off the highway in search of gas. The indicator was deep into E territory. With the road deserted and a deadline looming, it seemed as good a time as any to put the pedal to the metal and see exactly what the Lexus could do. After speeding two miles through the equivalent of East Bumblefuck searching for any service station, let alone one that was open, he heard a loud boom.

The car hurtled to the right, and he fought to regain control. His first instinct was to panic but thankfully, his driver's ed training came flooding back. He gripped the steering wheel and moved his foot slowly from the gas to the brake, gently applying pressure as he steered the hobbling vehicle onto what passed for a shoulder. His passengers awoke with a start, both from the noise and the initial jolt of the blowout, Carra with an "Oh my God, what's happening?" and Solomon with a long, sonorous howl.

Only after Jay had cut the ignition and rested his head against the steering wheel did he realize his body was bathed in sweat. He jerked back and checked on his passengers. Solomon had already nodded off again, satisfied that his meal ticket had survived another day, Carra had jumped out and was checking the front of the car. Neither knew how close he'd come to reliving the worst moment of his life.

"You must have hit something sharp because this tire is in shreds. Do you have a spare?"

He hung his head. "I did. Until I swapped it out a few weeks ago when I got a flat. I'm scheduled to get it replaced…on Tuesday."

The irony struck him hard. The only time Mr. Anal-Retentive relaxed and procrastinated, he'd endangered three lives. Make that four. Unless help came quickly, they might not make it to the terminal in time to rescue Helen.

Carra returned to the front seat and pulled her cellphone from her purse. "Figures. I'm almost out of juice. You have a charger for an iPhone?"

"Unfortunately, no. Mine's an Android. Tell me who you want to call, and we'll use my Samsung."

"I guess you should google 'towing companies near me.'"

He grabbed his phone. One bar. He sighed. Wherever they were, the reception was awful. Even repeated calls to the operator and 411 didn't connect.

"Should I get out and try to wave down a Good Samaritan passing by?" asked Carra.

"Wearing that?" Jay pointed to her trench coat. "You'll freeze your butt off and the road's deserted anyway. I'm going to wake Solomon and take him for a walk. While I'm gone, if more bars appear on my phone, want to reach out to a towing company?"

"Sure. Any idea where we are?"

"Here, I'll turn the ignition back on. You can check the

coordinates on the GPS."

Solomon reluctantly left the car, deigning to mark a few trees gracing the hell-forsaken wilderness in which they now found themselves. When he and Jay returned, Carra was thanking someone before disconnecting the call and handing him back the phone.

The bloodhound resituated himself in the back seat.

"So you got through? When will they be here?" asked Jay.

"Not sure you'll want to hear this. The towing company said they'd be happy to stop by when they open around eight. They'll tow us to the nearest service station to pick up a new tire, but since it's Saturday, it doesn't open until ten."

"Ten? You're kidding." His stomach fell as he realized what that meant. He'd miss Nana's bus completely, his one chance to prevent her from making a foolhardy mistake.

"No joke. So I called the local car rental place, figuring we'd leave the Lexus here and get it fixed later. Get this. There's one, single, solitary car rental firm in Wooster, which would have been perfect if they were open. Their answering machine says they're on vacation and thanked us very much for our patience and understanding. Then they offered the number of an alternate car rental place, but it's fifty miles away. What should we do?"

He threw his head back against the cushion in despair. "What can we do? We wait until eight and get towed to the service station. It's an excuse for a nap, anyway. You okay?"

"I have to go to the bathroom, actually."

He tipped his head toward the window. "There're some trees and bushes a few yards behind us. Solomon has already blazed a trail for you."

She slipped from the car, leaving him with his dog and his thoughts. A chasm lay between them, one of his own making, and he had to close it if they were ever going to share a friendship, much less a romance.

When she returned, his eyes were closed, and he waited until she made herself comfortable before addressing the elephant in the car. "Carra?"

"Mmm?"

"I'm sorry."

"For what, exactly?"

"For pretty much everything. For snapping at you at Helen's house. For accusing you of putting stupid ideas in her head. But most of all, for minimizing the importance of your job interview. If you like, I'll call the magazine and explain the situation."

"Well known in publishing circles, are you?" Her voice was rich with snark.

"You said it was *Sixty Years On*, didn't you?"

"I did."

"They've been after me forever to advertise. I could call, pull a few strings..." He swiveled to look at her, expecting to see a smile slowly spreading across her face. No such luck.

"That's not how I want to get this job. I want them to hire me based on my abilities. So thanks, but no thanks. I'll call myself and leave a message. Can I borrow your cell again?"

Strike two. He couldn't do anything right today. He handed it to her and watched as she googled the phone number and placed the call.

"Good morning, Ms. Oaks? This is Carra Quinn. There's been an emergency, and I can't make today's interview. I was hoping I could reschedule for anytime during the week, whatever's convenient for you. Please call me back at 845-555-2715. Thank you for your understanding." She disconnected and turned to him. "Hopefully we can find me a charger after we get towed so I can answer the call."

"Of course. I'm sure the service station sells them. If not, we'll take an Uber to somewhere that does."

They reclined their leather seats as far back as Solomon's presence would allow, and the car grew silent. Jay closed his eyes and assumed she had as well. Was this the time to mention what had been weighing on his mind? Who knew when he'd have another chance? If he helped her understand the truth, piece her life and her family back together, she'd have a wider support system. That was more important than ever, especially now that she'd lost the job at SALAD. It was worth a shot.

"Carra?"

"Uh-huh?"

"Funny thing happened at work the other day. This woman came to see me. She had a very sad story and a request. I thought since we've got some free time and you were so brilliant with the Dibble case, you might help me figure out how to handle it."

"Try me."

"The woman, let's call her Penny, had been a composer years ago. Rock and roll, classical; you name it. Very talented. Married probably a little two young. Two boys. A lot of pressure on her shoulders." He paused and when she didn't comment, he continued, "Whenever she'd be close to finishing a project, she'd get stuck. Being a perfectionist, Penny was very down on herself, made it worse than it needed to be. She turned to liquor and drugs—crack, meth, heroin, whatever she could lay her hands on—which helped her creatively for a short while. But when the buzz died and her block returned, she'd go on a bender, unable to stop herself for weeks at a time."

"Go on." There was a definite strain in Carra's voice.

"One day, Penny took her youngest son to a birthday party. Figuring no one would notice, she locked herself in the bathroom and shot up. When she stumbled out, she saw her child on the ground in the backyard. There'd been an accident, and someone had called the paramedics. Penny knew at that moment she wasn't good for her kids, not in her present state. She snuck out and walked for miles until she found a police officer. She asked him to get her to a rehab center, and she stayed there for months until she was clean.

"After that, Penny wanted to find a way back into her family's life, but she couldn't trust herself to stay straight, and her children's lives were too precious to risk. She granted her husband a divorce but kept in touch. Even after he remarried, she called every week to ask about the kids. She spent the next decade sober, following their lives but maintaining her distance, for their sake."

"So what's the problem?" The loathing in her voice startled him.

"Now that her sons are older, and she no longer considers herself a danger to them, she wants a reconciliation. She just can't figure out the best approach."

He opened his eyes and looked over. Carra was sitting upright, scowling.

"Wow, interesting. I only have one question," she said.

"What's that?"

"What the hell were you doing talking to my mother?"

If stares were daggers, he'd be lying prone at the morgue. "Your mother? No, no, you must be mistaken."

His weak attempt at feigned innocence incited her further. "Oh please, Jay. Don't play me for a fool. Her name is Daisy, not Penny, and she's a painter, not a composer. She had two girls, not boys, and there was no birthday party. An Akita attacked her youngest daughter in the park under her watch. I'd be happy to show you the scars sometime.

"Do you really expect me to believe she shared that story without mentioning we're related? I don't know how she got to you, but you can tell her to go straight to hell and leave me alone."

Nausea overcame him, his reward for having taken a chance that had gone terribly wrong. There was no turning back. He had to confess. "It was the day we had lunch at Perry Winkle's. She must have been following you. Once you left, she sat in your seat. Begged me to listen. The desperation in her eyes...I couldn't say no. So I heard her out. I'm sorry if I overstepped. I was trying to help."

"She's been trying through my sister Nikki too. The woman doesn't know when to quit."

"I thought if you understood why she didn't come back, that it was for your own good, maybe you'd give her a second chance. My grandmother said that at SALAD they call you the Queen of Second Chances. I thought you might extend the same consideration to your own mother."

"You were wrong. All I understand is you now know things about my life—like how it was affected by my mother's addictions—that I didn't know myself until this moment. It makes me feel naked, vulnerable. Please, let's not discuss this ever again."

Her bitterness was a chisel, carving out chunks of his soul. She turned her back and looked out the window, leaving him mentally scrambling for any way to repair the damage. The clock read six-forty-five. The towing company didn't open until eight. It was going to be a long seventy-five minutes.

Chapter Twenty-Seven

I turned from Jay so he wouldn't notice me shaking with anger. It wasn't him I was furious with; it was my mother. How dare Daisy Quinn follow me and attempt to insinuate herself back into my life?

Worse, Jay's story resurrected memories I'd long kept buried. My mother crying beside easels bearing unfinished paintings. Then nights out, followed by a flurry of activity. The times I'd ask Daisy questions and not understand her replies. Being a kid, I'd always assumed it was because I was too young, that my mother spoke on a much higher, creative plane. I believed that one day, if I explored my artistic self, I'd decipher that secret language. Now it appears the "creative code" was gibberish, the utterances of someone strung out on drugs. I felt stupid and betrayed.

I closed my eyes, willing myself to concentrate on something positive but even recent victories had fallen flat. All the good I thought I'd done at SALAD was a delusion. The great job opportunity at *Sixty Years On*—who knew if they'd allow me to reschedule my interview? Bea and Nikki, both mad at me. The real estate job would soon end, my one piece of good news in this deluge of disaster. Unfortunately, that meant no more salary, forcing Kiki and me to move back in with our families. She'd be furious, inconsolable. Unless something, anything saved me.

If only I could get the novel edited and sold. The royalties wouldn't be enough to pay the rent, but a published novel would infuse my resume with more credibility when applying for editing jobs. Too bad every time I tried to revise, I choked. Just like my mother...

Could that be it? Was I afraid of finishing the book because I saw what happened when my mother finished her paintings? Confusion, chaos, ruining the lives of everyone around her? Was that also why I kept men at arm's length, afraid to commit fully because when you loved someone, you suffered so horribly when they ultimately abandoned you?

Like my mother had abandoned me?

As angry as I was, another feeling came bubbling through. To my surprise, I believe it was hope.

I closed my eyes as the minutes ticked by but got no rest. At eight, Jay phoned the towing company and by nine, the three of us were sitting across the street from the garage, eating fried egg and cheese bagel sandwiches on the steps of a diner that wouldn't admit dogs. Solomon eyed our every bite with interest, having finished the burger Jay coaxed the cook into preparing during breakfast hours.

Passersby stared—not so much at me because my trench coat hid the flapper outfit—but at my less-prepared companion, whose Gatsby costume stood out from the overalls of the local factory workers. *Serves him right. Vengeance is mine.*

By eleven, the Lexus had a new tire, I had a new phone charger, and we resumed our journey—five hours behind schedule. Since there was no way to intercept Helen as she exited the bus, it alleviated some of the pressure.

I tried three more times to reach *Sixty Years On*, and when they didn't answer, I took the wheel, giving Jay a chance to grab some much-needed sleep. We kept within the speed limit and stopped more frequently to stretch our legs and walk Solomon. We even popped into a Walmart and picked up some cheap T-shirts and sweatpants, clothing comfortable enough for both travel and sleep. When we pulled into town around 9:00 PM, all we wanted was a hot dinner and some shut eye. We left Solomon in the car with the windows ajar and grabbed a booth at the Cracker Barrel.

While I scanned the menu, Jay scrolled through a hotel booking website and made a few calls, determined to locate a pet-friendly place to spend the night. When I glanced up, he wore a sheepish grin. "There's some religious conference in town, not many rooms available, especially ones that allow dogs. But I scored the honeymoon suite at the Walpole—the only room left. You okay with that?"

I gave him a silent thumbs up, wondering if any honeymoon suite, anywhere in the world, might feature two queens. My anger over his intrusion into my personal life had waned but not completely disappeared, and after everything we'd gone through over the past twenty-four hours, I wasn't sure how I felt about Jay sitting next to me, much less sharing a suite with one king bed. Maybe by the time we arrived there'd be a cancellation and another room would open up.

We practically inhaled our grilled cheese and tomato sandwiches, then bought a very spoiled Solomon another hamburger for his efforts—at what, I was still unclear. Energized by the unexpected treat, he barked sporadically at passing cars as we drove the thirteen miles to Fountain Square and our nearby hotel. Even though it was ten o'clock on a Saturday night, the business district was bustling with activity, giving the hound an abundance of targets to alert to his arrival.

With no luggage other than the toothbrush and toothpaste I'd picked up at CVS, and an oversized bloodhound whom we tugged inside—Solomon having recommitted to his normal state of lethargic indifference—we approached the unmanned check-in desk. Jay impatiently tapped the bell three, four, five times until a slender woman whose badge read, "Vanessa," emerged from the adjacent office.

"May I help you?"

"We have a room under the name of Prentiss."

Vanessa typed a few keystrokes into her computer then asked us to wait while she fetched her supervisor. She returned a few minutes later with a hyper and apologetic man named Eric, whose bulging eyes and spiky hair made him look like he'd just stuck a fork into an electrical socket.

"I'm so sorry, Mr. and Mrs. Prentiss. We would have prepared the honeymoon suite with the standard 'Romance Package' if we'd had more notice. I'm afraid there won't be any of the usual rose petals, synchronized massages, or, um, equipment."

I raised an eyebrow. "Equipment?"

Eric looked at me as if I'd grown a second head. "Yes, you know... the *equipment*."

I was tired but not too tired to let this go. "I don't understand. What equipment? Like a treadmill?"

Eric lowered his voice and whispered, "Dildoes, vibrators, handcuffs—you know. Sex toys."

Jay's face turned a bright shade of cerise while I swallowed my laughter and pressed forward. This was the most fun I'd had all day. "Eric, I don't suppose you've had any cancellations tonight?"

"I'm afraid not, no."

"So, this suite, does it have a living room with a couch?"

"More like a loveseat," he conceded.

"That's fine. If you give us a discount for the lack of equipment, we'll take it."

Eric held up a finger and retreated to the computer to do some calculations. "Would a $50 credit suffice?"

I nodded, grateful that this blip had lightened the mood. Jay just bit his lip and handed over his credit card to cover the incidentals.

"By any chance, would you have a guest who checked in under the name of Helen Sutherland?" I asked as Vanessa handed over two key cards.

"I'm so sorry, Mrs. Prentiss but I'm afraid we can't divulge the names of our guests. They trust us with their privacy."

Her curt answer nearly blew the scalp off Jay's skull, but he kept it together until we corralled Solomon into the elevator and pressed the button for the Penthouse Level. He obviously feared we might receive the same response from every hotel we planned to visit.

"It'll be fine," I said, trying to appease him. "I'll call from my cellphone so they won't know it's me asking again and request Helen's room. If they connect me, we'll have our answer. In the morning everything will look different. We'll be refreshed and ready to scour the town for your nana." Even if I didn't believe my own optimistic remarks, Jay's fury appeared somewhat mollified by the time we reached the room's double doors.

If Liberace had ever decorated a hotel room, it would have lost in the gaudy category compared to the Walpole's honeymoon suite. Everywhere we looked, there were miniature cupid statues, floral wallpaper, and carpeting, oversized tassels on deep purple velvet curtains, and chipped mock-crystal chandeliers. I dropped Solomon's leash and ran from room to room, mouth agape, taking in the horror of it all.

"Jay, Jay, come here, you have to see this," I called from the bathroom where a red, heart-shaped tub for two matched each of the double sink basins. In the corner, an oddly placed fridge, stocked with cans of André Brut champagne, ensured all guests would get so hammered they'd experience a bath they'd never forget or at least would drown trying.

"This absolutely puts me in the mood. To redecorate," he said, and we both burst out laughing, our earlier rancor forgotten for the moment. He pulled two cans of the world's cheapest champagne from the mini-fridge and handed one to me. "This will be a treat. Nothing says fine wine like a pop top."

We strolled back to the bedroom to find Solomon stretched out in the middle of the world's largest California King. "That's unfortunate," I said. "I call the loveseat. Where are you going to sleep?"

"You know, he does provide the perfect partition. I think if we shared the bed, it would almost be like we were sleeping in separate rooms."

We were each wearing T-shirts and sweats, and he was right about the distance. It seemed stupid to curl up on that unaccommodating Chesterfield settee when this inviting mattress beckoned, even if it was divided by an eighty-pound canine.

"I'm game, I guess." I chugged the rest of my drink. It left me warm and with a weak buzz.

"Let's do it then. I'll set my phone alarm for eight. There's someplace I want to take you before we start our Helen hunt."

I wasn't sure if it was the champagne or his awful pun, but we collapsed onto our respective sides of the bed, convulsing with laughter. He switched off the light, leaving us enveloped in darkness. Solomon's snores interspersed with the last of our giggles. Then only the dog's sawing remained, punctuated by an occasional unpleasant release of gas.

"Carra?"

"Yes?"

"You know I'm sorry about your mom, right?"

"You were only doing what you thought was best."

Another moment of silence.

"Carra?"

"Uh-huh?"

"You also realize that had you come back to my apartment last night, this scene would have looked very different."

"One can only hope," I responded. Solomon started running in his sleep, poking me with every lope. "Can I ask one favor though?"

"What's that?"

"Can we switch sides? Solomon's cantering is bruising my back."

We got up and walked around the foot of the bed, stopping only when we stood face to face in the dark.

"We seem to have reached an impasse," he said.

"You have a knack for pointing out the obvious."

He grazed my cheek with his palm. "Carra?"

"Jay?"

"I'm going to kiss you now."

"Thanks for the warning."

He moved the hand that had been caressing my cheek to the back of my head, then pulled me close as our lips touched. Quivering with desire, I ran my hands up and down his back, tracing the muscles in his shoulders. For once, this felt right. It was worth the risk. If I got hurt, I'd survive. It was better than not feeling at all.

"Jay?" I murmured.

"Uh-huh?"

"How hard would it be to push Solomon onto the far side of the bed?"

"Not easy, but for you, I'll try."

Chapter Twenty-Eight

Jay's alarm went off too early, considering our mutual lack of sleep, but to Solomon, the time of his morning walk was sacrosanct. Though exhausted, we determined it was better to accommodate him than to risk him relieving himself on any of the suite's priceless "fauxtiques."

"I'll be right back." Jay pulled on his sweats and tee. "Why don't you order room service while I'm gone? Somehow I've acquired quite an appetite." He threw me a wink. "Two fried eggs with bacon and wheat toast would be perfect. And coffee. Black." Solomon pawed at the front door, hastening Jay's departure.

I placed the order, adding some banana pancakes and tea, then ducked into the shower, leaving the heart-shaped tub for a return visit. As the water cascaded over my skin, I wondered how much of last night was due to Jay's true feelings, or if I should chalk it up to the André Brut. It had been memorable. I hoped it was also sincere and replicable.

Wrapped provocatively in terrycloth, I resisted the temptation to strut through the suite when I heard Jay and Solomon return. Best not to pressure the man; he had enough on his mind.

We scarfed down breakfast without too much chatter and headed out, packing Solomon into the rear, where he curled up against Helen's stolen dress.

"Where do we start?" I asked, fearing Jay might suggest visiting each of Cincinnati's hotels and threatening lawsuits until they turned over their precious guest manifests.

Instead, he said, "There's someplace I want to show you. A place I've never taken anyone before."

His attitude turned somber as he sped northeast on Route 50, following the signs leading to Mariemont. Just after we passed Linwood, he pulled onto the shoulder, cracked open a window, and exited the car, gesturing for me to join him.

"Should I bring Solomon?" I asked, figuring we were pulling over for a dog potty break.

"No, just you. I want you to see this."

He pointed, and my gaze followed his finger to a small cross made of rock, buried in the dirt next to a light post.

"I can't believe it's still here, but I'm glad it is." His eyes glistened. "Twenty-four years ago, my parents and I were driving along this road, heading to Bell Tower Park. We were going to meet some friends there for the afternoon." He paused, and I sensed what was coming next would not be pleasant. "Out of nowhere, a car jumped the barrier and collided with ours. Drunk driver. Our car spun out of control and slammed into this light post. The other car got hit by oncoming traffic, resulting in a twenty-car pile-up."

"Oh my God. How awful. No wonder the blow-out yesterday morning left you so stressed."

"The crash killed my parents on impact. The entire front of the car crushed them where they sat. The wreckage left me trapped, unable to move. I sat there for hours, crying, until the police finally found me. It took the jaws of life to get me out."

I didn't know what to say. I hugged him tightly, wishing I could squeeze the memories away. He ran his hand against my back but kept staring at the cross that marked their passing. "I'm so, so sorry, Jay."

"My nana took me in after that. I wanted to bring you here because yesterday you said I left you feeling naked and vulnerable. I thought if you saw this, knew something private from my past, maybe we'd be even, and you'd understand why keeping her safe is so important to me. Why I assumed you'd view having your mother back as a gift rather than a slap in the face. I'd give anything to have my parents with me again."

We embraced, swaying together by the side of the highway. Now I understood, not only why he tried to orchestrate the reunion and why he cherished his grandmother, but why he lashed out when things didn't go as planned. I couldn't imagine what he'd gone through, waiting hours surrounded by his parents' bloody, lifeless bodies. Who under those circumstances wouldn't structure a life where they remained constantly in control?

"Thanks for bringing me here. I understand your motivations now. I only wish I could make things better."

"You have. Sharing this with someone else is… liberating. Let's go. I want to show you the house where I grew up."

We headed northwest toward the East Walnut Hills and Woodburn sections of Cincinnati, pulling off onto Burdette Avenue, an upper middle-class street lined with newer townhouses. He stopped outside one with blue siding and white trim. "They've renovated the place since we lived here, but this was it. Let's invite the dog to stretch his legs before we hit the hotels."

Jay reached in and grabbed Solomon's leash. The bloodhound leapt from the car and suddenly stuck his nose high in the air, sniffing deeply. Then he went flying to the right, giant ears flopping. Jay ran behind, hanging onto the lead and fighting not to fall on his face. Solomon glued his nose to the sidewalk until he arrived in front of a gray house with a white porch where he stopped and bayed. Jay and I looked at each other quizzically, then ran up to the front door and rang the bell.

An older, African American woman with graying hair answered, wearing a housecoat and carrying a baby in the crook of her left arm. She glared at us oddly. "Yes? Can I help you?"

"I think you can," Jay blurted. "I'm searching for my grandmother. My dog led us to your door. Is Helen Sutherland here?"

"You must be Jonathan," said the woman, her face softening. "Oh my. I haven't seen you since you were yay high." She held her palm parallel to her waist. "Come in, both of you, come in."

Jay swept past her and scanned the living room, but there was no sign of Helen. Solomon, having fulfilled his accomplishment of a lifetime, stood by his side exuding an air of a self-satisfaction.

"Please excuse their rudeness," I said. "I'm Carra, a friend of Jay's. And of Helen's actually. She's a lovely woman."

"Yes, she is. I'm Emeline Shaw. I'm an old friend of Jay's nana. And this," she said, lifting the arm burdened with the infant, "this is P.J., my great-grandson. Say hello, P.J."

"Is she here?" asked Jay, obviously exasperated.

"She was here for a bit yesterday. Why don't you clear off some toys from the couch, and we'll all sit down and have a little chat?"

I did as Emeline asked, placing the rattles and balls into a wooden box at the corner of the room. But Jay wasn't ready to socialize. He walked through the house like an FBI agent hunting down a criminal, opening doors and peeking inside without permission. I finally walked over, took him by the arm, then forcibly led him to the sofa. Solomon settled at Jay's side and promptly dozed off.

Emeline came from the kitchen with a box of Oreos, which she set on the coffee table in front of us, then pulled up an easy chair for herself. The baby fussed and reached toward the table for his bottle, but once she placed the nipple in his mouth he quieted.

Jay was uninterested in small talk, and he made no attempt to hide it. "Why was Helen here? Where is she now? We have to find her and bring her home."

"Jonathan, calm yourself," cautioned Emeline. "Helen was here late yesterday afternoon. She was passing through town and made a point of stopping to say hello to some old friends. I was so happy to see her. She's looking so well. You must take wonderful care of your nana."

"Did she say where she was going next?" he pressed.

"No, Helen actually made a point of not telling me out of fear you'd try to hunt her down. She did mention spending some time with her friend, Troy. Did she ever tell you about him, Jonathan?"

Jay wrung his hands in frustration. "No, I never heard his name until a few days ago."

Gently bouncing the baby, Emeline sighed quietly. "Your nana met him years ago while she was working as a secretary. He was an accountant for the same company. Instant chemistry. That man was a gem. Never had a harsh word to say about anyone. Devout, church every Sunday. It was the first time I'd seen her happy in years. They planned to move in together, get married."

"What happened?" I asked, caught up in the tale's romance and suspense—the perfect memoir.

"That terrible accident, that's what happened. Troy wanted to stand by Helen, have the two of you move in with him and support you both. But Helen...she said it was better to get Jonathan out of Ohio, move somewhere different where he'd be able to forget, start over fresh. You all headed east the next month. I think she had cousins or something out that way."

"She gave up all her dreams." I marveled at Helen's sacrifice.

"That was her, always putting others first," Emeline said, nodding. "Anyway, she told me yesterday she'd been thinking about Troy, that her last chance for love may have passed her by. A little bird whispered in her ear that it's never too late to pick up where she left off. It got her to find him on the internet and write him a note. I guess we'll find out the rest of the story in time."

"Do you remember the name of the company he worked for? The church he attended? I can trace him through there, get his last name, find him online..." said Jay, grasping at straws.

Emeline stood up, the baby still in her arms, and looked sternly at Jay. "You will do no such thing Jonathan Prentiss. Your grandmother gave up everything for you. You will step aside now and let her gather up the pieces of her past and see what she can build for herself."

"But she's not well..."

"She's as healthy as I've ever seen her. She told me some rubbish about an unsteady gait and the doctor's warnings. They've been telling me the same thing for years and guess what? My thoughts are as clear as that bay window, and so are hers. You leave her be, Jonathan, or you'll have me to answer to." Then she smiled to show she meant no animosity. She was merely protecting a friend's wishes.

"Now, if you will keep an eye on this angel, Ms. Carra, I'm going to make you all some lunch to celebrate seeing Mr. Prentiss again. I have leftover meatloaf and mashed potatoes from last night. How does that sound?"

"It sounds wonderful, Emeline. Thank you for your hospitality," I answered for the two of us.

She put the sleeping baby in his cradle and disappeared into the kitchen.

"Are you okay?" I whispered to Jay.

He shook his head. "There's got to be something more we can do, not just leave her out in the world on her own."

"Sounds to me like she's doing fine. Your grandmother planned her entire route and scheduled her departure when she knew you'd be too busy to notice. She took the time to visit old friends, and even navigated the digital wilderness to track down a lost love. You should listen to Emeline here, have a little faith that your nana knows what she's doing. She did okay raising you, so she can't be too far gone." I elbowed him in the ribs. He allowed a grin to take hold. Hopefully I'd broken through.

Emeline summoned us to the dining room and set down two heaping plates. There'd be no need to stop for dinner tonight.

"What are your plans this fine Sunday afternoon?" she asked when the feasting slowed. "The zoo, the art museum? I don't know if you've been here before, Carra, but Cincinnati is a lovely city."

"I'm sure it is. But now that you've convinced Jay his nana should proceed on her adventure without him, I think we're going to drive back home. If we're lucky and the traffic cooperates, we can make it back by midnight. Right, Jay?"

He sighed, clearly resigned. "Right. I guess it's best all around. I do have work tomorrow."

I wish I did. No one from *Sixty Years On* had returned my call. Perhaps I'd try again on Monday and explain what had kept me from my interview. It was worth a shot. The Helen hunt would make a whopper of a first feature.

Chapter Twenty-Nine

As it turned out, the traffic did not cooperate. By eleven, they were still one hundred miles west of Rock Canyon. Jay had a choice: stop and buy caffeine pills or spend another night cuddling with Carra. To him, the choice was clear, and his companion didn't seem too upset with the suggestion either. They found a little motel outside Philadelphia that permitted pets, stopped by a late-night pizzeria for a few slices, then hunkered down for the night, happy to find themselves in each other's arms. The smaller, double mattress forced them to relegate poor Solomon to the floor. He expressed his displeasure by farting repeatedly before falling into a deep slumber.

Jay forgot to set his alarm. At 8:30 AM, they woke to the ring of his cell.

"Where are you?" Meggie demanded. "I have Mr. and Mrs. Vehring here, waiting to discuss their long-term care options."

Jay threw his head back against the pillows. "I can't believe it, Meggie, I completely forgot. I had an emergency this weekend and had to leave town."

"Yes, I forecast such an emergency arising when I saw you two dancing at the Lion's Club Friday night."

Jay grimaced at her impropriety. He'd have a word with her later that day. "I'll be there in a few hours. Can you ask them to come back?"

He heard Meggie's muffled voice relaying the question to his clients. "They said okay. Do you think you'll be here by two?"

"Not a problem." He disconnected the call.

"Issues at the office?" asked Carra.

"Nothing I can't handle. How does breakfast sound before we hit the road?"

"Sounds wonderful." Carra smiled, appearing refreshed after several hours of uninterrupted sleep. "Roll closer, and I'll grab a bite."

~ * ~

It was close to eleven, and they were twenty-five miles from the Rock Canyon border when Carra requested a bathroom break. The rest stop also interested Solomon, who pulled Jay yards from the car in pursuit of the perfect tree trunk to mark.

Distracted by the leash tug-of-war, he didn't check the Caller ID when his cell interrupted. "Prentiss."

"Jay, it's Adriana."

"Please, not now. We have nothing more to discuss." It was over. Why couldn't she get that through her head? Did he have to change his phone number?

"You've made that quite apparent. I thought you'd like to know that your little paramour from the other night, Carraway Quinn? She works for Rock Canyon Realty as a salesperson. I can email you a copy of her pocket card if you need proof. A real estate agent, conveniently working around all those elderly people with homes to sell, your nana among them. How interesting she took a job at the center, don't you think?"

If the news perturbed Jay—and it did—he refused to let that come across. "Why are you bothering me with this?"

"Because if she's with you, and I assume she is, romantic little getaway and all, she might be unaware that her sister is at the center today in her place. I guess one Quinn is as good as another when it comes to bilking people out of their homes. Just make sure Helen doesn't fall for the scam. It would be a shame for them to bamboozle her out of that lovely little townhouse you bought her."

"Are you finished?"

"Not quite. Since you never answered my messages, we missed the opportunity to have dinner with Senator Mitsky and his wife. Luckily, he's having a fundraiser tonight. It'll be a great opportunity to schmooze, and don't worry, I'll be there, but only as your publicist. Can I count on you?"

Jay saw Carra approaching the Lexus. His entire being vibrated with anger and a sense of betrayal. What had ever made him think this was going to work? What did he really know about Carra Quinn, other than their joint interest in his Visa card? Adriana had a good job, her own money, a sterling pedigree. More importantly, she still looked out for his interests and supported his political ambitions, no matter how badly he'd treated her.

Maybe he'd made a big mistake dismissing her so abruptly. "Yeah, I'll be there."

"Great. Be at the Water Club at 7:00 PM. I'll meet you in the lobby, and we'll go in together." *Click.*

Jay jammed the phone into his pocket and dragged Solomon back to the car. He wasn't sure which was more upsetting: that Carra was a real estate agent, or that she'd lied to him about her intentions at SALAD. All he knew was that his heart ached as if she'd ripped it from his chest and stomped it flat. Had she been at the center solely to con seniors out of their homes? From what he knew about real estate agents, especially from that firm, it was a good bet. They were the same people behind the Dibble sale. No wonder she knew so much about septic fields and leaking oil tanks. He settled into the driver's seat and gripped the wheel.

Carra got in and closed the door. He started the engine, put the Lexus in reverse, and slammed it into drive.

"Everything okay?" she asked.

"Fine. Everything is fine." He turned on the radio, eliminating the possibility of more communication.

He dropped Carra off at the Lion's Club around noon to collect her car, giving her an abbreviated kiss on the cheek. Then he sped home, showered, changed into fundraiser apparel, and fumed all the way to the office.

At work, he choked back his anger long enough to consult with the Vehrings, then sent Meggie packing, no longer willing to tolerate someone who spied on his movements and reported them to his ex-girlfriend. That still left him several long hours to ruminate over Adriana's accusations.

He thought he'd been falling for Carra and that she felt the same. Had she merely been using him for his money, the same way she'd been using SALAD to get new clientele? There was one way to find out. He called and invited her for afternoon tea at Julianne's Café. Somewhere crowded where she wouldn't make a scene. The four o'clock meal would leave him time to take Solomon home, then make it to the Water Club by seven.

Carra sounded so happy to hear from him. How fast would her attitude change once she heard what he had to say?

Chapter Thirty

I hummed as I dug through my closet, looking for the perfect outfit for afternoon tea. The earrings I already had–tiny mock-china teapots. He'd love them. As for the rest, I wasn't sure.

Kiki arrived home from work early, a reprimand at the ready. "I worried myself sick about you all weekend. All my calls went right to voicemail. Where were you? Why didn't you phone?"

I told her everything—being fired, chaperoning the dance, the mad dash to find Helen, the revelations about my mother, the blossoming of a new romance. It was a lot to take in all at once. Being Kiki, she zeroed in on the most pressing matter. "You've lost the SALAD job and Bea's job as well, since you can't deliver what she hired you for. The rent is due later this week. Will you have enough to cover it?"

There was no way I was going to let her practicalities decimate my good mood. "This month, yes. I'm going to call the magazine again, see if they'll give me another shot at the interview. But look at the bigger picture; I'm seeing someone. And he's caring and wonderful. Can't you just be happy for me?"

"Of course I can. To prove it, I'm going to warn you that the jumpsuit you're holding is all wrong. Wear something light, flirty, easy to remove. My advice is a button-down blouse and a miniskirt. Let him drool into his tea and rush to get you home."

"That's the spirit. I like this side of you better. Let me revel in my joy today, and tomorrow I'll worry about the rent."

I showed up at Julianne's Café a little early, eager for their scones with jam and clotted cream and, naturally, more time spent with Jay. This morning, his behavior puzzled me—how cold he seemed when he returned to the car. I chalked it up to pressure at work, compounded by the knowledge that Helen, his rock, might not be coming home any time soon. That had to be a hard pill to swallow. It was up to me to smooth the way, help him get over these hard times.

As usual, he was already at the table when I arrived, but he seemed off somehow, his expression subdued. We ordered almost immediately then I questioned what was bothering him.

"Carra, do you know where your sister Nikki was today?" He spoke in such a low voice I had to lean forward to catch every word,

"No idea, why do you ask?" Such an odd question. What was he getting at?

"She was at SALAD, working your shift. Do you know why?"

A chill ran through me. "You must be mistaken. She works at a rehab facility. What would she be doing at the center?"

"Hawking houses, that's what." His eyes were cold. Impenetrable. "I checked with a few members there. They said she asked them why they hadn't sold their homes and moved into assisted living. Apparently she has a real estate license, just like you."

His temper was back in full force, but frosty rather than burning with accusation. I could barely hear myself think over the pounding of my pulse. How had he found out? How could I explain this?

"Is that why you got me to fund all those innovations? To get the seniors on your good side so they'd trust you? Pull me into the scheme? I've enjoyed an excellent reputation in the community, but now, they're going to wonder if Jay Prentiss is in it with Rock Canyon Realty. You may have thrown years of good will down the drain."

Now anger overtook my upset. "If you'd let me get a word in edgewise, I'd be happy to explain."

He diverted his gaze but yielded the floor.

"First off, yes. My stepmother is a real estate agent who goaded me into getting my license and paid me to work at SALAD to make inroads into the senior market. And you're one to talk, Mr. I'll-Fund-The-Dance-For-The-Exposure. But, and this is a big but, I was never, ever able to bring myself to mention real estate to even one person. They're happy in their homes. Why dislodge them? I tried to break it to Bea, explain that no one had an interest in moving, but she kept prodding me. Once I realized how much I adored the job, I kept going back."

He looked skeptical.

"I hated the center at first until I considered the improvements I could make. Then it became fun. I liked the people, and they liked me. I felt fulfilled, exactly as you claimed you did after gifting Janet that dog and Bryan his computer.

"Judith fired me, best as I can figure, because my stepmother promised her a piece of the action if we sold any of her members' properties, and I wasn't fulfilling my end of the bargain. That's probably why Nikki is there now. Bea is like Angus with a marrow bone. She doesn't give up once she sinks her teeth in. You believe me, don't you?"

He sighed and looked down at his plate. "The problem is, your initial intention was to dupe these people, con them out of their homes. You implicitly agreed to it when you accepted your stepmother's job. I don't know how I can ever trust you again."

"Ask them." The neighboring diners turned their heads as I stood to leave. "You go ask every one of them, including Helen when she calls, if I ever mentioned real estate to them even once. If you don't trust my intentions, after all you've seen and all we've been through together, you're not someone I want to spend time with." I hit the table for dramatic emphasis, then ran out of the restaurant.

~ * ~

"It's over." I cried into Kiki's shoulder as we sat on the living room couch in our apartment. "I'll never see him again. Who cares? Who needs Jay Prentiss anyway?"

"I'll admit, banging the table in a crowded restaurant was a power move. But you said he has a temper. Maybe he could relate."

Squinting through tear-blurred eyes, I declared an end to my dating life. "I'll turn celibate, join a convent. Please call Our Lady of Perpetual Abstinence, see if they have an opening,"

Kiki patted my hand. "I wouldn't go that far. The habit would hide that voluptuous figure. Give him a few days to think things over. It wouldn't hurt you to simmer down either. Who knows, with a fresh perspective…"

"He didn't have enough faith to hear me out, to try to understand. I dropped everything to travel halfway across the country with him, in search of a woman who didn't want to be found, and I lost my dream job in the process. Just because I initially agreed to Bea's stupid plan, he's condemned me forever. It isn't right. Can't he recognize that life has more grays than blacks and whites?"

"From what you've described, no. He likes control in his life, remember? No surprises. He probably feels you pulled the rug out from under him by withholding information. Plus, you were targeting his nana, at least in his view, the one person he's most protective of. So give him the same amount of slack you're expecting in return. Call him Friday, see if either of you feel differently."

Kiki was probably right, but I was still on edge, my body twitching with rage. I needed to put things right. "Tomorrow I'm going to SALAD to confront Nikki. When I say goodbye to the seniors, I'll alert them to Bea's scheme and tell them Judith is in on it. I may not get Jay back—and who needs him—but at least I'll have done the right thing."

Chapter Thirty-One

As promised, Adriana stood waiting in the Water Club's lobby, thematically clad in an aquamarine A-line, tulle cocktail dress with a scoop neckline. Dazzling as always but then, that was her brand. She greeted him with a kiss on the cheek as if nothing had transpired between them. He marveled at her ability to overlook their lack of any lingering chemistry, despite his resolve to give it another go. In place of that connection was a growing knot in his stomach, warning him that everything about the evening felt hollow and opportunistic. In fact, he'd almost cancelled after his unpleasant encounter at Julianne's because his single thought as Carra stormed from the café was, *I've got to stop her. I can't lose her again.*

But he was a man of his word, and since he was there, he might as well make the best of it. Adriana escorted him into the main ballroom, the air heavy with political disingenuity. His stomach discomfort worsened from knot to tumor as he recalled why he hated these events. The attendees never chatted unless it furthered their personal agendas, and even then they'd forego direct eye contact in favor of staring over your shoulder in case someone more influential happened by. Not that he particularly wanted to converse with any of Mitsky's supporters, all brandishing conservative buttons promoting the NRA and the end of welfare and abortion rights.

Adriana flitted over to the bar and returned with a double scotch. "Down this, it will make everything flow easier."

Once satisfied that she'd partially assuaged his qualms through the magic of hard liquor, Adriana led Jay to Senator and Mrs. Mitsky and, as per her job description, gushed on cue. "Conrad, Jean, how lovely to see you. Thanks so much for inviting us. And this, as promised, is my client, elder attorney extraordinaire and future congressman, Jay Prentiss."

Despite Adriana's warning that Mitsky was a dullard, he struck

Jay as an "old boy" politician, paunchy and balding, but eternally eager to pad his constituency. His wife looked mousy and embarrassed, as if she'd prefer to be anywhere else.

"It's our pleasure, Adriana," the senator said, surreptitiously leering at her cleavage. "You're looking lovely as always. Nice to meet you at last, Prentiss."

"We're so sorry we had to cancel dinner last week," she continued. "Jay felt so, so awful but you know how it is when work calls. He's too modest to tell you himself, but the other day he rescued an old man being held hostage by his meth-crazed son."

Hearing the word "meth," the senator launched into his canned campaign speech, "Damn drugs. We need to ban them all. Especially that marijuana. Scourge of our youth. And that CBD? Not addictive, my ass. It's all garbage. So, this hostage situation, son. How did you free the poor bastard?"

Jay's face went hot with irritation. He'd specifically told Adriana that topic was off the table, that he didn't want to score points by capitalizing on someone's misfortune. Especially when he knew Garrison would be mortified if the story got out. "It wasn't his son; it was his son-in-law. And it's my friend Carra who deserves the credit. She's the one who sensed something was amiss and investigated further."

Adriana threw Jay an irritated look but tweaking her by bringing up Carra, her arch-nemesis, was his way of repaying her for mentioning Garrison. Regardless, his explanations were wasted on the senator and his wife. They'd ceased listening in favor of waving to a campaign contributor across the room.

Jay moved to leave, but the senator caught his arm. "Can we have a moment alone, Prentiss?"

"Of course," Adriana answered for him, then escorted them to a quiet corner of the room. "I'm his publicist. Anything you need to say to him, you can say to both of us."

Minsky put an end to that misapprehension. "Adriana, I appreciate the passion with which you protect your clients, but this is private. No offense, okay?" He winked, and she backed off to join his wife, Jean. Her expression made it clear she resented being dismissed.

"Let me get right to the point, my boy."

Jay noted the senator had twenty or thirty years on him, but he still resented being referred to as anyone's boy.

"You want something, and I want something. Let's do a little horse trading, son. What do you say?"

"I'm not sure what you think I want or what it is you'd like to trade." Jay hoped his dry delivery would put an end to the conversation.

"Cut the BS, Prentiss. You're well respected by the over-sixty crowd. I'm in a tight race to keep my seat in November, and a handful of senior votes could make the difference."

Jay did not like where the topic was headed. "I handle wills and estate-planning. How do you think I could possibly influence votes on your behalf?"

"A phone call here and there to your current and former clients or any geezers in the pipeline. A few positive words about my pro-senior agenda would do the trick. In turn, I'll support your congressional run next year. You're all your little lady talks about. Nothing subtle about that one; she can't tell the difference between a hint and a full-blown nomination. Nice piece of ass, though, you lucky bastard. And clean. A splendid choice for a congressman's wife."

"Clean?"

"You know. Pure American. No foreign blood."

Jay wasn't sure where to start. Defend the honor of his on-again, off-again girlfriend? Tell off the senator for his blatantly bigoted, anti-immigrant remarks? Or dissuade him from the notion he'd pimp himself out and muddy his professional relationships with political dogma to garner Mitsky's support? But no, this was not the place to make a scene. This was the senator's fundraiser; he was merely a guest. Best to be tactful, then discreetly take off.

"Senator Mitsky, with all due respect, yours is not a pro-gray agenda. You don't support the Assault Weapons Ban, even though my clients live in constant fear of their grandchildren being killed in school shootings. You want to end welfare benefits and insurance coverage for pre-existing medical conditions, which would at the very least saddle the elderly with enormous debt and, at the extreme, leave them choosing between death and homelessness. And you consider social security an entitlement though my clients have spent a lifetime paying into a program the government promised would support them in their old age. So how do you honestly expect my clients to support your candidacy?"

"Easy. Tell them they're confused, that my policies really are in their best interests. You're a lawyer, their lawyer. They'll listen to you."

"And when you win and you discontinue all their social programs? What then?"

Mitsky guffawed and hit Jay hard on the back. "What do you care? You're young. And people are aging into senior citizenship every day. When these folks kick, they'll be a whole new crop of them to take their place on your client list. What do you say? Do we have a deal?"

Jay stood speechless, gaping in disbelief. From the corner of his eye, he saw Adriana smile and give him a thumbs up. That's when he realized that when he agreed to come tonight, he'd done exactly what he'd accused Carra of doing. By coveting Mitsky's mentorship, he'd tacitly implied his support for the senator's conservative agenda, a platform Jay rejected with every fiber of his being. He'd consented because during a moment of weakness, he'd misled himself into believing the ends justified the means.

"I said, son, do we have a deal?"

"Senator, I'm afraid I've reconsidered. I can't back your campaign because my views and yours are diametric opposites. However, that little lady over there, the 'nice piece of ass'? I guarantee you if you tell her what you're looking for, she'll dig up a prospective candidate-slash-boyfriend to fill the bill."

He headed for the door, and Adriana's heels click-clacked behind him.

"Jay, what happened? Where are you going?"

He turned for what he hoped would be a last goodbye. "I'm going home. I can't back Mitsky's agenda, and I don't want his help."

"Oh, don't be silly. Sure, he's a little old-school. You don't have to agree with him to campaign for him. If you could be a little more flexible—"

He took off, leaving the rest of her sentence hanging in the air. He had one agenda now, and it had nothing to do with politics. Tomorrow he would go to Judith and threaten to expose her real estate scheme unless she hired Carra back, assuming she still wanted the job. Then he'd search for some way, any way, to win Carra back for himself.

Chapter Thirty-Two

It took every ounce of self-restraint to wait until one o'clock to drive to the center. I was practically crawling out of my skin, so eager for this confrontation with Nikki and Judith. Instead, I forced myself to look through Indeed for new job opportunities and finally reached Marina Oaks in Human Resources at *Sixty Years On* to reschedule my interview. She apologized, explaining they'd already filled the position but would keep my resume on file. With the job market as tight as it was, why had I expected anything different?

There was a surprise waiting for me when I pulled into the center's parking lot. Jay's dark gray Lexus was slumming beside the Fords and Chevrolets in the visitors' section. Was he here to ask members if I'd solicited their home listings? Or to scold Judith for exposing Helen to my insurgent teachings, which led her to flee town? Either way, I was not in the mood to tangle with him. Not yet. I slipped through the back door to avoid LaQueshia at the reception desk. No need to risk her alerting security.

I figured I'd sneak past Judith's office on my way to the rec room, since once she and I had it out there was no way would she let me say goodbye to the seniors. As soon as I entered, though, I noticed an eerie silence filling the hallways. No one was wheeling or hobbling around. Even the staff were mysteriously absent, including Judith who wasn't behind her desk sulking at some misplaced penny on her P&L statement. SALAD couldn't be closed, I reasoned. There were too many cars in the parking lot.

Then I heard a shout that seemed to emanate from the rec area, so I sprinted over and peeked inside.

The room was more crowded than I'd ever seen it, but rather than sitting and playing games, everyone had circled around something unfolding at its center. I pushed through the horde to get a better look. What I saw made the hair on my arms stand on end. It was Philip, Simon

Garrison's mustached, biker-type son-in-law, red-eyed and coked out, a pistol in his hand.

He held a terrified Nikki by the waist and alternated between pressing the gun to her head and threatening to shoot anyone in the crowd who tried to make a break for the door.

Judith and Jay were standing closest to the gunman, attempting to talk him down. I remembered his apocalyptic warning from our last meeting: "I'll get you, SALAD lady. Watch your back."

I should have taken him more seriously. That day had arrived but to my horror, instead of me, he'd grabbed my older sister.

"Hurting people won't make you feel better," Jay called from the sidelines. "Let me get you into rehab. They'll help you. I promise."

"All they'll do is lock me up. And it's this chick's fault. I had a good thing going, and she ruined it, and she's gonna pay." He turned the gun back on Nikki, this time against her chest.

Her eyes grew wide with fear.

At that moment, nothing mattered more than protecting my sister, no matter what the cost.

"She's not the one you want, I am." I pushed my way through the throng until I was within a few feet of Philip. "Let her go. Take me instead."

Confused, Philip looked at Nikki then back at me. Except for our haircuts and a few dress sizes, we looked like twins, especially to someone stoned out of his gourd.

In case he needed more convincing, I rambled on, "I'm the one who backed into your car. Called the police. Made you leave your drugs and guns behind. She's my sister and knows nothing about any of this. I'll trade places with her. See, I'm not armed." I held up my hands to prove I wasn't packing.

"What the hell are you doing, Carra?" It was Judith. Still scolding.

"The right thing. Philip, come on. Let her go. Take me."

He put his gun into the hand grasping Nikki's waist then reached out for me. Only when he'd locked onto my arm did he push my sister back into the crowd.

"How does it feel, SALAD lady?" he rasped into my ear. "Knowing everything is going to end. That these are the last people to see you alive. When I'm done with you, I'm going to find Simon and kill him too. Take over his house again. Restart my business. In the end, I'll be the winner. You'll be worm meat."

Someone must have texted the police. I could see four or five officers conferring at the back of the room, but they had yet to make a move. Familiar faces with worried expressions surrounded me as Philip butted the cold gun barrel hard against my forehead, his other arm tight around my throat. If anyone took a shot, I'd make the perfect protective shield.

Perspiration bathed my body, but my senses buzzed sharper than ever. I needed to keep my assailant talking, buy time until the police acted or until I figured out how to distract and disarm.

"This may surprise you," I croaked, "but Simon told me he was sorry I stopped you. He said he thought you deserved a chance to make it. That you're a good husband to his daughter. A good father to his grandkids."

"You're lying now, SALAD lady. You think I'm stupid, that I don't know crap when I hear it?"

"She's not lying," Jay hollered. "I was there, remember? Heard every word."

Philip launched into some inebriated tirade directed at Jay, rambling about new customers, better meth, and more expensive firearms, when I noticed Janet entering the room. She was pushing her way into the crowd with Angus, who was clearly sensing danger and barking wildly. Why was it whenever anything terrible happened to me, a dog was nearby?

Something terrible...a nearby dog...an idea hatched, petrifying as it might be. But what choice did I have? This had to work— blood red wasn't my most flattering color.

"When I interfered, I really *unleashed* a ton of trouble," I bellowed at the top of my lungs.

Philip grew quiet, befuddled by my non sequitur. I gave Janet a hard look, and she leaned over, fiddling with Angus's lead.

Philip was a time bomb, my heart's palpitations counting down the seconds until detonation. He cocked his gun, and my knees buckled, forcing him to pull me upright. "What the hell are you talking about, SALAD lady? Last words, better make 'em good."

I had two choices: risk a bullet through the brain or relive the biggest trauma of my life—the one that ultimately tore my family apart. I had to decide now, before he decided for me. "All I meant was you're a serious guy with a serious mission. It's not like this is *playtime, Angus!*"

A black canine bullet shot through the crowd. As the AmStaff bounded closer, I screamed, "Watch out, it's Cujo!" while simultaneously butting Philip in the head with the back of my skull and stamping my heel into his foot, exactly like they taught in my college self-defense course.

When the dog sprang into the air and pushed us to the ground, Philip was too stunned to pull the trigger. Through a flurry of tail wagging and tongue bathing, I felt the police jerking my assailant from underneath Angus and me. In the next second, they had him disarmed and cuffed.

Jay yanked the dog off me, then pulled me to my feet and held me like the world might cease spinning if he let go. "I'm so sorry, Carra," he babbled as I tried to regain my balance, having been body-slammed at twenty miles per hour by eighty pounds of musclebound terrier. "That was the bravest thing I've ever seen. Judith admitted everything. I should have never doubted you. Can you ever forgive me?"

"I will if you promise me one thing."

"What's that? I'll do anything."

"Never mention p-l-a-y-t-i-m-e again while I'm in the room."

Chapter Thirty-Three
One Year Later

It was our trial run. I was the client, Bea the salesperson. She thumbed through the catalog, describing the inventory page by page. "This is a toilet-seat riser. It puts less stress on your knees when you get on and off the bowl. If you need extra help, we can install the same grab bars by the toilet as we do in the shower." She looked at me for approval. I nodded, and she continued, "This is an auto-touch bedside table. We package it with mattress safety railings and adjustable bed frames. We can also install stair lifts, ramps for your front and back entrances, and even equip you with a scooter or wheelchair to help you get around."

It was a start. At least she was trying. Teaching an old dog new tricks was never easy, but luckily, Bea never failed to recognize a lucrative opportunity. I agreed to assist her real estate practice if she supplemented her property listings with products that helped the elderly age comfortably at home. I'd spearheaded the division, located the distributors, written and designed the marketing materials, and even coined the name: Why Don't You Stay? (Apologies to Bob Seger.)

Bea, nobody's fool, recognized that by offering prospects two alternatives—moving or adapting their home—and acting like a consultant instead of an opportunist, people were more likely to trust you, thereby doubling your chances of a sale. It didn't hurt that she'd taken a shining to our main distributor, Mr. Collins, and he reciprocated her affection.

For me, it was a part-time gig, enough to pay Kiki my half of the rent, though I rarely spent time at the apartment these days. I was busy writing and, even better, volunteering for the Jay Prentiss for Congress campaign. My publisher was releasing my first novel in a few weeks and the second was in the works. Once I'd realized how my mother's abandonment gave rise to the demons that were blocking me, the words flowed freely, and a publisher accepted my revised manuscript.

Even Jay's temper didn't bother me any longer since I realized it wasn't as bad as I'd first perceived; it was just something I'd blown out of proportion as a way to avoid intimacy.

The day had arrived, the culmination of a year of persuasion. Jay had finally convinced me to have lunch with Nikki and Daisy. He said he wanted me to forgive because that would help me to forget. My expectations were less lofty. I only wanted to confront and come to terms with the tragedy of my youth. But not alone. I told him if I was going, he had to go too. As my fiancé, he figured the family expected him there anyway. I told everyone I'd meet them at the restaurant. I had a few things to take care of first.

I made my weekly rounds, checking in on Janet, Blanche, Georgia, and the others, not to deliver trays but simply to say hello. Newly added to the list was Simon Garrison, who'd finally come out of hiding after hearing of Philip's arrest for false imprisonment and attempted murder.

Blanche Schmidt, now Blanche Gold, showed me her honeymoon pictures from Hawaii for the twentieth time. I didn't mind. I loved seeing her happy. Bryan, having grown bored with online classes, explained how he'd taken the leap and enrolled in community college. To his surprise, the younger students revered him for his courage and life experience. Even Michaela occasionally let me inside, trustful that I wouldn't touch any of her prized possessions.

Everyone raved about the improvement at SALAD since they fired Judith and Froy. Several of the seniors had pushed for me to take the job without realizing the enormous amount of education and training needed. Luckily, all were delighted with the newly hired staff— a lovely woman named Shannon Martino and her assistant, Chesterfield.

Shannon phoned me a few months into her employment to pick my brain on proposed projects for the center, prompted by requests from members who pressed for my return. I agreed to volunteer occasionally as Activities Czar, a playful twist on my original "Queen" moniker.

Following my visits, I placed my weekly phone call to Helen, who was happily living with her boyfriend Troy in San Francisco. After several long-distance conversations, Jay had finally accepted, and even supported, her decision to move on with her life. The couple planned to visit during the holidays to pack up her townhouse. Ironically, considering all of Jay's accusations that terrible day when we nearly broke up, she was the one who suggested I list the house for her. We planned to put it on the market right after New Year's.

Satisfied that all was well with my flock, I headed over to Perry Winkle's. Since it was where Daisy accosted Jay and begged for his help, he suggested it as the most appropriate venue for us to "become *re-acqua-inted* and start a clean *slate*." Tell a man a joke, he'll laugh for a minute. Teach a man to pun and he'll make others cringe for a lifetime.

Jay met me outside Perry Winkle's and gave me a supportive hug. Then he locked his arm in mine as I walked the longest journey of my life, from the front door of the restaurant to my mother's side, pushing through fifteen years of confusion, misunderstandings, and heartache. As we approached, I saw the hope in her eyes and my body went slack, sapped by a thousand different emotions, all urging me to reverse course. Jay squeezed my arm tighter, and I remembered the day he'd forced me to face my fear of Angus at the animal shelter. Ultimately, that dog had saved my life.

I wondered if this reunion would rescue me in a different way.

I leaned on him, as I had so many times over the past year, both literally and figuratively. My strength, my anchor. His response was as simple and as frustratingly logical as always: "Carra, a second chance is the greatest gift you can give someone. This time, that someone is yourself."

Turns out, he was right. That second chance was worth the effort. Take it from the queen.

Acknowledgement

Many thanks to all that made this book possible: first, to Savvy Authors, who ran the Autumn Pitchfest, where QOSC first caught the eye of Cassie Knight, and to my editor Lisa, the cover artist, the formatter, and everyone who worked hard to bring this novel to market.

As always, to my long-suffering family, who tolerate listening to the strategy behind every semi-colon and comma. To my late grandmother, Judith Ferester, sorry to turn you into an antagonist, but like you, the character is set in her ways.

Special thanks to Marian Rokeach, Marilyn Clarke, and the folks at the Northern Metropolitan Residential Healthcare Facility in Monsey, NY, who helped with my visit. While your facility does not resemble SALAD, observing the community and its activities helped my research greatly. Likewise, to Maddy, Sharon, Jean, and all the great people I met while volunteering at Meals on Wheels. Your rules are different than SALAD's, and I'm sure nothing happens to your meal recipients as they do in this novel, but my time there planted the seed, so thank you!

As always, a debt of gratitude to my critique group from HVRWA and special thanks to Elf Ahearn, my pre-submission editor extraordinaire, and to Mike Geraghty (not a hoarder like Michaela in the book!) who inspired me to break free of my COVID-19 writing paralysis and meet my daily word count. Above the call of duty, you tolerated my constant competitive posts on your Facebook page. Whatever it takes to get the book done, right? Your good nature and patience were much appreciated.

And of course, to my readers—thanks for making the leap with me from psychological thriller to Rom Com. Here's hoping it was worth the trip!

About the Author

To the average observer, I am a wife, mother, competitive trivia player, and a rescuer of senior shelter dogs. A select few, like you Dear Reader, know me as an author of sex, suspense, and satire. I am the president of the Hudson Valley Romance Writers, a board member of New York's Sisters in Crime chapter, and a member of ITW and MWA. In my free time, I teach writing as one of the Damsels of Distress and interview other authors at www.author-groupie.com.

QOSC is based in Rock Canyon, the setting for another one of my novels, *Expired Listings*. (That's where you can read more about the Realtor Retaliator Murders!). Unlike my other books, QOSC is a Rom Com, which is a genre departure for me, but during COVID-19, I decided it was more important to make people laugh than to unnerve them with a psychological thriller. Still, true to my genre-hopping nature, readers will find some suspenseful elements scattered about, as well as my usual punny sense of humor.

As in all of my novels, this book pulls from my life story, specifically my high school years volunteering at Glengariff Nursing Home, and later, at Meals on Wheels.

Please drop me a note and let me know how you liked it. I love to hear from readers. You can find and connect with me at the links below.

Website/Blog: http://www.dmbarr.com
Blog: http://www.author-groupie.com
Bookbub: https://www.bookbub.com/authors/d-m-barr
Facebook: http://www.facebook.com/authordmbarr
Goodreads: https://www.goodreads.com/author/show/15424118.D_M_Barr
Instagram: http://www.instagram.com/authordmbarr
Pinterest: http://www.pinterest.com/authordmbarr
Twitter: http://www.twitter.com/@authordmbarr

~ * ~

Thank you for taking the time to read *The Queen of Last Chances*. We hope you enjoyed this as much as we did. If you did, please tell your friends, grab another book by D.M., and leave a review. Reviews support authors and ensure they continue to bring readers books to love and enjoy.

Turn the page for a peek inside *Some Assembly Required*, where Ro Andrews, an overworked, undersexed, exasperated single mom, learns whether she can find love with Sam, a man allergic to chaos and crumbs, and make it stick, not sticky.

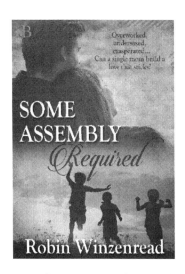

When new divorcee Ro Andrews moves her pack of semi-feral children to a run-down farmhouse, helping her brother restore the moldering homestead and living an authentic life—per the dictates of Instagram and lifestyle blogs everywhere—tops her to-do list. But romance? Hell, no. Between hiding from her children in baskets of dirty laundry, mentally eviscerating her cheating ex, and finding a job, Ro has a full plate.

Until she meets Sam Whittaker, a hunky Texas transplant with abs of steel and a nameplate that reads Boss. Clad in cowboy boots and surfer curls, this child-free stud has Ro on edge—and rethinking her defective Y chromosome ban. Somehow, this overworked, undersexed, exasperated single mom needs to find time to fall in love with a man allergic to chaos and crumbs and make it stick, not sticky.

CHAPTER ONE

As my young son's cries echo through this diner, I'm reminded again why some animals eat their young.

It's because they want to.

"Hey, Mom! Nick farted, and he didn't say excuse me!"

Normally when Aaron, my spunky six-year-old, announces something so crudely, we're at home, and his booming voice is muted by the artfully arranged basket of dirty laundry I've shoved my head into in hopes of hiding like an ostrich from a tiny, tenacious predator.

This time, however, Aaron yells it in the middle of a crowded diner in the small, stranger-adverse, southern Illinois town we're about to call home and, frankly, we don't need any more attention. Thanks to my semi-feral pack of three lippy offspring, we've already lit this place on fire, and not in a good way.

Despite our involuntary efforts to unhinge the locals with our strangers-in-a-strange-land antics, this dumpy, dingy diner, minus its frosty clientele, has a real comfortable feel, not unlike the ratty, stretched-out yoga pants I love but no longer wear because a) they don't fit any more and b) I burned them—along with a voodoo doll I crafted of my ex-husband (see my Pinterest board for patterns), after I forced it to have sex with my son's GI Joe action figure (see downward-facing dog for position).

Crap. I should have put the pictures on Instagram. Wait, I think they're still on my phone.

"Mom!" Aaron bellows again.

Right now, I'd kill for a pile of sweaty socks to dive into, but there's nary a basket of tighty-whities in sight, and that kid loves an audience, even a primarily rural, all-white-bread, mouth-gaping, wary one.

Frowning, I point at his chair. "Sit."

More than a bit self-conscious, I scan the room, hoping for signs of defrost from the gawking audience and pray my attempt to sound parental falls on nearby ears, earning me scant mom points. Of course, a giant burp which may have contained three of the six vowel sounds just erupted from my faux angelic four-year-old daughter, Madison, so I'll kiss that goodwill goodbye. I hand her a napkin and execute my go-to look, a serious I-mean-it-this-time scowl. "Maddy, say excuse me."

"Excuse me."

belch

Good lord, I'm doomed.

"Listen to me, Mom. Nick farted."

I fork my chef salad with ranch dressing on the side and raise an eyebrow at my youngest son. "Knock it off, kiddo."

"You said when we fart, we have to say excuse me, and he didn't." Finally, Aaron sits, unaware I've been stealing his fries, also on the side.

Kids, so clueless.

Nick, my angelic eight-year-old, is hot on his brother's heels and equally loud, "We don't have to say it when we're on the toilet. You can fart on the toilet and not say excuse me. It's allowed. Ask Mom."

Aaron picks up a water glass and holds it to his mouth. "It

sounded like a raptor." He blows across the top, filling the air with a wet, revolting sound, once again alarming the nearby locals. "See?" He laughs. "Just like a raptor."

I point at his plate and scrutinize the last of his hamburger. "Thank you for that lovely demonstration, now finish your lunch."

Naturally, as we discuss fart etiquette, the locals are still gawking, and I can't blame them. We're strangers in a county where I'm betting everyone knows each other somehow and, here's the real shocker, we're not merely passing through. We're staying. On purpose.

We're not alone, either. My brother, Justin, his wife, Olivia, and their bubbly toddler twins kickstarted this adventure—moving to the sticks—so we're eight in total. Admittedly, this all sounded better a month ago when we adults hashed it out over too much wine and a little bit of vodka. Okay, maybe a lot of vodka. Back then, Justin had been headhunted for a construction manager job here in town, and I was in a post-divorce, downward-spiral bind, so they invited the kiddies and me to join them.

For me, I hope it's temporary until I can get settled somewhere, as in land a job, land a purpose, land a life. When they offered, I immediately saw the appeal—the more distance between me and the ex and his younger, sluttier girlfriend the better—and I decided to move south too.

Now I can't back out. I've already sold my house which buys me time, but I've got nowhere else to go. Where would I land? I've got three kids and limited skills. Plus, I don't even have a career to use as an excuse to change my mind or to even point me in another direction.

In other words, I'm stuck. Whether I want to or not, I'm relocating to a run-down farmhouse in the middle of nowhere Illinois to help Justin and Olivia with their grandiose plans of fixing it up and living "authentic" lives since, according to Instagram, Pinterest, and lifestyle blogs everywhere, manicured suburbs with cookie-cutter houses, working utilities and paved sidewalks don't count. Unless you're stinking rich, which, unfortunately, we, most definitely, are not.

Let's see, Justin has a new career opportunity, Olivia is going to restore, repaint, repurpose, and blog her way to a book deal, and me…and me…

Nope. I got nothing. No plans, no dreams, no job, nada. Here I am, the not-so-proud owner of a cheap polyester wardrobe with three kids rapidly outgrowing their own. I better come up with something, and quick.

Where's cheesecake when you need it? I stab a cherry tomato, pluck it from my fork, and chew. The world is full of people living their dreams, while mine consists of an unbroken night's sleep and a day without something gooey in my shoes. I take aim at a cucumber slice, pop it in my mouth, and pretend it's a donut. At least I don't have to wash these dishes.

Across from me, Olivia, my sometimes-vegan sister-in-law is unaware I'm questioning my life's purpose while she questions her lunch choice. Unsatisfied, she drops her mushroom melt onto her plate and frowns. I knew it wouldn't pass inspection. She may have lowered her standards to marry my brother, but she'd never do so for food. This is why she and I get along so well.

Olivia rocks back in her chair and smacks her lips, dissatisfied. "There's no way this was cooked on a meat-free grill. I swear I can taste bacon. Maybe sausage too." Her tongue swirls around in her mouth, searching for more hints of offending pork. "Definitely sausage."

Frankly, I enjoy finding pork in my mouth. Then again, I have food issues. Though, if I liked munching tube steak more often, perhaps my ex wouldn't have wandered. The bastard.

Justin watches his wife's tongue roll around, and I don't blame him. She's beautiful—dark, luminous eyes, full lips flushed a natural pink glow, cascading dark curls, radiant brown skin, a toned physique despite two-year-old twins. She's everything I am not.

She tells me I'm cute. Of course, the Pillsbury Dough Boy is cute too. Screw that. I want to be hot.

Regardless, I expect something crude to erupt from my brother's mouth as he stares at his lovely bride, so I'm pleasantly surprised when it doesn't. Instead, he shakes his head and works on his stack of onion rings. "What do you expect when you order off menu in a place like this, babe? Be glad they had portobellos."

Across from me, she frowns. Model tall and fashionably lean, she's casually elegant in a turquoise and brown print maxi dress, glittery dangle earrings, silky black curls, and daring red kitten heels that hug her slender feet. How does she do it? She exudes an easy glamour even as she peels a corner of toasted bun away from her sandwich, revealing a congealed mass of something.

"This isn't a portobello. It's a light dove gray, not a soft, deep, charcoal gray. I'm telling you this is a bad sandwich. I'm not eating it." She extracts her fingers from the offending fungus and crosses her bangle bracelet encased arms.

Foodies. Go figure. No Instagram picture for you, sandwich from hell.

Fortunately their twins, Jaylen and Jayden, adorable in matching Swedish-inspired sweater dress ensembles and print tights, are less picky. Clearly, it comes from my chunky side of the family. They may be dressed to impress, but the ketchup slathered over their precious toddler faces says, "We have Auntie Ro's DNA in us somewhere."

I love that.

Justin cuts up the last half of a cold chicken strip and shares it with his daughters, who are constrained by plastic highchairs—which I can't do with my kids any more, darn the luck—and, in addition to having no idea how to imitate raptors with half-empty water glasses like my boys or identify mushrooms by basis of color like their mother, they are still quite cute.

Love them as I do, my boys haven't been cute for a while. Such a long while. Maddy, well, she's cute on a day-to-day basis. Yet, they are my world. My phlegm covered, obnoxious, arguing world.

Justin wipes Jaylen's cheek and checks his phone. "We need to get the bill. It's getting late."

I survey the room, hunting for our waitress. Despite the near constant stranger stares, this place intrigues me. It feels a hundred years old in a good, cozy way. The diner's creaky, wood floor is well worn and the walls are exposed brick, which is quaint in restaurants even if it detracts from the value in Midwestern homes, including the giant moldering one Justin and Olivia bought northeast of town. Old tin advertising posters depict blue ribbon vegetables and old-time tractors in shades of red and green and yellow on the walls, and they may be the real antique deal.

They're really into primary colors, these farm folks. Perhaps the best way to spice up a quiet life is to sprinkle it with something bright and shiny. As for me, I've been living in dull shades of beige for at least half a marriage now, if not longer. Should I try bright and shiny? Couldn't hurt.

Red-pleather booths line the wall of windows to the left, and a row of tables divides the room, including the two tables we've shoved together which my children have destroyed with crumbs, blobs of ketchup, and snot. Of course, the twins helped too, but they're toddlers so you can't point a finger at them especially since all the customers are too busy pointing fingers at mine.

Bar stools belly up to a Formica counter to the right, and it's all very old school and quaint, although I would hate to have to clean the place, partly because Maddy sneezed, and her mouth was open and full of fries.

Kids. So gross.

Three portly gentlemen in caps, flannel, and overalls overflow from the booth closest to our table and, clearly, they're regulars. They're polishing off burgers and chips, though no one is sneezing with his mouth open, most likely because his teeth will fly out in the process. I imagine the pleather booths are permanently imprinted with the marks of old asses from a decade's worth of lunches. Sometimes it's good to make an impression. The one we're currently making, however? Probably not.

Nearly every table, booth, and stool are taken. Must be a popular place. Or it may be the only place in this itty, bitty town. It's the type of place where everyone knows your name, meaning they all stared the minute we walked in because they don't know ours, it's a brisk Tuesday in early November, and we sure aren't local.

Yet.

Several men of various ages in blue jeans and farm hats sit in a row upon the counter stools, munching their lunches. A smattering of conversations on hog feed, soybean yields, and tractor parts fills the air. They all talk at once, the way guys tend to do, with none of them listening except to the sound of his own voice, the way guys also tend to do, like stray dogs in a pound when strangers check them out and they're hoping to impress.

Except for one of them, the one I noticed the minute we walked in and have kept tabs on ever since. Unlike the others, this man is quiet and, better yet, he doesn't have the typical middle-aged, dad-bod build. While most of the other men are stocky and round, square and cubed, pear shaped and apple dumpling-esque, like bad geometry gone rogue, he isn't. He's tall with a rather broad triangular back and, given the way it's stretching the confines of his faded, dark red, button-down shirt, it's a well-muscled isosceles triangle at that. Brown cowboy boots with a Texas flag burned on the side of the wooden heel peek from beneath seasoned blue jeans, and those jeans cling to a pair of muscular thighs that could squeeze apples for juice.

God, I have a hankering for hot cider. With a great big, thick, rock-hard cinnamon stick swirling around too. Hmmm, spicy.

This Midwestern cowboy's dark-brown hair is thick with a slight wave that would go a tad bit wild if he let it, and he needs to let it. Who doesn't love surfer curls, and his are perfect. They're the kind I could run my fingers through forever or hang onto hard in the sack, if need be. Trust me, there's a need be.

His body is lean, yet strong, and beneath his rolled-up sleeves, there's a swell of ample biceps and the sinewy lines of strong, tan forearms. It's a tan I'm betting goes a lot further than his elbows. His face is sun-kissed too, and well-defined with high cheekbones and a sturdy chin. A hint of fine lines fan out from the corners of his chocolate-brown eyes and, while not many, there're enough to catch any drool should my lips happen to ravage his face.

Facial lines on guys are so damn sexy. They hint at wisdom, experience, strength. Lines on women should be sexy too, even the stretchy white, hip-dwelling ones from multiple, boob-sucking babies, but men don't think that way, which is why I only objectify them these days. Since getting literally screwed over by my ex, I'm the permanent mascot for Team Anti-Relationship. I blame those defective Y chromosomes myself. Stupid Y chromosomes.

Regardless, it's difficult not to watch as this well-built triangle of a man wipes his mouth with a napkin. I wouldn't mind being that white crumpled paper in that strong tan hand, even if I, too, end up spent on the counter afterward. At any rate, he stands, claps the guy to his left on the back, and I may have peed myself.

The sexy boot-clad stranger pulls cash from his wallet and sets it on the lucky napkin. "I've got to get back to the elevator, Phil. Busy day."

Sweet, a Texas accent. How very Matthew McConaughey. Mama like.

A pear-shaped man next to him raises his glass. "See ya, Sam. You headed to George's this afternoon?"

"I hope so. I need to get with Edmund first, plus we have a couple of trailers coming in, and I've got to do a moisture check on at least two of them." His voice is low, but soft, the way you hope a new vibrator will sound, but never does until the batteries die which defeats the purpose, proving once again irony can be cruel.

And what the hell is a moisture check?

I zero in on the open button of his shirt, drawn to his chest like flies to honey, because that's what I do now that I'm divorced and have no husband and no purpose—I ogle strange men for the raw meat they are. Nothing's going to happen anyway. Truth be told, I haven't dated in an eternity and have no real plans to start, partly because I've forgotten how; just another unfortunate aspect of my life on permanent hold. I've been invited to the singles' buffet, but I'm too afraid to grab a plate. At this point in my recently wrecked, random life, I would rather vomit. Hell, I barely smell the entrees. I'm only interested in licking a hunk of two-legged meatloaf for the sauce anyway. There's no harm in that, right?

Where was I? Right, his chest, and it's a good chest, with the "oood" dragged out like a child's Benadryl-laced nap on a hot afternoon. It's that goood.

Of course, as I mentally drag out the "oood," my lips

involuntarily form the word in the air imitating a goldfish in a bowl. While I ogle this particular cut of prime rib, I realize he's noticed my stare not to mention my "oood" inspired fish lips, which is not an attractive look, despite what selfie-addicted college girls think. Our eyes lock. An avalanche of goosebumps crawls its way up my back and down my arms and, I swear, I vibrate. Not like one of those little lipstick vibrators that can go off in your purse at the airport, thank you very much, but something more substantial with a silly name like Rabbit or Butterfly or Bone Master.

That, my friends, is the closest I've come to real sex in two and half years. Excuse me, but we need a moisture check at table two, please. Not to mention a mop. Okay…definitely a mop.

For a moment, we hold our stare—me with my fish lips frozen into place, vibrating silently in my long-sleeved, heather green T-shirt and jeans, surrounded by my small tribe of ketchup-covered children, and him all hot, tan, buff, and beefy, staring at us the way one gawks at a bloody, ten-car pile-up. All too soon, he blinks, the deer-in-the-headlights look fades, and he drops his gaze.

C'mon, stud, look again. I'm not wearing a push-up bra for nothing.

Big, dark, brown eyes pop up again and find mine. All too soon, they flit away to the floor.

Score.

Damn, he's fine. Someone smoke me a cigarette, I'm spent.

I scan the table, imagining my children are radiating cuteness. No dice. Aaron imitates walrus tusks with the last of his French-fries, Nick is trying to de-fang him with a straw full of root beer, and Maddy's two-knuckles deep into a nostril. And I'm sitting next to Justin.

Figures. My big, burly, ginger-headed, lug of a wedding-ring-wearing brother is beside me. Does this hunk of burning stud think he's my husband? Should I pick my own nose with my naked, ring-less finger? Invest in a face tattoo that reads "divorced and horny?" Why do I even care? He's only man meat. After all, was he really even looking at me? Or Olivia? Sexy, sultry, damn-sure-married-to-my-brother Olivia? I whip back to the stud prepared to blink "I'm easy" in Morse code.

blink *blink* *bliiiink*

With a spin on his star-studded boots, Hotty McHot heads toward the hallway at the back of the diner, oblivious that my gaze is riveted to his ass and equally clueless to the fact that I have questions needing immediate answers, not to mention an overwhelming need to scream, "I'm single and put out, no strings attached" in his general direction.

Olivia pulls me back to reality with her own questions. "I mean, is it that difficult to scrape the grill before you cook someone's meal?"

She's still honked off about her sandwich, unaware I'm over here having mental sex with the hunky cowboy while sending my kids off to a good boarding school for the better part of the winter.

"I didn't have many options here," she rattles on, "even their salads have meat and egg in them. Instead of a writing a book, I should open a vegan restaurant. I was going to give them a good review for the ambiance, but not now. Wait until I post this on Yelp."

Eyeballing the room, Justin polishes off the last of his double-cheese burger. "Sweetie, we're moving to the land of pork and beef. Vegan won't fly here, and I doubt the help cares about Yelp. Did you notice our waitress? She's got a flip phone. Time to put away your inner princess and stick with the book idea."

Long fingers with bronze gel manicured nails rat-a-tat-tat on the tabletop. She locks onto him with dark, intelligent, laser-beam eyes. "Would it kill you to be supportive, honey bunch? You might as well say, uck-fay u-vay."

Apparently channeling some weird, inner death wish, Justin picks up an onion ring, takes a bite, then pulls a string of overcooked translucent slime free from its breaded coating. He snaps it free with his teeth, then offers it to her. "Your book is going to be great, babe, and it will appeal to a larger audience than here. Remember the goal, Liv. As for me, I'm trying to keep you humble. No one likes high maintenance."

The limp, greasy onion hangs in the air. She ignores it, but not him. "Okay, this time, sweetie, I'll say it. Uck-fay u-vay with an ig-bay ick-day."

Jaylen looks up from her highchair and munches a chicken strip. "Uck-fay?" she repeats through fried poultry. "Ick-day?"

Behind her an older woman, also fluent in pig Latin, does a coffee-laced spit-take in her window booth. I hope she's not a new neighbor.

Justin chuckles and polishes off the offending string of onion. Olivia stews. Time to implement an offense. Clearly, we need an exit strategy.

Out Now!

What's next on your reading list?

Champagne Book Group promises to bring to readers fiction at its finest.

Discover your next
fine read!
http://www.champagnebooks.com/

~~~

We are delighted to invite you to receive exclusive rewards. Join our Facebook group for VIP savings, bonus content, early access to new ideas we've cooked up, learn about special events for our readers, and sneak peeks at our fabulous titles.

Join now.
https://www.facebook.com/groups/ChampagneBookClub/

Made in the USA
Middletown, DE
23 December 2021